THE BIG BOYS
NEVER FIGHT FAIR

A chill shot up my spine. Something was wrong. I started to turn, too late. Someone grabbed me from behind and in one swift motion pinned my arms back and slammed me down hard across the hood of the Jeep, crushing my face against the cool metal. I heard a car door open, then shut. A voice said, "Flip him over."

The same hands yanked me free and with a deft twist flung me back against the Jeep. I barely had time to focus on the face in front of me when the second guy, coming out of nowhere, drove a knee into my crotch. It was a glancing blow, my inner thigh taking most of it, though my whole body seemed to explode and I pitched forward.

THE
HERCULES
TRUST

CLARKE WALLACE

toExcel

San Jose New York Lincoln Shanghai

The Hercules Trust

For information address:
toExcel
165 West 95th Street, Suite B-N
New York, NY 10025
www.toExcel.com

Published by toExcel, a division of Kaleidoscope Software, Inc.
Marca registrada
toExcel
New York, NY

ISBN: 1-58348-122-2

Library of Congress Catalog Card Number: 98-89851

Printed in the United States of America

0 9 8 7 6 5 4 3 2 1

to my son Marc

". . . just as legitimate art prices have escalated wildly, so has the market for stolen art. What was formerly a pastime for solo crooks has expanded to include whole networks of thieves who often steal to order, with fencing operations whose contacts are intercontinental. To serve the insatiable greed for art, galleries, private collections, archeological sites, museums and churches here and abroad are being steadily stripped of their treasures . . ."

1

Obviously I hadn't been expecting him.

I'd spent the early afternoon skiing the upper half of the mountain in a snowstorm, and when I finally made it down—there he was. I told him bluntly that I'd come to the Laurentians to get away from old acquaintances, not to renew them. It did little good, but then, what did I expect, that he'd shrug and walk off into the blizzard? Not Gerry.

After fifteen years you'd have thought he might at least have played it low-key, a pat on the shoulder, a little let's-bury-the-whole-damn-thing-and-get-on-with-it. But that's not Gerry's style either. Hell no. He has to make a production out of everything. Give him a booster button and he'll give you a stage show.

It was Friday, around three o'clock. I'd left my friends tearing up great chunks of snow in the deepest powder of the season. Actually I didn't leave them. I lost them. Or they lost me. Either way, it wasn't difficult under those conditions. What was difficult was the almost vertical Kandahar, the run I'd chosen on a whim, or death wish, to bring me down the mountain.

But I'd made it. Not, mind you, with the reckless abandon of someone who knows what he's doing, yet with enough sticky determination to get me down the damn thing without the usual ugly spills. It called for a drink.

The lounge of the Chalets des Voyageurs, part of the Tremblant complex, fitted snugly into the base of the mountain. It was a full house, bedlam in fact. I'd managed to make it inside the main door, but only just, when an arm drifted by carrying a tray of draft beer. Its owner was lost for the moment in the crush of bodies. Taking it to be a waiter on the other end of the arm, I plucked a draft neatly off the tray, yelling for him to add it to my tab. He didn't hear me, but then, I didn't hear me, for in that second a voice sounding unmistakably like the late Humphrey Bogart boomed across the room. Others heard it too. Chatter fell

1

off a couple of decibels. There it was again. Bogie calling for a waiter. People were clapping. They wanted more. They got more. Jimmy Stewart, drawl, broken speech, and all. Then Boris Karloff ordering a Bloody Mary brought down the house. Hair bristled on the back of my neck. I started for the door. Bogie again, this time from the wheelhouse of the *African Queen*. I'd almost reached the exit when Bogart's voice switched to some-one less familiar. "Hey, Stone, where the hell are you going? I thought you always got off on free entertainment!" This brought more cheers, even though this character wasn't as recognizable. It was to me. It was *my* voice.

His name was Gerry Hope-Warden, plain old Gerry Warden when I first knew him. We'd been friends at school, the same school where he'd begun with imitations of the teachers. When the joke wore thin, he had sense enough to switch to celebrities and later to politicians. Much later he would pop up regularly on television, not as a comic but rather as New York's young critic-at-large, discussing such meaty topics as Art in Perspec-tive, or maybe Art in Your Basement; in Your Hall; in Your Attic. Art in Disguise. Heady stuff. In spite of myself, I'd watched his career grow. He had done well for himself. Of course, it hadn't hurt that he was one of the most prominent art collectors in New York State. Just like his father.

By the time he reached me, the bar was back to its noisy self. I made my hasty little speech about being in no mood et cetera, et cetera, but most of it fell on deaf ears. Just as I was really warming up, he shrugged, bellowed *"Scotch"* in his own voice, and wandered off to look for another waiter. Well, so much for waiting fifteen years to get something off my chest. My heart wasn't in it by this time anyway.

Two Scotches-on-the-rocks.

"Okay, what did you think of the impersonation?" He had to shout.

"Bogart, Stewart, or Stone?"

"Stone."

"Uncanny," I shouted back. Bloody right it was uncanny. Harvard. Business-admin finals. He got on a let's-imitate-Stone kick. Before I knew it, he had my mannerisms, my voice down pat. He'd phone on nights before an exam. I'd hear *me* saying, "Hi, this is Philip Stone. Have there been any messages?" Funny. I got a supplemental that year.

He was watching me now, over his Scotch. I had the feeling

he was on the lookout for any new mannerisms I might have picked up over the past fifteen years. He grinned. "When did you first know it was me?"

"Karloff and the Bloody Mary. A Warden original." I sipped at my Scotch, letting the ice rest against my upper lip until it tingled. Then I took the glass away. "How did you find me?"

The grin was still intact. "Heading for the door."

"Naturally," I answered. Not that I believed him. On the other hand, I really didn't give a damn.

"I'll be gone in the morning."

I felt better. "You've had a chance to ski, then?"

He hadn't.

By now, the upper lifts had been closed by the storm, so we made two runs down the Flying Mile on the lower section.

I'd never be a top skier, he told me afterwards, unless I quit enjoying it. I should attack every goddamn slope as if qualifying for the U.S. National Ski Team. I propped my skis and poles against the wooden rack and told him the U.S. National Ski Team was getting along well enough without me.

It was four-thirty. We avoided the lounge, picked up a couple of beers in the adjoining cafeteria, and plunked ourselves down at an empty table. It was beginning to feel like old times. He unzipped his yellow nylon jacket, hooked his goggles around his arm for safekeeping, and slopped beer into his glass.

The matching outfit looked good on him, expensive, nicely tailored. He'd worn pretty well for his thirty-eight years. A little graying at the temples, telltale lines around the mouth. I should talk. As kids in Westchester County, people often mistook us for one another, same height, same age, same coloring. Well, almost the same coloring. His fair skin blossomed into a rich deep tan come summer, while mine turned an ugly red. I envied him. My eyes were brown, his blue, and our temperaments varied as much. I'd taken the ups and downs of youth to heart while he treated them with indifference. Later he learned to use people like me. I guess I was aware of it, but he had still been my best friend.

He'd noticed a collection of black-and-white photographs in the hotel lobby, winter landscapes, ski scenes. My name was on them. I nodded over my beer. In college once I had taken a photo of him playing football. I'd caught him beautifully coming through the line. He'd never forgotten it. Same old touch, he told me now, but I was still a lousy businessman. Those blowups

3

would fetch twice the price. Taking photographs was part of my new image, I lied, neglecting to mention I'd since pawned my camera down in Montreal to buy cross-country skis.

Early last December I had wandered by Tremblant Lodge, eighty miles north of Montreal, near the village of St. Jovite, to find the hotel short of cross-country ski instructors. Management hired me out of desperation, even without the customary work permit. Now I was teaching wilderness survival as well. Three nights a week, half an hour after supper, in the Ping-Pong room. Gerry smiled. A smashing success? Of course. I invited him for tonight, guaranteeing his presence would double the usual attendance. We both laughed, bought more beer, and were well on our way to one hell of an evening when he spoiled it. I had a feeling he would. Sooner or later he'd bring up Sarah, and he did.

We had remembered something amusing about the past, I can't remember if it involved her or not, when his laughter suddenly dissolved into sobs. I couldn't believe it. I leaned forward, aware of the silent stares around us. He was weeping into his hands and muttering to himself. I caught broken phrases, a breakdown, fights, threats. The hands dropped, leaving behind a swollen tragic face. Now she was gone. How long ago? Three weeks, almost. He hadn't stopped looking for her. Then it struck me. Surely that wasn't why he was *here*! "You came to Tremblant thinking she was with me?" I watched the eyes close, the head nod. Jesus, I thought, the irony of it. I hadn't seen Sarah for years. I told him now, but he was off again, rambling on, something about being in too deep . . . if she only knew the danger she was in! I grabbed his arm, but he pulled away. *What* danger, I wanted to know, but his head sagged down onto his arms again.

I got the poor bastard outside, propped him up on a sheltered bench, and clomped off into the storm. It didn't take long to learn that Gerald Hope-Warden had been given one of the more exclusive cottages out back. Number twelve.

It was almost dark now. Skis were mostly gone from the racks outside the Chalet. The fresh air had done Gerry some good. He gave me a sheepish grin, apologized for screwing up, and wondered if I'd point him toward his cottage, wherever it was. I'd do one better, I said, and take him there.

Snow obliterated the path leading to the log cottages set back from the main complex. They were only fifty yards away, but the trek seemed endless in the storm. Finally I stopped to check my bearings, only to have Gerry complain lustily about my poor sense of direction. He belched and pushed by. Fighting the urge to let him go and find his own damn way, I followed. I couldn't see him now. I couldn't see anything. I yelled, took a few giant steps, and yelled again. Nothing. Well, not quite nothing. From somewhere I heard a sort of muffled blurp-blurping sound which I couldn't place.

I stumbled over him not long after, facedown, mostly buried. I chuckled, thinking he sure couldn't hold his liquor like the old days. Fine mess you've got us into, Ollie, I muttered, none too soberly myself, and knelt beside him. I nudged him, and when he didn't respond, I reached down into the snow, grabbed what turned out to be a shoulder, and pulled back hard. He came out of the snow then, rolled and flopped backward, almost into my lap. I glanced down. "Oh, my God," I whispered, because his face was gone. In its place was a pulpy mass of stringy flesh matted together with chunks of frozen, bloodstained snow.

2

The call woke me shortly before eight o'clock the next evening. I had been up all night and most of the day over Gerry's death and had only now managed a few hours' sleep.

"Stoney? Oh, thank God. Are you all right?" It was a woman's voice. "It's me, Sarah."

"Sarah!" Hearing her now was a shock, a voice out of the past. "Sarah," I shouted, propping myself up on my elbow. "Where are you?" The line crackled. "Sarah?"

"I can hear you, Stoney. I'm in New York, with my father-in-law. I've been away, but I'm home now. Was he . . . really murdered?"

I leaned back against the pillow, wondering what to say. "Yes, he was. Jesus, I'm sorry. But are you all right? Gerry was worried." I was trying to picture what she looked like now.

"I'm okay, really, Stoney." The line did funny things again. Then her voice: "Have they any idea who might have done it?"

"No, not that I know. Listen, Sarah, Gerry said you'd disappeared. Nobody knew where you were. So how did you find out he'd been killed?"

"A friend."

"And how'd you know to call me?"

"The story was in the afternoon papers. And on TV. They said you were with him. You of all people, Stoney. I don't understand. Why was he with you? Why was he killed? What's going on?" Her voice was going higher.

"Sarah!" I yelled into the sputtering phone. I heard muffled voices, then hers again. Calmer now. "I'm sorry, but I just can't believe it."

Not knowing what to say next, I opted for the usual "if-there's-anything-I-can-do . . ." and left it hanging.

"Yes." She paused. "Yes, there is. I have to talk to you, Stoney. You were the last one to see him alive. I hadn't talked to him for . . . it doesn't matter how long. And now . . . Could you please come down for the funeral? I would appreciate it so much."

"Look," I said, "maybe you could have someone down there send me the arrangements." I found myself hedging. "I'll see what I can do."

Her voice crackled in my ear. "Thank you, Stoney. I'm sorry to . . . Good-bye." The line went dead.

Sleep didn't come easily after that. Each time I closed my eyes, I found myself staring down at Gerry, or what was left of him. It had been late morning before someone had driven me over to the St. Jovite police station to sign the lengthy statement I'd made earlier and to identify the corpse. There hadn't been much to identify. Blood-spattered yellow nylon jacket, a few strands of hair. The rest, I wouldn't want to talk about. A grisly business. For the moment, I needed something even more than sleep. I needed a drink.

The winsome young thing at the reception desk intercepted my dash for the bar to press a small, solid brown envelope into my hands, confessing it had been left for me yesterday. In the confusion, she'd forgotten to pass it on. I assured her nothing could be that important, not even small brown envelopes, and continued my dash for the bar.

It was crowded, yet quiet. That suited me just fine. I waved to Gaston, the oversized French Canadian bartender, found an empty table, and was barely seated when a large cognac splashed down

6

before me. I raised the snifter and swallowed. The fiery amber liquid burned a hole clear down to my boots.

Next, the envelope.

I tipped the contents onto the table, a sheet of paper wrapped around what seemed to be those leatherette folders you associate with traveler's checks. I opened the paper to find it was a typewritten note from Gerry. An eerie feeling—reading a letter from a dead man.

Stoney,

You are probably reading this after I have left. No matter. What's important is this. I came looking for Sarah, but after asking around, I found you haven't been seen with anyone fitting her description. So much for my hunch. I had made other plans should this arise. It involves a favor. I'm in trouble—how much trouble, I don't know. But retaliation might involve Sarah. She is in danger, but I couldn't get it through her thick skull. Worse if anything happens to me. It's too complicated to explain now. You'll just have to believe me. And there's a further problem. Emotionally Sarah's in left field. I worry for her. She needs someone she can trust. Like you. You have never been far from her thoughts, despite what happened. Stoney, you are the only one I can turn to. Now, if you haven't already, look in the envelope, and then read on.

I looked inside the now-empty envelope, then realized he was referring to the traveler's checks. I chose one packet at random. Seconds later my hands were visibly trembling. There were five small folders containing checks of varying denominations. American currency. Ten thousand dollars. What spooked me was the signature on each upper-left corner. *My* signature.

These checks are for you. I did a little digging back in New York. I know you're broke, that Jane got the house, everything. Custody too. What in God's name did you do to be nailed with such lousy visiting rights? Hump the judge's housekeeper? And now about the checks. They were purchased with cash, making them only mildly counterfeit. The forgery cost me almost as much as the sum total, so they ought to be good. You'll validate them in the usual spot with your real signature, so what the hell?

7

Stoney, I'm asking you to find Sarah and see that she's safe. After that, keep in touch, okay? Please, don't let me down. Or her.

Gerry

It was madness. And so bloody unfair. A lot he'd ever cared about letting me down. But three days later I headed for New York.

3

I caught the early Tuesday morning flight from Montreal, leaving enough time at the other end to freshen up at my hotel and reach the funeral home by eleven. I hadn't counted on a delayed departure and a shortage of cabs at La Guardia. Besides, my timing was off. My contrary mind insisted on dredging up the past; Sarah had suddenly become a major distraction.

We had met in our early teens at a friend's cottage in Vermont. She was all legs, my weakness at the time, freckles, and brown eyes. Her name was Sarah Ann Hope. From Nattick, Massachusetts. She was a year or two younger than I was, looked a year or two older, and acted it. Sarah Anne knocked me out. She climbed trees, j-stroked a canoe, and loved to neck. With anybody. Someone else would introduce her to sex, but then, someone else would introduce me to sex. So we were even. Later came Harvard. Sarah was enrolled in design while Gerry and I took business admin. Sarah and I picked up where we left off, on a grassy knoll overlooking the Vermont cottage and Lake Champlain, leaving Gerry to exhaust himself with the prettiest coeds on campus. In our final year he quit playing the field and settled for a blond. That she happened to be Sarah Anne Hope made little difference to him. Nor, God knows, to her. Over the years, I put the hurt behind me. I fully intended leaving it there. Until now.

I arrived at the Burbery-MacLeod Funeral Home thirty minutes late to find the lobby wall-to-wall with three-piece suits. Dark grays and navy blues were in season. A worn sheepskin coat, turtleneck, and rumpled corduroy pants were not.

8

A nervous little man in a jet-black toupee that stuck out like a jet-black toupee appeared at my elbow.

I said, "I'm here for the Hope-Warden funeral."

He eyed me warily. "Ah, yes," he whispered, "we are running somewhat late, as you can see. . . ."

"Then I'll have a word with Mrs. Hope-Warden. She's expecting me."

He wrinkled his brow. "Ah. Ah, yes. And you are Mr. . . . ?"

"Stone."

Heads turned. Smiles. I tried to think of a Stone who turned heads. I couldn't.

". . . yes, Mr. Stone. If you would kindly wait here." He had no sooner disappeared than the two large oak doors off to the left opened. The chapel beyond was banked with flowers. We started moving forward.

I had almost reached the doors when those ahead suddenly shifted to one side. Two gents in their funeral best were escorting a forlorn little guy out of the chapel. He kept assuring them that he was a close friend of the family. He was also drunk, though from the looks of him he probably wouldn't have caused trouble if they'd have let him be. As the three came by, I stepped out and neatly slipped an arm around the old guy's shoulder.

"Well, well, Uncle George," I crooned, deftly turning him back toward the chapel. After all, a friend of the family is a friend of the family, even if he did smell like a bourbon factory. "Mrs. Warden will be so pleased that you could make it."

He gave me an owlish grin. "Uncle Hershel," he muttered. "Hershel Nesbitt."

I gestured for forgiveness. "Uncle Hershel, of course. It's been some time." I turned to our friends. "I'll look after him," I said, then quickly found two empty spots in the last row. Once settled, I looked around us.

The low-ceilinged chapel was packed. Corporate suits filled the pews shoulder to shoulder on either side of the main aisle. Beyond was an ornately carved wood railing, and beyond that the coffin of gleaming mahogany and brass handles. Flowers were everywhere. So was the morbid music playing over our heads. I couldn't see Sarah, and figured she was in the corridor with the family waiting for the service to begin. The family. On her side a mother and father, divorced long ago. On his, a mother who had been killed in a boating accident when Gerry was five or six, leaving Harold to raise his only son. I was trying to picture Sarah's mother and father when Hershel stirred beside

9

me. "They're waiting for Sarah," he said in a whisper loud enough to distract those around us. "I tried to tell them she wouldn't be here, but they wouldn't listen."

I sighed. "Okay, okay, let's just see how they handle it," I replied, only to find he was staring at me as if we hadn't been properly introduced. "What's the matter?" I asked.

The old man's eyes were bright, despite the dark hollows around them. "You're Stone, aren't you, son?" I nodded. He went on, "She told me to look for someone not like the others. Not like Hercules." Heads turned. I was about to shut him up when a hand touched me on the shoulder. One of our friends warned me "for the last time" that if I didn't keep the old buzzard quiet, we'd both be out on our ears.

As it turned out, Nesbitt knew what he was talking about. Sarah didn't appear when Harold Warden slipped silently in the side door of the chapel. He was still a tall, aristocratic man with a mane of white hair and tanned skin who looked a decade younger than his seventy years. She's late and the service has to begin without her, I reasoned, watching the family gather in front of the coffin. Harold, the minister, a woman, from her looks Sarah's mother, then her father, Andrew Hope, if I wasn't mistaken. It was their last name that Gerry had added to his own for hyphenated color: Hope-Warden. That Sarah had refused to be anything but "Sarah Warden" had always been his social thorn, according to the gossip columnists. Six solemn-faced men in dark suits, whom I took to be the pallbearers, stood off to one side. But no Sarah. As the music swelled into a slow rendition of "Nearer, My God, to Thee," I poked Hershel Nesbitt. His eyes popped open.

"What the hell's going on?" I hissed. "Where *is* Sarah?" The boys were back. I didn't wait for Nesbitt's answer. "Come on," I said, "let's you and I get out of here." I wasn't really in a mood for a funeral anyway.

The Nesbitt Art Gallery was housed in a small, cluttered shop off West Houston in Greenwich Village, sandwiched like an afterthought between two massive brick warehouses. The cabby and I carried Nesbitt inside, found a well-worn couch in a curtained-off back section, and stretched him out.

Before he'd passed out, Nesbitt had told me Sarah had been in Colorado when Gerry was killed. She was back there now, having left yesterday morning. Where in Colorado? Nesbitt's answer was one long snore, which left me frustrated and pacing about the gallery thinking that surely to God she could've stayed in town long enough to bury her husband. Besides, what about me?

As I scribbled a note to Hershel saying I was off to check into my hotel and what about a late dinner, something else occurred to me. I needed money. I was close to being broke. What funds I had would pay for a hotel room, with just enough left over for return air fare. As for the traveler's checks, carrying them with me was bad-enough; cashing them was forgery. Then I remembered a modest account I'd kept for emergencies. I'd never closed it and thought that with any luck it might have some loose change floating around in it. Worth a try.

The account was with Greenwich Savings, Fifty-third at Madison, four blocks from where I had worked in the family business. I told the teller I wanted to close out my account. The number, she asked, without looking up. I couldn't recall it. She glanced at me. Prim, bespectacled. The name, then? I told her. I watched her fingers flash across the computer keyboard, caught a slight irritation in her eyes, and saw her repeat the process. Then a third time. Finally she glared at me as if it were my fault and hurried away. Well, maybe it was my fault. The account could be empty, or worse, overdrawn. I was ready to skip it when I spotted Miss Prim quick-stepping it back with reinforcements, Edwin O. Blake, the assistant manager, who blushed as he told me I had one great sense of humor. I thought as much.

I was ushered into a glass-paneled office and waved into a chair. Only when Blake was seated behind his desk did he press the issue. Had I indeed told the teller, Miss Watkins, to close out the account and pay me the residue in cash? I had indeed. Blake, watching me closely, giggled and fired off, "Mr. Stone, you must be kidding," leaning across the desk to push a button on his intercom. He wanted the Philip A. Stone file, he said flatly, then sat back.

The statement arrived. Blake shoved it across the table. A glance at the long column of figures spread over six pages was enough to convince me the account wasn't mine. I told him so. His face went a pasty white. He aimed a finger again at the intercom and changed his mind. He had me give him a sample of my signature, then launched himself out the door under full sail. Meanwhile I picked up the statement to study it more closely. The name at the top of the first sheet was mine. Stone, Philip Andrew. The address was deleted. After "Business Address" was "Finland House Building," but it was crossed out with a

_ 11

notation, "See file data." Next, the deposit and withdrawal columns. Very busy. I flipped to the last page and ran a finger down to the final balance. The account was credited with more than a million dollars.

My first reaction was blind panic. The second was a little more realistic. My name must have been cross-filed with someone else's account. I looked up. Blake was in the doorway clutching a thick file. He was all smiles.

For what seemed hours we pored over the accounts, sifting through documents, letters, statements of quarterly earnings, taxes paid to the Internal Revenue Service, debits, credits, receipts of generous donations to museums, art galleries, the Red Cross. Among these receipts was one for fifty thousand dollars assuring me a life membership in something called the Hercules Foundation. Hershel Nesbitt had mentioned that name at the funeral. It didn't make sense. But then, neither did all this money. And how could I tell the Greenwich Savings assistant manager that this was somebody's idea of a joke? I'd have to explain how my signature got on *every* document. The perfect forgery. Don't ask *me* how they got there, I could hear myself saying to Blake, 'Ask a dead man.' What the hell had Gerry been trying to do, set up a Philip A. Stone Charitable Fund? Not goddamn likely.

Blake was holding out a letter. Another signed by me. It was dated six weeks ago and outlined how I wanted the account handled, what I expected from the bank, and so on. It mentioned that because I was traveling extensively until further notice, the bank would be furnished with a contact, should any confusion result from the account transactions. I pointed to this portion of the letter. Blake assured me the man had called subsequently and left an address where he could be reached. I interrupted. "You've had no reason then to contact Mr. . . ." I let my voice trail off, hoping Blake might fill in the rest.

Blake smiled. "Gerhard Hegler? Why no, no Mister Stone."

We were finished. I took several more stabs at finding out who this Hegler guy was, but didn't. Out of curiosity I asked Blake how much money had originally been left in the account. He shuffled through the papers and drew out a single sheet. The total had been twenty-six dollars, eleven cents. I grunted, dug out a packet of Gerry's traveler's checks, and signed enough to give me six hundred dollars.

12

4

By six o'clock I had checked into the Algonquin Hotel on West Forty-fourth Street. I was given a Cardgard to Room 204, that slip of plastic that is quickly replacing room keys these days, as well as the bag I'd dropped off en route to the funeral. Clutching both, I threaded my way nostalgically through the crowd and climbed aboard the elevator.

My room was high-ceilinged in the European tradition, and comfortably old-fashioned. Once free of my overnight canvas bag and sheepskin coat, I placed a call to room service, stripped, and poured myself a hot bath. Naturally enough, I was climbing into it when the martini arrived. Carrying it back to the bathroom, I found a spot for it in the soap dish and sank down into the hot water, then closed my eyes.

It had been quite a day. No Sarah, but I was rich, in a perverse sort of way. The money intrigued me, as did Sarah's disappearing act. I tried to connect the two but gave up quickly and sipped on my martini instead. A million dollars. Of course I couldn't touch it. Assistant bank managers aside, the money wasn't mine and I wasn't quite ready to add embezzlement to my list of misdemeanors, which for the moment began and ended with forgery. But one had to eat, which reminded me of the note I'd left Hershel Nesbitt regarding dinner. Poor old soul. I remember thinking at that time he didn't have the sad, gaunt face of a steady drinker, despite the dark eyes. I wondered now if he had merely been fortifying himself for the chore of attending the funeral.

The martini glass was empty, the bathwater cool. As I toweled myself dry and ambled into the bedroom. I tried to figure out why in God's name Sarah hadn't shown up. We'd meant a lot to each other once, especially during those teenage years when everything seemed a crisis. We'd been buddies, not just friends. She was bright, fun, dependable, at times resolutely stubborn. Not the Sarah who'd later walk away from a husband's funeral. Unless she'd changed. How would I know? In fifteen years our paths had crossed only once, which hardly gave me license now to judge her. Then let things be, I told myself. She'll work it out her own way.

I called Hershel. His line was busy. Next I ordered up another martini and searched the phone book for the Hercules Foundation. It was't there. Directory assistance didn't have it either. What about calling my ex-wife? Jane Muir now. She prided herself on slaving her buns off for any outfit accepting volunteers, a work ethic you could easily trace back to Junior Leaguers. Jane knew every organization along this line and would probably know Hercules well. But I decided no. Phoning her meant rekindling a hassle neither of us needed.

Meanwhile, my second martini arrived. I sipped on it and tried Hershel again. Still busy. Directory assistance's batting average hadn't improved; it had no listing for a Gerhard Hegler. This brought to mind *my* batting average. My score was worse. No Sarah, a whopping bank account I couldn't account for, and traveler's checks forged, ridiculous though it seemed, with my own signature. Whatever was going on, I didn't want any part of it. So it wasn't hard to come to the conclusion, as I finished off my martini, that Philip A. Stone would be on the early-morning flight back to Montreal. And Uncle Hershel would be the first to know.

I finally reached him around eleven o'clock that evening. He sounded somewhat better, not much, and apologized for his morning's atrocious behavior—his words, not mine. He'd yet to find my note, and when I said my good-byes, he didn't take them lightly. "And what about Sarah?" I chose the wrong tack by insisting she was a big girl now. "She's a troubled woman, Mr. Stone," he fired back, "and if I weren't such an old man, I'd be out in Colorado seeing if I could be of some help. Isn't that what friends are for?"

"Listen," I said, "I'm the friend who came here because she asked me to. She's the friend who couldn't be bothered to wait for me."

"Please, Mr. Stone, you've come this far . . ."

I could feel myself giving in again. "Where can I find her?"

5

It was early when I crossed the empty lounge and entered the Algonquin's Rose Room. Its only occupant, seated at a table near the far wall, glanced up from his plate and waved his fork. "Breakfast, Mr. Stone?"

A waiter appeared, noticed me, and nodded cheerily. I pointed to what's-his-name and sauntered over.

"I'm Jim Agostino," he said, finishing a mouthful of eggs and bacon. He thrust out his hand but I waited for him to discover it still held a knife. He smiled and said, "Sit down," motioning me toward a chair opposite him. When I didn't, he added, "I'm with the Federal Bureau of Investigation." I sat down.

He was in his early forties, maybe less, with black curly hair, deep-set eyes, and a nose pushed to one side. His rumpled gray suit fit my mental picture of what FBI agents should wear, but possibly I'd watched too many late-night shows.

"How was the funeral?"

I looked at him warily. "Fine," I said, "just fine."

"I hear you were with the poor bastard when he got it."

I nodded. The waiter stopped at our table. I pointed at the agent's plate. "The same," I said.

"You only came for the funeral."

"Yes."

"And now you're heading back. To Canada."

I didn't answer.

The agent leaned forward, cradling his coffee in both hands. "Mr. Stone, we have a booking for you. La Guardia to Dorval Airport, in Montreal. Eight-fifty-five. Air Canada."

I sat back. "I don't even hear so much as a 'please'?"

"You won't." The grin was as lopsided as the nose, but the combination gave Agostino a certain charm.

"I won't?"

He shook his head. "To be truthful, Mr. Stone, I doubt if what we're doing to you is strictly legal, but it is in your best interest."

"I'll call my lawyer."

15

"Sure. From Dorval. You've been working illegally up there, but we've arranged with Immigration Canada for a work permit for you. It's good as long as the ski season lasts. You have your passport?" I nodded. "Show it at the immigration office at Dorval. They'll give you the permit."

I was getting annoyed. "You talk as if all this is a foregone conclusion. What if I decide to stay?"

Agostino sighed as he put down his cup. "Suit yourself. We'd probably charge you with, say, cashing forged documents, something like that." He was watching me closely. I kept my eyes on his, though I could easily have brought up last night's martinis. "However, if you leave now, we wouldn't do anything."

I said nothing.

He went on. "Look, Stone, do yourself a favor. Forget about our little chat, okay? Go back to Tremblant. What's this, the middle of February? You've got a good two months of snow." He opened his mouth and shoved in a large piece of bacon, following it with a forkful of egg. If he was through, I wasn't.

"What the hell is this all about?" I asked. "I've been minding my own business."

Agostino grunted as he chewed. When there was enough room in his mouth, he said, "Bullshit. You turn up at a funeral where you weren't invited in the first place."

I cut him off. "Sarah Warden asked me to come."

Agostino grinned across the table at me. "She wasn't even there, Stone. But let me continue. You disrupt an important funeral by clowning around with a poor little drunk, then insist on dragging him out of there in the middle of the bloody service. And *that*, I take it, is minding your own business."

The waiter was coming over to our table with a large glass full of lumpy, brown, vile-looking liquid. He placed it down in front of me. I could have sworn he was doing his best not to smile. "What's this?" I asked.

Agostino answered. He sat back, pushing his own plate away from him. "Fresh prune juice. The pits are left in. To give it body. You're having what I ordered, remember?" He stood up and slipped into a weathered leather coat I'd noticed draped over a nearby chair.

I watched in silence as he began doing up the buttons. How the hell had this—what was his name?—Agostino come across the traveler's checks? He hadn't mentioned them specifically, but it was no subtle hint that he meant business. How much more did he know? He must have seen the confusion written all over

16

my face, because he said, "Now, look, Mr. Stone, we're not out for blood, just a little cooperation." His smile showed a slight gap between his front teeth, to go along with his busted nose. "Enjoy yourself back in the Laurentians," he went on. "I might drop up there one of these days to see how you're getting along." The smile widened. "Any excuse for me to get back on skis." He turned away, but stopped near the white pillar in the middle of the room. "By the way, about your friend Hershel Nesbitt," I stiffened. "He was found beaten up in his gallery last night, around midnight."

Jesus, I thought, pushing myself slowly away from the table, it couldn't have come long after we'd talked. "Is he all right?" Agostino shrugged and continued on. "And why Hershel?" I yelled after him.

"How should I know?" he shouted back over his shoulder. "Maybe somebody doesn't like the company he keeps." I stood up to follow. "Don't forget La Guardia, Mr. Stone, eight-fifty-five, which doesn't leave you much time." His voice trailed him out the dining-room door. "Pick up your ticket here in the lobby, compliments of the FBI."

Air Canada's jetliner flight to Montreal left on time, taking with it my canvas bag but not me. Meanwhile I was scrambling aboard United's morning flight to Chicago, then Denver. All during the flight I tried to convince myself that the FBI agent had been making suggestions, not threats. Besides, this little detour was for an old man who couldn't make the trip himself. At least that's what I told myself.

6

The speed of the Corvair 537 slackened as it banked to the right, slipped over the snowbound ridge, and dropped to the runway spread out on the small plateau below. Then the scut-scut sound of its tires striking the frozen tarmac. Above my head a loudspeaker crackled. A voice announced our arrival at Yampa Valley Airport, serving Hayden and Steamboat Springs.

Of the dozen or so passengers on board, I was the only one who got off at Yampa. The others were going on to Aspen and

17

Vail. I stood at the corner of the airport building watching the Corvair trundle back down the runway, then turn and pause. The plateau seemed even smaller from here, the mountains hemming it in on all four sides. I had a funny feeling that there wasn't enough room for such a takeoff. The plane had used up a good half of the strip in seconds and still showed no signs of lift-off.

"Looks like the little bugger'll never make it," drawled a voice beside me. I grunted, but didn't look around. My eyes were glued to the Corvair. "Yep," the voice went on, "she'll get real skittish any moment and lift her pretty little arse off as neat as . . . there." Air showed beneath the belly as it shot into a steep climb that carried it well clear of the far ridge. I watched until it was swallowed up by the intense blue sky.

"Looking for transport, mister?" The same voice. I turned to find myself staring at Yampa Valley's answer to the lean, rangy cowboy: tall, broad shoulders, slim hips, battered stetson, and grin spread wider than three states. "Steamboat, huh? Any hotel in particular?"

Yes, I told him, Steamboat would be fine. No particular hotel. No luggage? No luggage. No skis? No skis. Only a fool comes to a ski resort in winter without booking ahead. This conversation went on even before we ambled by the luggage room, into the main waiting area, and outside again past a chain-link fence to the parking lot. I might have asked why we hadn't just walked around the building, but didn't bother. It had been that kind of day, two different airlines, an hour stopover in Chicago, a four-hour wait in Denver, and by New York time it was close to my bedtime. Or felt like it. Finally he stopped to ask if I had any preferences in hotels, and I took a stab at Sarah's hotel, the Thunderhead Inn. "Nice," was his only comment.

His name was Carl Henry "Bo" Jacobs, and his taxi the eighth wonder of the world. It had its beginnings as a Dodge limousine until, as he put it, "My friends decided it wasn't impressive enough, so they welded a custom Merc body into the middle of it." He grinned and patted it proudly. "Hop in."

I had six doors to choose from—along one side alone. I picked the seat next to the driver. Jacobs got in and slapped the steering wheel out of sheer affection. "But they weren't satisfied," he went on, talking about his friends, "so they shoved a jesus-big eight-cylinder Caddy engine under the hood, slapped on a couple of coats of black paint to hold her together, then turned her loose." I watched as he thrust the key into the ignition and gave it a sharp forward twist. All eight cylinders exploded at once,

18

sending a shiver down its entire length. "That was eight years ago," he yelled over the racket, "and she hasn't quit since."

In the next fifteen minutes Carl Henry Jacobs added a whole new dimension to the word "terror" as we dropped down into the Yampa Valley. Curves, icy patches, railroad tracks, potholes, all absorbed with the accelerator flat on the floor. Meanwhile, I was given a boisterous, irreverent verbal introduction to the local inhabitants, to Steamboat Springs, the Yampa Valley, Rabbit Ears Pass, and downtown Howelson Hill, site of America's first ski jump. He spoke of the Sleeping Giant ridge, the infamous Hole-in-the-Wall Gang slipping in from a Wyoming battle in the 1890's, of the late Buddy Werner, the skiing legend, killed by a cascading avalanche in the Swiss Alps, 1964, of the shock later on when the citizens of Steamboat woke one morning to find its beloved Storm Mountain had, by act of council, been renamed Mt. Werner, causing a rift among townsfolk that still lives on.

We hit the flats. I jokingly asked what was holding us back. Jacobs roared with hurt pride. "A goddamn stove and fridge, that's what, in behind us." He was right. I could see them in the space behind the rows of seats, lying on their sides. Jacobs went on, "I couldn't wrassle those mothers by myself, so I'm figuring on settling you in somewhere, which shouldn't be a problem. I know this town. Then I'll pick up a couple of guys at the hotel to help me." They were for an old widow out at Buffalo Pass. When I mentioned seeing a highway marker pointing off to Buffalo Pass, he nodded. "Yup, that's the place, all right. Ten miles out into nowhere." It took me the next three miles to convince him that he and I could deliver the stuff. Which we did.

It was dark when we finally pulled up outside what Jacobs described as his "favorite watering hole," the stolid Harbor Hotel on Steamboat's main street, Lincoln Avenue. We clomped into the dingy paneled bar where Jacobs insisted first on introducing me to every living soul in the place, then buying the drinks. The beer flowed. Soon we were "Bo" and "Stoney." I kept reminding him about my need for a hotel, but he waved it aside until I couldn't give a damn. Neither could his friends, who were busy arguing about the price of beef, the invasion of sheep, the cost of feed. Bo and I discovered we had many things in common: a lack of enthusiasm for parking meters, politics, taxes; a love of the outdoors (I'd found a soulmate; like me, Bo believed in fishing for trout in streams rather than lakes), our

19

love of autumn. Of fresh air. A few more beers and nostalgia caught up with me. I rambled on about New York, the good times, the frozen rinks, the hot dry summers spent on my uncle's farm in Vermont. Carl Henry couldn't believe it. I was a farmer? Sure, if being a farmer between the ages of seven and eleven counted. Hell, he said, once a farmer, always a farmer. We drank to it. Then we got around to him.

Born here in the Yampa Valley, Bo had quit chasing an education in ranch management at Colorado State, in Fort Collins, to settle down on the abandoned family homestead with his wife, Betty, a Denver-born nurse. They raised kids, two girls, two boys, and cattle, at last count several hundred head. He was also part-owner in a local snowmobile franchise, a small downtown motel, and owned outright a one-vehicle limo service. And what about me? Well, I said, I came here tracking down an old lady friend.

I wanted to go on, but by now my mouth and my brain weren't on the same wavelength. It must have been obvious, because Bo patted me on the shoulder and told me not to worry. "You may not know this, Stoney, but a few drinks at this here altitude can do strange things to you flatlanders. Give it a couple of days and you'll be drinking me under the table. For now, I figure we've got about twenty minutes to get you a bed."

I awoke to hear a toilet flushing. I was in bed, fully clothed. Struggling to pull myself up against the solid headboard, I called out, "Hello!" A door opened and a pert young face under long bleached bangs appeared, then the rest of her tucked neatly into faded jeans and a denim shirt. She was smiling.

"Hi, mister. I'm Anna, hotel staff. I came in here earlier to tidy your room. I didn't want to disturb you, but my lunch break is soon and I wanted to clean your bathroom at least." She made a face. "It must have been some night, huh?"

I tried to smile, then looked past the wood railing leading down into a small living room on a slightly lower level than the bed. In the far corner was a metal fireplace and opposite it a large glass window filled with sunlight. I could almost hear my eyeballs creak as I shifted them back to her. She said, "I could bring you some aspirin . . ."

"No . . . thanks, Anna," I said, watching her move toward the door. "There is one thing, though. What hotel is this?"

She laughed then and her eyes twinkled. "The Thunderhead Inn, of course. God, you must have had some night. Didn't anyone warn you ·about the altitude?" I closed my eyes, and

20

when I opened them, she was gone. My brain ticked over. The Thunderhead. Sarah's hotel, I thought, as the phone beside me started ringing.

"Stoney!" bellowed a voice that sent shock waves clear down to my toes. 'It's Bo, Bo Jacobs. How're you farin'?"

"Well, I'm dressed," I said, glancing down at my socks. "Look, Bo, I'm sorry about last night . . ."

"Shit, Stoney, *you're* sorry! Betty's been on my back all morning for not taking better care of you."

"Anyway it was fun while it lasted." My head was pounding. "How the hell did you ever get me into the Thunderhead?"

There was a pause. "You really want to know? We carried you in the front door. Me and some of the boys from the hotel. You told me in the limo that's where you wanted to stay."

"You're kidding. Jesus, the last thing I remember was hanging on to the limousine."

"That's when your lights went out. By the way, how's your friend?"

"I'll let you know. When I find her."

"Fair enough." He paused. "Now, none of your horseshit, but I had my son Billy run a jeep up to the hotel parking lot for you. He was told to leave the key under the seat. I hope he did. Anyway, it's old, the canvas top is ripped, and you can't see through the plastic side windows because they've yellowed. But the little bugger goes like a fart in a hurricane. And what's left of the paint is original army green. It's yours while you're here." I started to thank him. "Forget it," he said, "you're a friend. And if you can keep tomorrow night open, fine. Betty and me and some of our friends get together at the Harbor Hotel every Friday, after bowling. She wants to meet you. To apologize for *my* behavior. Keep in touch huh?" The line clicked. I looked at my watch. It was noon. I dialed the front desk, asking if Mrs. Sarah Warden was registered in the hotel. I was told politely to hold on. The seconds ticked by. At last a voice said, "I'm sorry, but Mrs. Warden checked out last week. To return to New York." I muttered "Thanks" and hung up. I swore to myself, knowing it was possible she hadn't come back here at all.

Not to be deterred, I spent the next hour working my way alphabetically down the list of hotels I'd found in the Yellow Pages. I had two left when I reached the Village Inn. Yes, Mrs. Sarah Warden was staying there. Room 631. I took a deep breath as my call was transferred to the switchboard operator. I repeated the number. The phone rang once, then twice more. After half a dozen rings the operator suggested trying the Robber's Roost bar. She wasn't there either. About to let it go at that, I asked where I'd find the Village Inn. She asked where I was staying. I told her. She chuckled. "We're the tall building just across the square from you, sir."

With this settled, I felt better, though no one told my headache. Fresh air, a look around the resort, was what I needed, but first I removed the packets of traveler's checks I'd pinned for safekeeping in the two inside pockets of my sheepskin coat, shoved all but one in a Thunderhead Inn stationery envelope provided for guests, wrote my name and room number across it, and dropped it off at the main desk. I stayed around until it reached the safe, then stepped outside.

It was a beautiful day. The sun was bright; I could already feel its warmth against my face. As I walked out from under the cantilevered overhang of the hotel entrance, I found myself staring up at the mountain which climbed straight up to a cloudless blue sky.

I toured this new complex called Steamboat Village, removed from the old town of Steamboat Springs by four or five miles. Here stores, shops, and bars catered exclusively to the skier. Hotels like the Thunderhead Inn and Village Inn gave its clientele easy access to the many lifts scattered along the base of Mount Werner, itself laid open by a myriad of trails and slopes twisting their way down its side.

I did a bit of shopping too, picking up some shaving gear, undershorts, turtlenecks, Levi's, and a few other things. Then a small leather suitcase and a pair of Justin cowboy boots, with walking heels. Back at my hotel room, I shaved for the first time in twenty-four hours and lit a fire in the small fireplace. Only then did I phone the Village Inn. Still no answer from Room 631. I left a message where I could be reached.

I spent the early evening hauling logs from the balcony to fuel my small fireplace, or dozing on the couch. By nine-thirty hunger got the best of me and I slipped down to the hotel dining room to eat my way through snails cooked in garlic and roast duckling smothered in orange sauce. By eleven I was ready to tackle the local nightlife.

First stop was the Robber's Roost. It was packed, raucous, and fun. But then, so was the Hole-in-the-Wall, the Sundance, and somewhere down the line, Cassidy's. At the Whiskey Barrel I bumped into a smiling Anna, the room maid, who didn't recognize me at first, "because I've never seen you standing," she shouted in my ear.

"And I've never seen you in a dress," I yelled back in hers. It was calico and cut low. She was drinking a Coors. I joined her. Like so many others who flocked into the Colorado ski resorts, she had dropped her winter semester, in this case at a Nebraska university, to work the hotel circuit, spending every free moment skiing. "That is, when I'm not dancing." I asked her about nightspots I might have missed. She told me several of her favorites, adding that if I was heading into town, not to miss the Cave Inn, on the highway. She had a couple of hours to kill before her boyfriend finished working the bar, and suggested coming along so I wouldn't get lost. I declined her offer, assuring her that she'd have more fun right here. Giggling, she kissed me on the cheek. "See you in the morning, Mr. Stone."

The jeep was everything Bo Jacobs promised—old, drafty, forlorn. It brought back memories. The two years I'd spent in the army back in the sixties, memories best forgotten. It came complete with its own snowdrift piling up behind the driver's seat, directly below the tear in the canvas. I found the key under the seat and slipped it into the ignition on the dashboard. One twist and I found myself sitting behind the wheel of the noisiest jeep in Colorado.

The Cave Inn was just that, a grotto of simulated rock made dingy and foreboding by a flood of funk-blue light. I found a stand-up bar. By feel.

The place was packed. And noisy. A fresh blast of disco rock broke through the room and I was swept up by a bunch rushing for the dance floor. Just short of it I broke loose. I was lifting the Coors to my lips when through the crowd I saw Sarah Anne Warden.

I caught the flash of her long blond hair, the closed eyes, and the parted lips before she disappeared among the other dancers. I saw her again, closer now. Perspiration was running down her neck and between her breasts, only partially covered by a loose denim shirt. Jeans clung to her thighs and buttocks as her body undulated to the beat of the music. Jesus, she was still beautiful, though hardly the woman I'd expected to find in light of what had happened.

The next dance was a slow number. Sarah's partner was a young guy maybe in his early twenties. He was tall, tanned, and solid. The two of them hardly moved as they danced, arms

23

wrapped tightly around each other, their bodies and faces pressed close.

The music stopped. I watched them pause, then pull reluctantly apart.

A few minutes later I'd worked my way around to the far side, where I spotted them sitting with friends at a table well back from the dance floor. I was only a matter of yards away when her head bobbed up and our eyes met. I smiled. As if on reflex, she smiled too, then quickly looked away. A pause, and suddenly her eyes swung back and the mouth dropped open. "Stoney!" she screamed and, jumping up, scrambled between the chairs and into my arms.

We held each other tight. She was trembling, and when we drew back her eyes were brimmed with tears. "Philip Stone," she whispered, "it's so good to see you. You will never know how much." The music started. "Let's dance," she said, taking my hand. It was another slow song. I let go, pulled off my coat, and dropped it over an empty chair. With a strange smile, Sarah took the beer out of my hands and set it on a table.

Sarah drifted into my arms and I felt her hand slip high up across my shoulders. Our cheeks touched briefly, as did our hips. She was warm, moist, sensual. She pulled away slightly. "Stoney, I'm sorry about New York. I just couldn't stay." Her eyes had tiny crow's feet in the corners, the face deeply tanned.

"You look beautiful," I said, "for someone in mourning."

She gave a sudden sharp laugh, and pulled me close. "The same old Stoney," she murmured in my ear. Then she changed the subject. "You look good, even mildly attractive. You'd been putting on weight the last time I saw you."

The music stopped. I half-expected her to start back to the table, but instead she stood beside me, holding my hand. She was looking across the floor. I followed her gaze. It had stopped at the kid. "What do you think of him?" she asked.

I didn't answer. I was looking at the striking woman the kid was obviously sharing a joke with. She was thirty-five, maybe, brunette, and was laughing now with dark eyes that brightened her whole face.

"He's definitely your type," I said at last. "Tall, lean, athletic." I quit before I got to "a spitting image of the young Gerry Warden."

Sarah swung back to me. "Well, aren't you going to say it? 'My, my, isn't he about half your age?' "

24

I caught something terribly vulnerable in her look and shrugged. "I really hadn't noticed."

The music again. Her arm tightened around my neck, and as her cheek touched mine she said, "Apart from your macabre sense of humor, Philip Stone, you are still very sweet."

"You're only seeing my good side," I answered. My instinct was to be gentle. She gave me the impression of delicate china, the kind that cracks for no reason, just when it's looking most beautiful. "For instance, I could say I'm worried about you and I'm not alone." I felt her stiffen, and in the process swung her against the next couple. In avoiding them further, I stepped on Sarah's toe.

She said, "Ouch." Then, "Now, *that* feels like old times." I eased her gently away from me, but she averted her eyes.

"Don't change the subject. Your old friend Hershel Nesbitt feels the same. He thinks you're in deep trouble. That's partly why I'm here." She said nothing. "Gerry was worried too. He wanted . . ."

A hand touched my arm. The kid was standing beside us, partly annoyed, partly hurt. Sarah pulled eagerly away from me. She wrapped her arms around him and introduced us. "Philip, this is Terry Samuels. Terry, this is Philip Stone, an old friend." "Nice to meet you." "Yes, nice to meet you, too. You're itching to dance with Sarah, I suppose." "Yes, yes, thank you, ah, sir."

My God.

Music, rock, bodies, suddenly exploded around us. I ducked for the safety of the tables and dropped into an empty chair next to my coat. When I reached to retrieve my beer from the table, I found the same woman, opposite, watching me with mild curiosity. She looked somewhat out of place in a soft gray sweater and matching slacks, though she was just as beautiful up close. She smiled. I grinned back. "Hi," I yelled. She said something I missed, so I leaned across the table. "I'm a friend of Sarah's. Philip Stone."

She looked surprised. "I am also a friend of Sarah," she shouted back. "I am Monique Brosseau. And you are who? Philippe?"

"Yes, I am Philip. Or 'Philippe,' if you wish." I liked the way she pronounced it. "You're French, no?"

She nodded vigorously. "I am French, yes. Come, you sit beside me. The music is very loud."

25

I shook my head. "Sorry, I can't hear you. The music is very loud . . ." We both laughed.

The table was littered with beer bottles and empty glasses. We decided to find less mess and more quiet by retiring to a small bar deep in the recesses of the "cave." Over beer, her preference for the moment, I asked what a Frenchwoman was up to here in the wilds of Colorado. Monique had been to New York on business, seeking markets for French glass products, when she had a sudden urge to see the American West and improve her English.

Monique explained that she and Sarah had met in the Denver Airport, during the customary wait for the Steamboat flight. Two women traveling by themselves, they soon discovered they shared similar interests, in the arts, travel. When was this? About a month ago. To Monique, Sarah seemed in need of a friend.

"And so did I, Philippe," she went on. "Sarah had reservations at one hotel and I at another, but we found they were not far apart. Suddenly one day she was gone and I thought, well, that is friendship in America. Here today and, boom, gone tomorrow." Monique smiled and lifted her glass. "Then she was back and I knew something terrible had happened. But she wouldn't tell me."

So I did. "She needs a good friend like you," then, I added. "She seems to have found more than one."

"You mean Terence?" she said, tilting her head to one side. "He is a nice boy, very charming. So are his friends. Do you know about them?" I didn't. "They are students from the University of Colorado, in, where is it, Boulder? Yes. They are here to compete in ski-jumping on Saturday against teams from colleges in Utah and Wyoming. Sarah met Terence the night she returned from New York. They have been very close since."

It was intermission when we returned to the others. Taking me by the arm, Sarah introduced me to Terry's three companions and their dates, local girls. I ordered a round of drinks, and sitting down beside Monique, found myself talking to the kid, Collins, on my other side. I asked if booze and late nights were part of the training program. His face broke into a grin. "Are you kidding, mister? If the coach caught us here, he'd have our balls for bookends." He paused to glance down the table toward Terry and the others. "Hell, no, this is our last fling. Tomorrow we knuckle under. The goddamn competition is Saturday." My sentiments exactly. It wasn't hard to guess who'd talked the guys into meeting the women here.

The evening was beginning to sour. Pushing my beer aside, I stood up to wish everyone good night and good luck. Sarah tore herself away from necking with Terence to blow me a kiss. As I reached for my coat, Monique grabbed my arm, but her words were drowned out by the music, which had started again. I leaned in close to her, aware that I was filling my lungs with the musky scent of her perfume. "Do you want a lift?" I shouted over the din. She nodded. So I grabbed up her sheepskin coat from a chair and swung back to the others. Sarah and Terry were already dancing. Monique and I waved, which brought a grin from Sarah, who made a little "tsk-tsk" gesture with her fingers. Monique turned quickly to me. "What does this mean, Philippe?" she asked, making the same motion with her fingers. I laughed out loud. "It just means that Sarah is up to one of her little games. It's called Mix and Match." From the puzzled look on Monique's face, I knew she didn't understand.

I was dozing off for the umpteenth time in one of the Village Inn's deep leather chairs when Sarah and Terry came plowing in through the front door. The clock on the reception desk showed it was four A.M. Terry saw me first and stopped. "What does he want?" he asked Sarah. I pulled myself slowly out of the chair and pointed toward the elevators, away from the watchful eye of the night desk clerk.

We reached the elevators. Sarah was leaning on Samuels, her eyes fixed on me. She was drunk.

I said, "I'll take her up, Terry," and pushed the button. "You can wait for me here. I won't be long." He looked confused.

Sarah's arms tightened around him. "He's coming up to my room."

I ignored her. "Tell me, Terry, how many nights have you violated curfew? Two? Three? And what if you get caught, just once? Let me guess. The shit hits the fan, huh? In other words, you break curfew once, and you're off the team. *If* you're caught." I waited, watching his hands clench. The color was draining from his face. "You're staying in this complex?" I asked, my voice softening.

Sarah answered. "No, in town. The Rabbit Ears Motel. Opposite the Hot Springs Pool."

I pulled the key from my pocket and handed it to him. "There's an old jeep parked outside. Start it up, and I'll be right down." Sarah reached up and kissed him on the lips, whispering

27

she would see him tomorrow. Then she let him go. He left without looking back.

"You really are a bastard," she said, once we were on the elevator. She swayed against me and held on. "Don't be hard on him."

"*Me* hard on him." I laughed. "What about you? Jesus, have you ever seen those jumps young Samuels flies off? They're killers, Sarah. The kid needs all his mental faculties, his concentration, to say nothing of physical strength, to make it down in one piece. So he breaks all the rules, even drags his friends into it, just because he's infatuated with you. And you say I'm not to be hard. . . ." The elevator stopped, the doors slid open.

Sarah was just as messy as she'd been in college. A tailored ski outfit in bright yellow had been abandoned on one of the two double beds, along with a turtleneck, socks, and underclothes. Sarah sat on the other bed, her legs drawn up, her head resting on her knees, clutching a glass half-filled with straight Scotch. She'd been a light drinker when I'd known her. But then, hadn't we all. She watched me as I sat down beside her on the bed. A glint came into her eyes. "How was Monique?" she asked.

I shook my head slowly. "I brought her back here to the hotel, we had a nightcap in the Sundance, danced a few bars, and I dropped her off at the elevators."

She made a face. "You disappoint me. I remember seven years ago when you—"

"Let's talk about you," I cut in, wanting to get through to her. "Samuels must know you're a week-old widow. What does he think? Does he know you're going down the pipe, breaking up into pieces a little at a time, even willing to settle for something as short-lived as an orgasm, if it shuts out reality? Or are you just going through the motions, Sarah? Dysfunction. Isn't that the word for it?" I was watching her carefully, hoping to break through, but she just sat there sipping the Scotch, her eyes vacant. I could feel the kid down in the jeep, tearing himself apart, wondering what we were doing together. So I went back at her.

"Sarah, listen to me. Something is eating you from the inside. You're running from it, but unless you face it, all hell's going to break loose. Gerry told me you were in great danger. That's why he wanted me to find you. Me, of all people." I leaned close to touch her face with my fingers. The skin was moist with tears. "In your own way, you loved him, didn't you, like he loved you. And do you know *why* he came up to Tremblant? Because

28

he thought you were there with me." I had her by the shoulders now, aware that I too was shaking. "And I saw him die, Sarah. That's what you wanted to know, how he died. Well, it was a fucking mess, believe me. You should have seen what was left of him . . ."

Suddenly Sarah broke. It began with a low groan; then she was pounding me with her fists. I grabbed her and held on, encouraging her to let it go, let it go. She kept repeating over and over how she hated Gerry. Her arms went around me as sobs racked her body. I had been working up to this moment; now I pleaded with her to tell me what was going on, what danger she was in. "Trust me," I whispered again and again. I took a wild guess. "New York. Before the funeral. You ran away from something, didn't you?" Her head nodded against my shoulder. "What did you find out, Sarah?"

For a moment I thought she had fallen asleep, because the tension was ebbing from her. Then her head moved and she whispered, "I know why Gerry was killed, Stoney. I found out why! But please, don't ask.I don't want you to get involved."

"Who did it, Sarah? Do you know that?"

"Y-yes. Hercules. They did it."

A shiver bolted down my spine. "The Hercules Foundation? Who? Sarah?" I shifted her slightly, to find her eyes were closed.

I covered her with a blanket. Her glass was lying on the carpet, unbroken. I placed it on the night table, then sat down beside her.

Being this close brought back memories of a young woman worried about a certain bluntness to her nose, nostrils too flared, a lower lip too large. In those days I was asked to pass judgment. Taken altogether, I would say, these combined to make her as beautiful as the Goddess Diana, a goddess that the Almighty had surely reproduced, then quickly made these slight adjustments to so as not to be accused of infringing on copyright. At this she would hoot with laughter and hug me, much as she had tonight at the Cave Inn.

Now this same woman was living a nightmare I couldn't possibly imagine. Reason enough for her to try to block out the past.

I was fascinated by the accusation that "Hercules" was responsible for Gerry's death, without doubt the same Hercules Foundation which had signed me up, for fifty thousand dollars, as a lifetime member. And how did this Gerhard Hegler fit in? It

29

shocked me how deeply I was becoming involved in something I knew so little about. Maybe Sarah and I both needed help.

I found Samuels sleeping on the passenger side of the jeep. I brushed the windshield free of snow and climbed in. The ignition key was still in his hand, so I pried it loose and switched on the engine. The racket woke him with a jolt, as I am sure it did half the population of Steamboat Village. His face looked pasty, probably from the cold, because he was only wearing denims and a ski jacket. We were on the road leading down to the highway however before he was wide-awake enough to talk. "Hullo," he said, giving me a sheepish grin. "How's Sarah?"

"She's fine," I replied, keeping an eye on the road, already partially blocked by drifts.

The highway was just ahead. I took my foot off the gas. "Which way, left or right?"

"Right, please." He paused. "And thanks."

The phone woke me from a deep sleep. It was Bo. "What the hell are you doing stayin' in bed on a day like this? It's after eleven."

I muffled a yawn. "What makes you think I'm still in bed?"

"Because I'm here at the front desk and my friend says you haven't left your room. Even for breakfast."

"Who's your friend?" I asked, slipping out of bed. I carried the phone down the two steps and across the small lounge to the window. The sun was dazzling and my balcony buried in snow. Beyond it the mountain and trees and skiers looked like a postcard. I thought of my camera equipment sitting back in the Montreal pawnshop. Not that I didn't have more pressing matters to think about.

"Stoney? Wake up."

"Sorry. Who's your friend, and how much snow fell last night?"

"More than a foot, and my friend's the desk clerk. He checked you in the other night." I heard a chuckle. "Such as you were. Another's in charge of reservations. Willy. We were swappin' lies when it struck him that you phoned the desk yesterday asking about a woman. A *Mrs*. Sarah Warden. Willy told you she'd checked out last week. He describes her as blond, thirty-five. Very sharp lady, and pretty. Well, the point is, one of the guys here spotted her last night at the Cave Inn." I started to tell him I found her there myself, when he said, "But there's more,

30

Stoney. Want to have a coffee in the bar behind Reception? Willy'll let you in.''

I turned away from the window. "Give me five minutes," I said, adding, "That's where I found her, by the way, at the Cave Inn.''

Bo was sitting at the deserted bar in his stetson, a down vest pulled over a thick plaid shirt, wrestling with a huge plate of flapjacks and sausages. He hadn't shaved. Next to him was another plate of flapjacks and sausages.

His "g'morning" lacked the usual Jacobs spirit. "That's yours," he said, pointing to the second late. I hauled myself onto the neighboring bar stool and reached for the syrup. "The toast and coffee's coming," he went on; then, in the same breath, "Stoney, I don't know what's goin' on, but you've got problems. Big problems.''

"Tell me about it," I said. I waited while he finished off a mouthful of food.

"I was called out to Yampa airport just now to pick up a couple of dudes who'd flown in by private jet. They were slick guys. Y'know, everything in place, suits and ties all nice, leather coats with fur collars. Easterners. No smiles." He managed a grin. "No offense, Stoney, but we get people from the East out here that I'll swear have never cracked a smile in their goddamn lives. Anyways, it took me three trips to get their gear aboard old Bessy. Jesus, they might have carried their own small suitcases, but hell no." He glanced up from his plate. "Are you listening?''

"Sure." I was thinking of Agostino and his remark about "any excuse to ski." "Did one of them have a pushed-in nose?''

Bo shook his head. "No, but they were big bastards. Sturdy. Anyways, they sat behind me and 'round halfway back one with a mustache leans over and starts talking about Steamboat Springs being popular with Eastern skiers and how was the skiing. And what about the food. Mexican influence, he'd heard. So fine. I don't mind fieldin' questions like that, but then they start getting personal. Nice limo, they say. They don't suppose I've paid it off yet, and was I in the market for a little spare cash. Then the other guy asks did I pick up a fare three or four days ago. He described her real well, and asked where I might have left her. I told him, 'Mister, I pick up a lot of fares and one blond looks just like another.' Which is horseshit, Stoney, because I remember faces, particularly this one, because she looked as if she'd been shot out of a cannon and missed the net. She'd been crying

31

real hard and her eyes were soggy with tears. She was my only passenger Monday afternoon, and all the way from the airport she apologized, but said she couldn't stop cryin'. Finally I said, 'Lady, what you need is a good strong cup of coffee.' She looked at me through those tears, Stoney, and told me she sure could use one. Y'know, I liked her then. She had a lot of guts for whatever was troubling her. I pulled in at Ernie's truck stop on the highway and we drank coffee and talked. About nothing much. Just talked. Finally she made tracks for the ladies' washroom, then to the pay phone. She came back to say a friend at the Village Inn was arranging a room for her."

"It was Sarah Warden, wasn't it?"

He nodded. "But it meant nothing at the time. Then this morning a fifty-dollar bill came floating down over the seat. Those bastards offered to double it if I locate her by suppertime. I tossed the bill back, telling them point-blank that people come out here to forget their troubles. They sure don't need me sticking my nose in where it doesn't belong. I dropped them off at a place on the ridge here, called the Timberline. Just as I pulled up, one of the guys scribbled a couple of names on a piece of paper and dropped it over the seat. He said it was worth two hundred bucks to know where these people were, before six. I didn't even look at it. I told them I operated a limo service, not a bloody missing-persons bureau. At Timberline I just dumped their baggage out and buggered off."

"And you came down here," I said, feeling as if I didn't want to hear any more.

Bo sipped his coffee. "Yup, to see how you'd made out. That's when Willy mentioned you'd been askin' about this Sarah Warden. I nearly crapped. I skittered out to the limo and got the paper. Mrs. Sarah Warden's name was on that paper, Stoney." He paused. "And so was yours."

This was the part I didn't want to hear. I said nothing. Bo went on. "At first I wondered why these two guys would corner me. Simple. Who'd know better of comings and goings if not the limo driver. So I began thinking of Mrs. Sarah Warden. So maybe the lady's pissed-off husband sends these two yahoos out to explain to my friend Philip Stone that it isn't wise to sniff around a man's wife."

I told him I wished it were that uncomplicated, telling him briefly about Gerry's death. "I came out here to make sure she doesn't do anything foolish," I said, "like pitching herself off a cliff. Sarah and I go back a long way."

32

Carl Henry shook his head. "Jesus, I can sure open my mouth and put both feet in. Boots and all. I'm real sorry, Stoney."

"Forget it," I said. "Besides, it's comforting to know someone's taking my interest to heart. Now, can we find out who these turkeys are?"

"No problem. I'll check as well to see if they listed a business address when they signed in."

"Could they be cops?"

Bo grinned. "Tell me you're on the lam."

"Not quite," I replied, almost choking on the irony of it. "Could they be?"

"Since when did cops fly around in their own Lear jet? My gut reaction is, no. But I might be able to dig something out of the local police. A deputy . . ."

"I appreciate it, Bo, but not for the moment. If we can get the names first, that would be a help." I ran a forkful of flapjacks around the plate to soak up the syrup, but stopped it short of my mouth. "I suppose you also have friends working at the Timberline?"

"Nope"—he laughed—"a nephew."

Another five minutes and breakfast was over. I walked Bo to the main entrance, thanked him for the jeep and the information. He brushed it aside, saying if I really wanted to repay him, I'd show up at the Harbor Hotel—"leastways, just to please Betty."

I promised.

7

The news that Sarah and I were on someone's most-wanted list didn't brighten my day. It sounded to me like Agostino's handiwork, despite the pair's arriving by private jet. Hadn't he insisted I go back to Canada? And when I hadn't shown . . . well, he was about to prove that the FBI had long arms. But I was even more concerned about Sarah's conviction that this Hercules outfit was behind Gerry's death. Suppose it was true? And just suppose that it was this same Hercules who'd panicked her into leaving New York? I reached for the phone, then stopped. Before frightening Sarah, I'd put a call through to Agostino to find out if he'd turned anybody loose on us.

33

A woman answered. "Federal Bureau of Investigation, may I help you?" I wanted Jim Agostino, but I wasn't sure which department he was in. She said, "I'm ringing Division Twenty-seven for you now, sir." I started to ask her which branch Division 27 covered. Too late. The line clicked·and I heard a man's voice. Again I asked for Agostino, only to learn he was out for lunch. I said it was urgent. "Then try Reuben's. The deli. Or Casey's." I told him I was calling from out of town. Then I should leave a message; Jim wouldn't be long. After some hesitation I gave him my name and hotel number, thinking to myself how this bit of news wouldn't make Agostino's day. I thanked the guy and was about to hang up when I said I hadn't realized that "Jim" had switched departments. He hadn't, I was told. "Jim's been with art theft for the past nine years." I heard myself say, "Art theft?" but the connection was already broken.

Art theft. The words tumbled over in my brain. Where had I read recently that international law-enforcement agencies placed art objects next to drugs as the world's worst trafficking problems? Art thefts reached fifty million dollars annually in the U.S., a great deal more in Europe. Objets d'art. Paintings. Some alone worth millions. At the time, the article had reminded me of Gerald Hope-Warden, in his latest reincarnation as art historian and collector, and I'd recalled wondering if he or his father had ever had any of their paintings stolen. And now I found myself imagining, with everything that had happened in the past week, that Gerry could have been the victim of some sort of stolen-art conspiracy. Well, why not? Why else would the FBI art-theft department be tied in with the murder of a prominent art figure? Right then it struck me. Sarah! Was *this* the danger Gerry had anticipated? I grabbed the phone and dialed the Village Inn. Unable to reach her there, I tried the Rabbit Ears Motel, to drag Terry Samuels away from a team lunch.

"Stoney!" he yelled in my ear, then dropped his voice. "Can't talk. Team lunch. But listen, it's cool. Really. But close. Thanks, huh?"

"My pleasure. Look, have you any idea where I might find Sarah?"

"Did you try the bar at the inn? If she's not there, then she's skiing Werner. All day. Look, I'm sorry, but I can't talk." I wished him good luck and cradled the receiver.

I needed skis. Good ones. In the Storm Hut, I carried on like a visiting oil sheik. Yes, I'll take those ski boots, these bindings,

34

that outfit. Poles, gloves, sunglasses, sweater. Rossignols to replace the same brand I'd left in Canada. Yes, and I'll pay by traveler's checks.

Chalk it up to expenses.

By two-thirty I'd covered much of the upper mountain from Priest Creek to Buddy's Run and Sunshine Peak. The new skis felt good, the edges digging in nicely when I hit the rugged little pitches of Cyclone, Tornado, and Twister. But still no Sarah. Worrying more for her by the minute, I stopped long enough at the mid-mountain Thunderhead restaurant, a cantilevered structure of glass and wood, to find she wasn't there. Outside again, I was snapping my boots down into the bindings when I heard someone call my name. I looked up to find a group of skiers coming up from the direction of the gondola. Among them was Sarah, molded into the same yellow ski outfit I'd seen on her bed the other night. She was waving at me.

"Hi," she said, stopping opposite me while the rest went on. She looked great, her loose hair windblown. "The sun is turning your face red."

"Your nose is peeling."

"I'm sorry for last night. I'm not in very good shape sometimes."

"I understand."

"Yes, I think you do."

"You've been skiing alone?" She nodded. "Where's Monique, then?"

"She's taking a private lesson."

I leaned on my poles. "Tell me something. Last night you mentioned the name Hercules. What does it mean?"

She turned away.

"Well?"

"The Hercules Foundation. It's a group of private art collectors and museum curators." Her voice wavered. "Powerful people in the art world."

I moved in close to her. "Last night you told me that Hercules was responsible for Gerry's death." I paused. "Can you prove it?"

The muscles around her mouth tightened. "I don't know." She jammed her poles down hard into the snow and shot forward. I swung my skis around and took off after her down a short steep run. I caught up to her at the lift. We lined up for the double chair and got on.

She sat motionless with her poles held rigid across her lap as

35

the chair swung us upward. Slowly the heavy whirring noise of the lift machine grew faint and we were swept up in the silence. Only then did I speak.

"Sarah, for Christ's sake listen to me. Two men arrived here today looking for you. Don't ask me how I know, just believe it. Now, do you have any idea who they might be?"

"They might be police," she said, tilting her head back to catch the sun. "Hershel Nesbitt wanted me to go to them. We had an argument about it the day before the funeral. That's when I came back here. To get away." Her eyes closed.

"And you think these guys are police, sent here to persuade you to come back and talk?"

"Yes, I suppose so."

I watched the fir trees slipping beneath us. "You must have a lot to tell."

She looked at me then with eyes that held steadily onto mine. There was no fear in them, no panic. When she spoke, her voice was steady, resolute. "Stoney, I came here to break with the past. I'm not stupid enough to think I'm in hiding. If the police or Hercules wanted to find me, it wouldn't be difficult. But I'm beginning a new life for myself. I don't want to discuss my past with anyone. You included." A smile played in the corners of her mouth as she leaned forward and kissed me on the cheek. "I'm glad you're here, Stoney. Your concern touches me. Our past is something I don't want to forget." She pushed her cheek against my shoulder. "Let's ski now, okay?"

"Okay," I said, seeing in her some of the grit Bo had mentioned.

For the next few hours Sarah and I lost ourselves on the open glades of unpacked snow cresting the top portion of Mt. Werner, schussing and snaking down through the powder to stop breathless at the base of the uppermost lift, which would scoop us up for another run, then another and another. Unused to this altitude, I stopped frequently and sucked in air to cool my lungs. Once Sarah tut-tutted me, and removing my sunglasses, produced a plastic tube from her jacket pocket. The contents, a thick white sludge, she spread on my face. "I got a bad burn the first day out," she said, screwing the lid back on the tube. "That sun is a sneaky little bugger." Then we were off again, in search of fresh powder.

But the skiing ended too soon when the upper lift closed for the day, leaving us the long run to the bottom.

We were there now, leaning on our poles and breathing hard,

feeling the exhilaration, the fatigue of a good afternoon ski. Snow clung to our wet faces, to our eyebrows behind the glasses, to our hair. "Warden," I told her, "you're a damn fine skier." She grinned at me. "Stone, flattery will get you nothing but a free drink. I'm buying." I accepted.

We'd stopped outside the Storm Hut, where I bought two small silver decals with "Ski Steamboat!" stamped across them. The same sort had been put on my skis when the bindings were installed. Sarah had noticed them and thought them fun. I stuck these two new ones on her skis. She laughed and promised to be forever grateful.

We parted then, planning to meet at the Village Inn lounge in twenty minutes. I hobbled back to my hotel to free my feet from the agony of the new boots. Leaving my skis and poles in the hotel locker, I went on to my room, to find a note from Bo pushed under the door. Two names were scrawled on it. Not recognizing either, I shoved the paper in my pocket, changed into my snow boots, and left.

The Robber's Roost was packed with après-skiers. I stood in the entrance across from a noisy country-rock group who was contributing more than its share to the bedlam inside. Unable to spot Sarah at first glance, I stepped in and moved between the tables, hoping she might see me. She hadn't yet. Then I saw her, toward the back of the room. I'd already started in that direction when I noticed something was going on. People around me were standing up to see what was happening. I quickly shouldered my way forward. She was screaming angrily and struggling against two people who were pinning her to the chair. It seemed that everyone around Sarah was trying to calm her, but when she saw me, she screamed my name, broke away, and flung herself at me. I grabbed her and held on. I asked some guy next to me what had happened. He pointed to the two guys who were already moving away. "They were just talking to her, like, when she started carrying on. They tried to calm her, mister, that's all."

I tried to get a good look at them, but it didn't matter. The mustache on one of them was enough. Their names were the same as the ones written on the note in my pocket, or I was a donkey's uncle. As for being cops? Phooey.

Sarah was still sobbing when we reached her room. I wanted to find out more about the pair, what they had said. But this wasn't the moment. She needed some time to think, she said. A quiet evening on her own. I asked if she'd be all right. She said she would. And anyway, Terry had promised to drop by later. I told her I'd see her tomorrow and went down to the lobby to phone Bo.

"Those are the dudes, all right, Stoney. Corry and Fleck. Accordin' to my nephew, the guy with the mustache is Alonzo Fleck. The other, a William Corry."

"From?"

"Their reservation came through Horizon Imports, New York City. Mean anything?"

"Not that I can think of. Anything else?"

"No, but he said he'd keep an eye on them."

"Fine, Bo, but tell him not too close an eye. I don't trust those bastards."

"Fair enough. Listen, I tried to reach you earlier, when I dropped off the note."

"I went skiing," I said.

A chuckle came over the line. "Couldn't resist it, huh? Sometimes I regret not learnin' to ski. Anyhow, now that you've worked up a healthy appetite, why don't you slide your butt out here. We're just sitting down to dinner." I begged off, saying my legs were stiffening up and I was heading for a hot bath. "Then you should drag that same butt of yours down to the hot-springs pool." I'd heard of it. Opposite the Rabbit Ears Motel. "Ya, just this side of town. You're still planning to meet us at the Harbor Hotel 'round ten o'clock?"

"You bet," I replied, sounding more like a Westerner every minute.

Before leaving the hotel, I called Monique, who told me how much she had enjoyed last evening. I said the feeling was mutual and how was the ski lesson. She had added a few more bruises to her derriere, but she was coming along nicely. I suggested a swim in the hot-springs pool to ease her aching muscles, a good meal, and drinks with some friends.

"It sounds lovely, Philippe, but I have made already other plans. I am sorry. Another time, perhaps." Another time, I promised.

I left the hot-springs indoor pool before my body registered medium-rare—soothing though the experience had been—and drove down Lincoln Avenue to a little restaurant known as the Gold Mine. It came highly recommended by a young lifeguard at the pool, who also vouched for the burritos with ham and the cinnamon-apple pie. I wasn't to be disappointed.

Lingering over the meal, I listened idly to conversations around

38

me, mostly about skiing, and found myself lost in my own thoughts. Sarah mainly, and Agostino. He hadn't returned my call, which meant tracking him down tomorrow, Saturday or not. Between the burritos and pie, I phoned the Village Inn, but there was no answer from Room 631. A good omen. She would be with Samuels, who would lift her spirits. Tomorrow would be time enough to worry about the visitors from Horizon Imports.

It was snowing heavily when I stepped out of the Gold Mine shortly after ten o'clock. I brushed enough of the snow away from the jeep's windshield so I could see where I was heading, climbed in, and swung it back up the street. Soon the Harbor Hotel's red neon sign came flickering out of the storm and I turned down the alley marked with a sign saying "Hotel Parking in Rear."

I found an empty spot in the last row next to the fence, backed in, cut the engine, and got out. I was closing the door when a car pulled up a few feet in front of the jeep. Unable to see the driver clearly, I shouted, "Sorry, I'm not leaving. I just arr—" A chill shot up my spine. Something was wrong. I started to turn, too late. Someone grabbed me from behind and in one swift motion pinned my arms back and slammed me down hard across the hood of the jeep, crushing my face against the cool metal. I heard a car door open, then shut. A voice said, "Flip him over."

The same hands yanked me free and with a deft twist flung me back against the jeep. I barely had time to focus on the face in front of me when the second guy, coming out of nowhere, dove a knee into my crotch. It was a glancing blow, my inner thigh taking most of it, though my whole body seemed to explode, and I pitched forward.

I lay motionless in the snow, on the verge of vomiting. When I couldn't, I reached for the jeep and slowly began hauling myself up by the door.

Corry and Fleck? Who else.

"Sorry, Mr. Stone," came a voice from behind. "My friend and I only want to impress on you that what we have to say must be taken seriously."

"Good for you," I gasped. "but you could have impressed me just as easily without the knee."

"Ah, but that isn't my style. Whenever something bothers me, I like to get it out in the open."

I was almost standing now as I clutched the plastic window. I'd have to stall them, praying that someone might come along and get the police. "Sure," I answered, surprised at the effort it was taking to get myself upright, "in the open, as in an empty parking lot."

He ignored the remark. "What's bothering me at the moment is your old friend Mrs. Warden. She won't take *her* responsibilities seriously. We talked to her about the problem in New York last week. We thought she understood. Obviously we were wrong, because she gave us the slip. And now, here she is back at her old tricks."

"What do you want me to do," I muttered, leaning against the plastic, "scold her and send her home?"

A round blunt face sporting a thick mustache appeared close to mine. Alonzo Fleck's, to be sure. "We expect more than that, Mr. Stone. Mr. Warden left a lot of things undone. It's up to Mrs. Warden to carry on where her husband left off." His face clouded. "*Where* he left off is of interest to a great many people."

"So you've been hired to put the muscle to his widow."

He shrugged. "Think what you will, Mr. Stone. The point is, much time has been lost, valuable time. It's our job to have you and Mrs. Warden back in New York no later than tomorrow. We have a plane at Yampa airport, and I expect you to have her on it by noon. If you don't, the consequences won't be pretty. And believe me, Mr. Stone, we're not amateurs." The face disappeared. "William."

Again my arms were pinned behind me, by Corry. I struggled, only to feel the grip tighten like a vise. The smiling Fleck removed the jeep keys from my pocket, then got in and started the engine. Next came the grinding of gears, and suddenly the jeep bucked forward, slamming into the front-left fender of their car. More grinding gears as Fleck reversed the jeep just enough to clear the other car. The keys were put back in my pocket. Fleck looked pleased with himself. "Now, Mr. Stone, to impress on you that we don't take our responsibility lightly," he said, with a nod to Corry, "it's your turn."

Bo found me crawling up the side of the jeep.

"Stoney!" he shouted, dropping down beside me. "One of the guys we had a beer with the day you came just told me you were out here drunk and hollerin' for me. He'd just come to his car." He was staring at me. "Je*sus*, you're not drunk. Somebody's been kicking the shit out of you."

I closed my eyes against the pain, describing to him how I'd had the shit kicked out of me *after* being kneed in the crotch.

40

The pair had taken their time working me over, first one holding me up, then the other. No lead pipes, no baseballs. Just well-aimed kicks, under the kneecaps, behind the knees, to the joints, elbows, hips, and punches under the ribs, the spongy area of the lower back. Blows that finally could inflict no more pain. Then they'd driven away.

"Corry and Fleck?" Bo asked when I finished. I nodded. "The mouthy bastard with the mustache and the other guy who just sits there."

By now we had me leaning up against the jeep. I was saying, "Corry just doesn't sit there, believe me," when a coughing spell sent a spasm of pain down to my heels. I gripped the edge of the jeep until it was over. "C'mon, let's get me back to my hotel."

"Hold on, Betty's bringing our car around from the Safeway lot across the street." He brushed the snow off me. "She'll insist on taking you to the hospital when she finds out you're not drunk." Then he tried to hold me up under the arms, but even that was painful. I insisted on getting around to the passenger side; he insisted the other car would be more comfortable. "Besides, we got to get you to the hospital. Suppose you're bleeding inside?"

I grunted. "It wasn't that kind of beating. They want me alive."

We had worked me past the front of the jeep and by the battered fender. I told Bo to look at it. He told me he had better things to do and yanked the flimsy door open with a free hand. "I'll put you in this tub, but we're heading for the ranch, not your hotel. Je*sus*. Betty'll carve me up for breakfast when she finds out what happened. I'm supposed to be looking after you."

"Leave her to me," I said, wincing as we worked one leg past the jeep's door frame.

Bo grinned. "Goddamn right I will."

I stiffened badly during the ten-mile drive to the Lazy J Ranch. The blinding storm had slowed us down to a crawl, and by the time we stopped I was fighting off tears of pain. Betty had wheeled the other car in beside the jeep and had my door open before Bo could get around. I found myself staring at a compact, pleasant woman with dark hair whose features were mostly hidden under the hood of tan parka. She stared at me, curious; then her eyes widened. "Carl Henry," she exploded, "this

41

friend of yours isn't drunk, he's in pain!'' We told her what had happened.

She scowled. "He goes to the hospital. Right now." Bo came to my rescue. The last four miles had been the hardest on me. Over the broken road. And it would only mean going back over it. We waited for her answer.

Betty made a clucking noise. "All right. But if I feel he warrants hospital treatment, neither of you will argue?" Bo nodded, for both of us. "Fine," she said. "Then I'll go ahead and open the doors and get things ready."

"What's all this just-leave-it-to-me stuff?" he growled, helping me down into the snow.

"I owe you one," I muttered between clenched teeth.

By three o'clock in the morning I was a new man, at least new enough to move about under my own steam. I owed it all to Nurse Jacobs' magic fingers. I found her alone in the kitchen, drinking coffee. She was wearing jeans and a loose knit sweater.

She pointed to the chair next to her, then at me. "Is this the man we brought in here and stretched out on this very table?"

I sat down slowly. "The same. Thanks to you."

It was thanks to Betty, for once I was on the table, her fingers went to work, probing every inch of my body, feeling for damage. That she found nothing didn't surprise her. I'd been worked over by pros, she said, who knew how to inflict the most amount of pain with the least visible injury. Working emergency in a Denver hospital had shown her that much; victims crippled without so much as a mark on them. She discovered only one outward sign of the beating, a small, slightly discolored bump behind my left ear, but under the hairline where the knockout blow wouldn't be readily noticed. A little thud on the mastoid bone, she said, and out I'd gone. She told me this while probing my eyes with a small key-chain flashlight to make sure I could move the pupils in both directions smoothly. Her verdict: no apparent concussion, though I would feel dizziness for a few hours.

Next came the massage to help prevent further stiffening, and then I was ordered into an ice-cold bath for twenty minutes, to reduce the swelling and pain. After this I could dress myself *and* walk unaided, at least to the kitchen.

I leaned on the table, feeling sorry for myself. "Where's Bo?"

"He's outside, though heaven knows what he's found to do at three o'clock in the morning. He never stops, that man." She glanced at her cup, then at me. "I'm sorry. Coffee, Stoney?" It had been "Stoney" from the start. I watched her move to the stove. She had let her hair down and it came almost to her waist. She turned around and smiled. "Cream and sugar?"

"Black," I answered, hoping it might sustain me long enough to make it back to town. I wanted to see Sarah while I could still move.

Betty was helping me into my ski jacket when Bo came in the door. He was covered in snow. "You're not leavin'?"

"He won't stay," Betty said quietly.

Bo shook his head. "You'll be lucky to get through. It's getting worse."

"That's all I need," I said. "But thanks. I was having trouble doing up the zipper of my jacket. Betty wasn't amused. She took over, after making a face at me. I apologized to Bo for the damaged fender, saying I would have it repaired.

Bo said, "Don't worry none. I took a look at it. The fender'll fix easy. The headlight was busted, so I replaced it." He paused. "But I can't help wonderin' why those yahoos would ram their car with the jeep. They've left a bit of their red paint behind." I left the question unanswered.

In the silence that followed, Betty slipped an arm through mine and guided me to the door. "You'll begin to stiffen soon," she said. "When you do, take another bath. And another after that. If it gets really bad, we're here." Suddenly she reached up and kissed me firmly on the cheek. I kissed her back. Then Bo and I battled our way out to the shed.

"You look like the goddamn ghost of Christmas past," Bo shouted at me as we stepped inside.

I grunted and looked around. We were in an old driving shed lit by a single bulb hanging from a hand-hewn beam. The jeep and Chrysler were nearby, both cleaned of snow.

I drew in a deep breath. "Can I make it to town?"

"If you don't stop."

I walked around the jeep and got in. Bo followed. "In your condition, I'm willing to bet you haven't strength enough to keep this tub on the road. Provided you can *find* the road." He paused, then motioned me over. "I'm coming with you."

"Nope, you'll never make it back. But thanks." I closed the door and fumbled for the key. When I looked up, the large shed doors were wide open.

Starting off in a blizzard wasn't bright, but I couldn't wait until morning. Nor could I shake off the ugly feeling that somewhere, someone had only to nod and *thump*, Philip A. Stone was laid out in a hotel parking lot in Steamboat Springs, Colorado. That same, possibly unemotional gesture had in effect torn me off the sidelines and launched me into a game where I didn't know the rules, let alone the principal players. Frankly, it pissed me off, and no bloody Colorado blizzard would keep me from the one person who knew what the hell was going on. Besides, I had no reason to believe that the same bastards who nailed me wouldn't come down just as hard on her.

It was five-fifteen when I stumbled into the lobby of the Village Inn. Surviving the gut-wrenching drive through blinding snow and drifts tall enough to bury me and the little jeep alive was a miracle in itself. Now I was paying for it. I could scarcely move.

A wave of dizziness sent me reeling into the rack of house phones. I grabbed for it and hung on, waiting for the dizziness to pass, then slowly picked up the nearest receiver and dialed 631.

No answer. I tried again, letting it ring a dozen times before giving up. I managed to reach the hotel operator next and asked for Monique Brosseau. The line clicked. I waited, feeling my whole body slowly turn to concrete. My eyes were closing and I was drifting away when I heard a voice. "Yes? 'Ello? 'Ello?"

"Monique?"

"Yes? Who? Philippe?"

"It's me," I answered slowly. Monique, I . . . I need help. I'm down in the lobby." She found me still clutching the receiver.

I opened my eyes. She was beside me, barefoot, in jeans and what looked like a man's pajama top. I said, "I hope . . . I'm not interrupting anything." Her face came close to mine. I wanted to touch her, but my arms wouldn't move. I told her of aching all over, of a barroom brawl because I didn't want to bother her with the truth. Her eyes went sad and her fingers touched my face.

We were on the elevator, her arms wrapped around me, her head pressed against my chest. I could smell the freshness of her skin drifting up from inside the pajama top.

Motion stopped. Doors opened. As we started down the corridor, my legs wobbled. Her grip tightened, but I remember reeling heavily against the wall.

Motionless again. I was on a bed, naked except for a towel across my thighs. The pain returned. Monique was beside me, her thighs barely covered by the pajama top. She was on the phone talking softly. When she saw I was awake, she slipped her hand over the mouthpiece. She said, "A moment ago you insisted on talking to Sarah." I didn't remember. "I have her now, but she won't talk to you."

I struggled to sit up. "Where is she?"

A murmured conversation followed. Then: "She's at the Rabbit Ears Motel for the night."

My arms felt like two lead weights. "Let me talk to her." I couldn't get my arm off the goddamn sheet.

Monique shook her head. "She won't. She's afraid you're mad at her for not staying in." She was back on the phone, smiling. To me again: "She wants you to know Terry was in bed early, not to worry about him."

"That's just fine," I said, "but tell young Samuels he'd better not let her out of his sight." She was muttering into the mouthpiece, then blushed. But Terry Samuels' protection *wasn't* enough! I grabbed for the receiver, caught it by my fingers, and jammed it against my mouth. "Sarah!" A buzz floated round in my head. I fell back swearing to myself. "What the hell did I do that for?"

Monique's face appeared above mine. "Because you care about her," she said, putting a hand on my chest. I glanced up at her. Light from the bedside lamp spilled across her dark eyes, making them glow. I heard her say, "Don't give up on her, Philippe. You are her only contact with reality."

I found myself staring at the pajama top. It was partially unbuttoned, showing the roundness of her full breasts. Her eyes met mine. With effort I brought up my hand, slipping it past the fabric. Her skin felt warm. She shivered. Her breasts were large and firm. I let my fingertips move slowly across the smooth surface until they reached the nipple. It began to swell under my touch.

Her eyes closed. She sank forward. Our mouths groped hungrily for each other. Tongues touched, explored. I felt the hand on my chest glide down my body and flatten on the towel. I could feel myself harden beneath it.

45

Her hand left the towel. The fingers touched my lips. "Philippe," she whispered, "tell me, it was not a barroom brawl that injured you. You have been badly beaten."

I kissed her nose. "Yes. Two of them. Methodically."

"Yes. Then you need a bath to soothe the muscles."

"Later," I murmured, rubbing the underside of her breast.

A sigh rose in her throat. "You know what will happen. We will make love together and we will fall asleep. When we wake up, you won't be able to get out of bed. Or walk. The muscles will have tightened." I grinned at her. "I said something funny?"

I removed my hand and pulled her gently down on top of me. Our cheeks touched. "Yes, you said something funny, but it sounded so good. Do you think maybe you could give me a massage before the bath, then?"

"You bet, m'sieu," she whispered in my ear.

Monique announced that my bath was ready. I opened one eye as I lay on the bed. The massage had left my body tingling. "I hope it's deep," I said, easing myself off the bed. She came over to help me, only to scurry off when we reached the bathroom door. I dropped the towel.

Cold water again. I was freezing and mumbling obscenities when I heard her say, "May I come in?" She was in the doorway, all legs, clutching a glass and a frosted green bottle of Rémy Martin.

"Yes, do," I muttered.

She sat down on the side of the tub and filled the small glass. I gulped down half and settled back, feeling numbed by the cognac's fire. Aloud I admired her sleepwear.

"I have had this a very long time," she said. I watched her hand touch the water, then sink down to my knee. The sleeve of the pajamas went with it. "A friend loaned it to me once when I had nothing else to wear. It was so comfortable, he let me keep it."

"The bottoms too?"

"No, he wore those."

Her fingers were on my thigh.

"You kept the best." My voice trailed off as her hand closed around my shaft. Our eyes locked together. I reached out, slowly unbuttoned the rest of her pajamas, and cupped a breast in my palm. The nipple had already hardened. I rolled it gently between my thumb and forefinger before dropping my hand down along her body. I touched her legs. They yielded. My fingers burrowed

46

into the silkiness of her pubic hair, seeking first the soft folds of moist skin and finally the tiny nub of her clitoris. For a while we stroked each other, our eyes never wavering. At last I removed my hand, and taking her shoulders, eased her over the side. She was on top of me now. The overflow gurgled.

Forgetting the aches, the pain, the tenderness around the groin, I pulled her down on me, pressing my open mouth on hers. At last she sat up, straddling my legs. Her hair was soaked. I reached up to touch the wet garment where it clung to the protruding breasts, the belly, the hips. She was kneeling over me now as I held myself upright between her thighs. Her eyes closed. From her throat came a low growl and she sank down, driving my erection deep inside her. Our lovemaking that night had just begun.

I awoke to find Monique curled up beside me, her head on my chest, an arm flung across my stomach. I felt her naked body next to mine, its warmth penetrating my skin. Once during the night I'd awakened to find her massaging the muscles of my legs. She had been worried lest they stiffen while I slept. After making love again, she'd insisted on another cold bath—together. Later, shivering beneath the blankets, we shared our pasts.

Monique had grown up in Paris. She'd been educated at a lycee and then the Sorbonne. She had never married. She lived in an apartment, alone, on the Ile St. Louis, a neighboring island in the Seine a stone's throw from Notre Dame Cathedral. She was born in Paris? No, in a small town to the south. Oradour-sur-Glane.

Now me.

I had been with the family business in New York, a consulting firm specializing in personnel training. It had been a foregone conclusion that once my two brothers and I, one older, one younger, left college, we would be part of it. Not partners, just part of it. Father, the old bastard, we'd always figured was next to God. So had he. I had joined the firm reluctantly. It grew too fast, branching out into psychological testing of clients' prospective employees. Tension, overwork, then drink, led to a wife who rightly complained of never seeing me. She'd never complained of what such work brought us, though. Membership in the local country club, winter vacations down south. A large home. We grew apart till there was nothing left to hold on to. Except Jessie and Sybil. Separation, divorce. Jane kept the house. And our daughters. During the divorce I was in lousy shape. I had been for some time. My family worried about what a divorce would do to the Stone name. "Philip makes a habit of tarnishing the family name every six years or so." My younger brother, Pete, had said it, the one who had always hankered after what was mine. On the last day of court, I handed him his latest hankering, the vice-presidency of Stone Inc.

Later, a chance meeting with Sarah Anne Warden on a busy New York street turned into a drink in the blue bar of the Algonquin Hotel. And an affair that lasted all of eighteen hours. End of story.

We slept.

I was on the verge of drifting off again. Suddenly I lifted my head. The room was dark, but the window was covered with heavy drapes. I'd closed them myself. Easing Monique's head onto the pillow, I slipped awkwardly out of bed and jerked back the curtains. Sunlight poured into the room. *Sunlight!* Jesus, the deadline, the goddamn deadline. Fleck and Corry. My watch was on the bedside table. It was after eleven-thirty. Wasn't I to have her on their plane by noon? I grabbed the phone and asked the operator for the Rabbit Ears Motel. There was no answer in Terry's room. They were on their way to the hill. I knew I'd never make it. *Why* hadn't I done something last night? Maybe Agostino could help.

Leaving Monique asleep, I was dressed and downstairs at a pay phone within three minutes. What the hotel switchboard didn't know wouldn't hurt it. My call to New York got no further than the FBI operator, who told me only a skeleton staff operated on weekends.

"Is Jim Agostino among them?" I asked angrily.

"Among whom, sir?" came the bored voice over the line.

"Among the skeletons, for Christ's sake. . . . Well, is he?"

A pause. Then: "I'll check the roster." Another delay. "No. No, sir. I could leave him a message. He'll pick it up first thing Monday morning."

"That's not good enough. My name is Philip Stone. I need him now!" It was quarter to twelve. "Forget it," I said, and slammed down the receiver.

I found Sarah at the Howelsen Hill ski-jump site, buried knee-deep in fresh snow and surrounded by hundreds of spectators on the knoll halfway up the slope. She was chatting excitedly with those around her.

"Sarah!" I shouted, fighting my way up through the deep

snow and the crowd. I reached her. "Sarah, we've got to get out of here." I felt her sudden coolness. "Just trust me. I'll explain later."

I had her by the arm now, but she yanked free. The hysteria was surfacing again.

"I'm staying right here, Stoney," she snapped at me.

"Don't be stupid," I shot back. "Corry and Fleck have come to take you back to New York."

"I know. I told them yesterday in the bar I wouldn't go."

I took a deep breath and let it out slowly. "Sarah, they beat me up last night."

Her hand went to her mouth. "Oh, God," she moaned.

"Things are only going to get worse. We have to go to the police. Here in Steamboat."

Her face softened. "Stoney, I'm sorry, but I just can't. It is my life now. For the first time in years."

Our eyes held for a moment longer.

I looked away. Corry and Fleck would have to wait.

We were on a knoll. From here it dropped away sharply to form the jump's landing area. Above us to our left, some twenty feet, the ramp ended at the takeoff point. This ramp continued on up the hill, cutting a narrow swath through the snow-laden firs, to stop at the crest of the ridge. Spectators packed the sides of the hill that formed this steep landing zone and below it the wide fenced-in runoff area. Beyond this was an open stretch of flatland fanning back to the Yampa River. Past it was downtown Steamboat, still digging itself out from last night's storm.

Behind us now a loudspeaker came to life. A broad drawl announced the start of the second jump. The crowd around us went silent. Heads turned uphill.

A figure appeared high on a small platform adjoining the ramp, hands clamped on the side railings, skis shifting back and forth. The starter waited beside him, his hand poised above the competitor's back. Then it touched him. A resounding *thwack* of the heavy skis striking the main ramp echoed into the surrounding trees.

We watched the first jumper—Reed, from the University of Utah—crouch, his elbows touching his knees, hands clasped at the ankles. As he gathered speed, he flexed his body.

He was halfway down the ramp, a bent figure whose large goggles obscured his face. Sixty miles an hour looked to be no exaggeration as he streaked down and hit the point of takeoff.

In this split second Reed drove his body both upward and

forward, his hands dropping back along his sides, the palms turned downward. At the same instant, a grunt from him shattered the stillness. Along with it came the high-pitched crackling sound of the wind tearing at the skintight suit.

The jumper rose up above the line of trees, his torso bent slightly, legs straight, the tips of his skis forced back by the pressure of the air. Quite suddenly he was well over the landing area and coming down fast. The backs of his skis touched first, one just ahead of the other, the legs bent, the arms spread out to the side. The crowd clapped. Reed hit the runoff, slipped his skis neatly into a snowplow, which stopped him close to the fence.

I hardly noticed the next few jumps. I was too busy looking over my shoulder. Noon had come and gone. Monique's arrival brought me back. I tried to make excuses, but she cut me off, saying not to worry.

Terry was next. He took his place and waited for the starter's tap on his shoulder.

In spite of myself I was drawn into the excitement. Sarah hardly moved, her eyes locked on the figure high above us. Monique clutched my arm.

Suddenly he was off. A perfect form in a perfect jump. The crowd caught its breath. We watched him land far below in what would be the longest jump of the first round.

By the beginning of the second and final round I was starting to relax. Two hours had passed since Fleck and Corry's deadline, and I had yet to spot either of them in the crowd. We were working our way along the knoll to the rope marking off the jump area when someone called my name. It came from the spectators on the other side of the snow-packed strip. I saw the stetson first above the heads. Bo was below it, and next to him Betty. I waved back, explaining to Monique that he was the friend who lent me the jeep. Her face lit up. "The one in the cowboy hat? Mon Dieu"—she laughed—"he looks very like he would own such a vehicle." I gave her a squeeze. When I looked up, I found Sarah watching us. She glanced quickly away.

The next three jumps included Number Eleven, Terry's friend Collins, whom I'd met at the Cave Inn. He landed with a respectable eighty-four meters, plus an announced fourteen points for style. A guy from Utah followed him, wavered on takeoff, but corrected himself in time to avoid a bad fall.

Terry was now waiting in the slot. We could see him sliding his skis back and forth with casual ease. The loudspeaker barked,

"Samuels, University of Colorado." Terry bent low and sprang forward.

In seconds he exploded off the ramp to soar into space, so close we could see the skin around his mouth forced back against his teeth by the pressure of the air.

It was another picture jump, controlled, unwavering, and he was still climbing. You could feel the tension grip the spectators.

He was at the height of his jump, hanging there, suspended in that hairbreadth of a second before being drawn back to earth, when suddenly the skis shot apart. The crowd gasped. His head and shoulders dropped between his spreading skis. Too late to recover. Arms, legs, skis, were everywhere as he plummeted earthward.

It was the back of his neck that struck the hard-packed snow first, his weight then driving him down the length of the steep landing zone, the body rolling, flopping, spinning into the runoff enclosure, the skis already ripped from his boots.

At once I tore myself free from Sarah's paralyzing hold on my arm, ducked under the restraining rope, and plunged headlong down the slope, falling over myself, half-running, half-dragging my now aching body toward the still figure. I was caught up in one terrifying moment, hearing nothing but my own labored breathing until I dropped down beside him.

Terry's long legs were bent back, his arms jammed under him as he lay twisted on his side. Yanking off my gloves, I quickly felt along his neck for a pulse. There wasn't one.

Feet came pounding up behind me. A voice shouted in my ear. "What the hell d'you think you're doing?" A beefy little guy wearing an "Official" armband stuck his face down close to mine.

"I want a stretcher," I barked, "and the police." His jowls shook with indecision. Then he nodded and took off. I got back to Terry.

Gingerly I rolled him over on his back. Blood was trickling from the low corner of his mouth, staining the snow a deep crimson. But my eyes were riveted now on his chest, where the numbered bib had disintegrated into a cavity of shredded flesh.

Tearing off my ski jacket, I covered his chest, then gently closed his eyes.

I gazed down at him. The message was all too clear. Those bastards would stop at nothing.

God knows how long I knelt over Terry. Probably seconds.

51

Then someone touched my shoulder. "Stoney?" Bo came into focus.

"He's dead," I heard myself saying, "the kid's been shot."

His eyes widened. "Jesus!" he whispered, "Corry and Fleck?"

"I'm sure of it. They—"

Bo cut me off. "We've got company."

I glanced over my shoulder. Sarah had dodged an official and was stumbling toward us. "It's Sarah," I gasped. "For Christ's sake, get her out of here."

Without a word, Bo stepped around me and started across the snow. Grim-faced, she tried to outmaneuver him. He moved incredibly fast, scooped her up over his shoulder, and in a dozen paces disappeared through a break in the snow fence.

An emergency toboggan swung in beside Samuels. Two young ski patrollers came with it. One started fussing with the toboggan's canvas cover while the second began removing the coat. Both ignored me.

"Leave it," I said. "Load him onto the toboggan as is. Now."

The guy opposite me shrugged. "Sorry, mister, we gotta check him first."

I leaned forward, dug my bare hands under Samuels, and started to lift. "Either we use your toboggan or I'll carry him myself." Neither moved. "Fine," I said, gathering up Samuels. "The whole goddamn town can watch you both refusing to help." They looked at each other, then at me.

With several officials running interference for us, we hauled the toboggan through the crowd to a first-aid hut nearby, bundled it inside, and closed the door. I stepped aside.

A little guy in flimsy spectacles suddenly burst in, glanced about, then drove a quivering finger toward the two wide-eyed patrollers.

"Harvey, Dennis," he screamed, "who in God's name told you to remove the injured man from the hill? Who?" Neither wasted a moment nodding to me. Old Spectacles spun around, almost tripping over the toboggan. "You? Who in hell are *you*, mister?" He didn't wait for an answer. "You two boys get Sheriff Bachman. Now!" he yelled, carolling in high C. They didn't have to be told twice.

When they were gone, he shuffled around to the far side of the toboggan and hunkered down beside Samuels. He was having difficulty keeping an eye on both of us. I said, "Why don't you wait for the sheriff?'' But he didn't. His eyes left me and settled on Samuels. I counted to five before his head jerked up.

"Why, this young man is dead!''

As if on cue, the door swung open and a large barrel-chested man in a stetson and worn sheepskin windbreaker, a heavy holster slung low on his hip, strode in. He was followed by two pared-down replicas of himself. The ski patrollers squeezed in behind them.

Sheriff Bachman's chiseled features and sheer size dominated the room. With one sweeping gesture he acknowledged old Doc Jenkins, sent a deputy scurrying to block the door and the other to guard the toboggan. The same gesture ended, arm extended, palm up, pointing to me.

"ID,'' he drawled, clamping his tired gray eyes on mine. I reached for my wallet, removed the plastic sleeve with my Social Security and driver's license, and passed it over.

"Doc,'' he said, thumbing through the papers, "these two patrollers here tell me the young jumper is dead. Is that right?'' Jenkins nodded vigorously. "With bullet holes in the region of the chest?'' Again a nod. Bachman turned to me. "You're a little light on credit cards, Mr. . . . ah . . . Stone. A lack of credit cards usually means a bad risk. Are you a bad risk?''

"A lack of credit cards could also mean a person doesn't want any,'' I answered.

Chuckling to himself, he shoved the plastic sleeve into his pocket and got down to business. "Who gave you the authority to move the jumper, Stone?''

"It was my idea.''

"Dennis and Harvey tell me you insisted on removing the kid, against their better judgment.''

"That's true. They thought he'd just been injured. I knew he was full of bullets. I thought of only one thing. Get him out of there before word got around he'd been hit by a sniper. I didn't want several thousand people to panic.''

"You know Samuels?''

"Yes.''

"How come you reached him first?''

"I'm not sure. I remember the moment he lost control. It didn't look right.''

"How do you mean?''

"He didn't fall right. A guy jumping ahead of Samuels lost his stable position in flight. I watched him. He struggled all the way down, to do something about it. Terry had a good jump

53

going for him. When he lost it, he didn't even try to save himself. At that speed, at that height, you'd work like hell to get it back. Unless you couldn't."

"So you come to his rescue. A one-man scout troop." Bachman looked at me for a moment. "And if I asked you who's behind the shooting?"

"Two guys from New York named Corry and Fleck. They're staying at the Timberline."

Bachman's raucous laughter echoed around the room. "So you've got everything wrapped up, have you? What did you say those dudes' names were?"

"Corry and Fleck."

"Corry and Fleck. Those names might ring a bell."

"Why?"

"Damnit, Stone," he bellowed, "how should I know? I hear a hell of a lot of names in a day. Some ring bells, some don't." He patted his pocket. "Yours, I won't forget. And by the way, I'll probably be layin' a charge of obstruction against you."

Before I could say anything, he'd turned to Old Spectacles. "Doc, do me a favor and hustle this kid out of here in an ambulance, as if he's just badly injured. Run him up to the hospital."

I cut him off. "Sheriff, they have their own plane. At Yampa airport."

He eyed me suspiciously. "What are you tryin' to do, Stone, frame somebody? Frame two somebodies? Look, I promise I'll look into it, but right now I've got a body on my hands." He pointed to the door. "Beat it. I'll see you later in my office. You can pick up your ID and stuff then. In the meantime, I'll decide whether or not to press that charge."

"Look," I said. "There's someone else who can fill you in better than I can. He's James Agostino, with the FBI. In New York. Tell him about Corry and Fleck."

"Sure, Stone. In fact, why don't I just turn the whole investigation over to you, huh? Where are you staying?" I told him. "And can anyone around town vouch for you?"

"Sure," I replied. "Carl Henry Jacobs."

Bachman erupted with laughter. *"Bo Jacobs?* Not that sonofabitch!"

8

It was about six o'clock when I parked the jeep outside the sheriff's office and settled back to wait for Carl Henry Jacobs. With a moment or two to relax, I felt the stiffness begin to track me down again. But physical discomfort was the least of my worries.

I'd left Bachman organizing his troops in the first-aid hut below Howelsen Hill, driven directly back to my hotel, and called the ranch. Bo answered. He assured me that Sarah was fine. With Monique's help, Betty had calmed her down. A mild sedative had put her off to sleep. He wondered how I had made out. I mentioned Bachman's possible charge of obstruction. When Bo heard that I was to report to Bachman, he insisted on going with me.

The second call was to New York, again to the FBI. This time I refused to hang up until the switchboard woman promised to phone Agostino at home, asking him to reach me either at the hotel or in care of the sheriff's office. I'd waited then for half an hour, giving him time to phone back, then, disgusted, driven the twenty-six miles to the Yampa airport. I wanted to see what sort of plane Fleck and Corry had flown here. After getting directions from someone in the main building, I found it, a sleek little Lear jet. Twin engines. Horizon Imports had money.

I had returned to town then, bitter that things had gone so far, so fast. Not that Fleck hadn't warned me. But killing a kid to make a point that Sarah and I weren't cooperating, for I could see it no other way, was pretty strong medicine. Obviously we needed help, from the FBI. Protection. However, first things first. I'd want Fleck and Corry off our backs—by tying them in with Samuels' murder or at least with my beating. The key lay with the sheriff. With Bo backing me up, there was a good chance of us winning round two.

"You're late," snarled Bachman, standing in his doorway hitching up his pants and gunbelt. He pointed at me, then jerked a thumb toward his office. "Stone, in. Carl Henry, butt out." I went in. Bo followed.

Bachman's room was cramped and stuffy, its walls festooned with charts, maps, and "Wanted" bulletins. Behind the heavy oak desk was a large Smith & Wesson poster promoting its latest arsenal for crowd control, in living color: rubber bullets, gas guns, projectiles, and other such pleasant little items. Fascinating. As for the rest of the room, a cyclone couldn't have caused more damage, with boxes, books, clothing, open files strewn everywhere. I took refuge against a filing cabinet while Bachman lowered himself into his chair, then began shuffling through the mess on his desk. At last he leveled his gaze at Bo. "Jacobs, you're not invited, or didn't I make myself understood?" Bo stared back from under his stetson. Bachman grunted and turned to me. "Mr. Stone, I'm not pressing charges. How's that?"

I swallowed a cheer. "So you've talked to the FBI. To Jim Agostino?"

"Well, no. I . . . I couldn't see the point."

"You *didn't* contact the FBI?" Sidestepping a chair loaded with boxes, I came up to his desk and leaned across it. "Sheriff, you don't seem to understand. Something's going on around here, something big. It involves the pair from New York. Bad enough that they killed the kid, but it goes beyond that. Now, Agostino . . ."

Bachman shrugged off a yawn and shoved a tired pair of cowboy boots up onto the corner of the desk. His look was sympathetic. "Like I said, Mr. Stone, I couldn't see the point. Let me explain." With that he bellowed, "Hofstetter, bring me today's accident report."

Bo and I traded glances as Hofstetter, a deputy I recognized from the first-aid hut, trudged in, nodded at Bo, and handed a file to the sheriff. Bachman dismissed him and thumbed through the batch of blue papers. "Here it is," he said finally, jabbing it with a stubby finger. Picking up his glasses from the table, he went on, "Two guys came in here this afternoon asking for the sheriff because they felt uneasy not having reported an earlier hit-and-run. They told me that last night 'round nine, some yahoo smashed into their rented car in back of the Harbor Hotel, then lit out. They gave chase, but lost him in the storm. Well, sir, they didn't realize how much damage was done till they saw the car this morning in the daylight." Bachman tossed the file on his cluttered desk and glanced up at me. "Funny thing, Mr. Stone, is their names. They introduced themselves as Corry and Fleck."

I knew what was coming next.

"Now, correct me if I'm wrong, but weren't those the guys you said were involved in that boy Samuels' death? But they couldn't have been. Unless you're tellin' me I'm a liar, Mr. Stone. Y'see, both Corry and this Fleck were detailing the hit-and-run at the moment I got the call about the trouble at Howelsen Hill." The glasses went into his khaki shirt pocket.

I stalked back to the filing cabinet, remembering how Bo and I at the ranch that night had puzzled over why the jeep had been rammed into the car. Now we knew. What better place to be when a murder's committed than cuddling up with a sheriff? Which left one ugly little question unanswered.

"Then there's got to be a third guy," I said, swinging back toward Bachman. "A hit man."

He shrugged his large shoulders and turned to Bo. "The pair described the vehicle that hit them as a jeep, Carl Henry. Army green. You have a jeep, huh? Army green?"

Bo's expression didn't change. "It should be. It's army surplus. Like a dozen others round the county."

"Do any of them have red paint on the right-front fender?"

Bo tugged at his stetson and stood up. "Maybe mine does. It's just down on the street. Why don't we all go have a look. You, me, Hofstetter, Stoney here."

For a second I thought Bachman might take him up on it. But after removing his boots from the desk, he leaned back against the chair. "Too busy. Besides, Corry and Fleck should be here any moment. The killing busted right into the middle of them signin' their statements." Bo was fidgeting with his hat. "Something the matter, Carl Henry?"

"Nope," he said, "but if you're done plaguing Stoney here, I'll run him back to the ranch. Betty's waiting on us for dinner." He gave my arm a tug as we stepped out into the corridor. "Keep walking," he whispered. "Just keep walking. Those bastards, those cunning bastards . . ."

"Stone!"

It was Bachman. I told Bo to go on, so he could move the jeep away from the front of the building.

I turned around. Bachman was in his office doorway, arms folded across his chest. "You might be interested in the preliminary report on young Samuels." When I didn't answer, he went on, "I learned from the Boulder police that the kid had been hustling drugs on campus. They figure he'd been holding back too much of the profits."

"That's utter crap, Bachman," I yelled down the corridor, "and if you won't listen to me, it'll be your ass they'll nail to the wall."

I came away trying not to look like a competitor in a hundred-yard dash. The jeep was still there. Bo was leaning against it with his hands shoved in the pockets of his vest. He was covering the crumpled fender with his rump.

"So much for winning round two," I said, more to myself than to Bo, as I searched for the ignition key. "Now, let's get out of here."

Bo didn't budge. "Easy, Stoney, that's what the sonofabitch wants us to do. Panic. It's always been his game: Drop a little bomb, then sit back and watch everyone go berserk. Besides, those two yahoos won't show."

The key was in the back pocket of my jeans. "How do you know?"

"Because they've already told him everything. It was only a bashed fender, after all. Knowing Bachman, he'd just tell them the department would keep an eye out for the jeep, and send them on their way. Just the same, imagine those dudes showing up like that. They bust you up, then turn it around as an alibi. Smart. But like you said, there's one fucking great hired gun floatin' 'round at the moment."

I handed him the key. "That's why I want to go out to Yampa airport. No hit man would drive into a town that could be sealed off at either end." We got into the jeep.

"So you figure he flew in?"

"That's what I think. And if we're lucky, he may not have flown out yet."

"What if he is out there?" Bo said a few minutes later as we swung onto the highway. "Hasn't anyone ever told you that these guys *kill* for a living?"

"I don't want to get chummy, I only want to know if he's still here." I paused. "It's a long shot, but maybe we can narrow it down to a dozen, half a dozen planes arriving in the past twenty-four hours." Bo looked skeptical. I was beginning to lose my patience. "So, what do we do? Wait for Bachman to get off his ass? If we find something, he'll *have* to. In the meantime, Fleck and Corry might be tracking Sarah down."

"Okay, okay, but I got news for you. Hit men don't hang around. They fuck off. Fast as their little feet will take them. You've got a point, though. The airports are our best bet."

58

"Wait a minute," I said. "Airports? There's more than one?"

"Sure. A smaller one. Steamboat airport. Rocky Mountain Airways uses it. Only good for short takeoff and landing. Plus private stuff."

"Where is it?"

"Northwest of town. Five miles from here. Hold on."

We swung into the next gas station, bounced across the uneven snow, and stopped within inches of a service-bay door. "I'm gonna let the phone company save us a lot of work," Bo said, climbing out. "Sit tight."

Waiting for him, I couldn't get my mind off Terry's death. What, I wondered, could be so important that the kid had to die? Surely it was something more than unfinished business.

Bo was back, a grin spread wide across his face as he slipped in behind the wheel. "First off, Stoney, we can scrub Yampa airport. Only the bigger commercial flights were using it all day. Smaller craft were scared off by the storm. And no one left Yampa on the late-afternoon Frontier flight to Denver. The gal says the only real action out there was some guy pokin' around."

"That was me," I said. "I wanted to see what Fleck and Corry are flying these days."

Bo grunted and jammed the gear into reverse. We did a four-wheel pirouette and shot out onto the highway again.

Bo had also phoned the ranch. Sarah was sleeping still, "and your other friend and my wife are into the sauce, so everything's good. I told Betty to bolt the doors and bring Calhoun inside."

"Calhoun?" I shouted over the engine noise.

"Ya. Our German shepherd. One hell of a watchdog, so don't worry none about the women. By the way, I called ahead to Steamboat airport. We're expected."

During the short drive, I was amazed to learn that Bo had never flown.

"I climbed a tree once, Stoney, and that's about as high as I ever want to get, believe me. Unless it's liquor-induced." He slowed and pulled onto a rough section of road.

Darkness struck us between the highway and the airport, coming as it will in mountain areas like the snap of a finger. At last we pulled up beside a small hut illuminated only by our headlights. The engine gave a last struggle, a whine, then stillness. I got out and closed the door. We started through the snow toward the hut, when a couple of grunts broke the silence. Then came a string of unbroken curses from our right, away from the hut.

Bo yelled, "Pops? Pops Struble?"

At first I could see nothing. Then, as my eyes grew accustomed to the darkness, the forms of planes took shape, clustered about a solid dark area. Bo said, "C'mon, he's over in the hangar."

More curses. Bo called his name again. Then: "Carl? Carl Henry? I'm in the hangar. Git yoreself over here'n help me wrassle this lame-brained, snot-nosed bastard of a plane inside afore I boot the sonofabitch clear into the next county." A pause. "Carl Henry? Ain't you hearin' good?"

We stopped. Bo shot back, "It's not my hearing that's no goddamn good, Pops, it's my seeing. Turn the bloody hangar light on before my friend and I clothesline ourselves on a wing out here."

Suddenly light streamed across the snow, outlining a nest of small aircraft lashed down around us. From behind a plane partially blocking the hangar door a figure appeared cursing and stomping his feet.

Pops Struble was the airport's eighty-five-year-old watchman. He was a grizzled old guy, wrapped in what seemed an ancient buffalo coat. His face was razor-thin, the eyes quick and catlike. His handshake was incredibly strong, like the language he heaped on the plane in the entrance to the hangar. "And starin' at it won't get us nowheres," Pops said, eyeing us both. "It'll take pushin', if yore up to it." Bo grunted and poked around to find the trouble. The back of the plane's ski was caught under some loose planking.

"I ain't never seen a one-eighty so clumsy to handle on the ground," he was saying when we finally got the prop in clear of the doors. We stepped outside while Struble rambled on. "I've told management a thousand times I was hired t'watch them planes, not shunt them all over the friggin' map."

"That's the spirit," Bo replied, winking at me. "Hey, did you find the stuff I phoned about, by chance?"

The old man's grin was all gums. "Sure did, Carl Henry. It's waitin' in the office. Now, you two git. I'll be along."

We had come to look at listings of daily arrivals and departures; we found them in a tattered ledger on the counter.

For the next hour we sifted through the arrivals column. restricting ourselves to entries made within the past day and a half.

By the end of the hour we'd set aside thirty names. We kept those from out of town, or better still, from out of state. Some were chosen simply from gut feelings. In this area Bo and I didn't always agree, as with one guy from Gallup, New Mexico. Pops had come in from his rounds, muttering about the cold, when he heard us arguing. He listened for a while and finally said if we were looking for a pilot that had never been here before, the one from New Mexico was a bad choice. Everett Lyndahl was the mayor's second cousin, on his mother's side. This prompted us to show Pops our list of thirty, asking him to eliminate anyone who might have used the airport facilities previously. He reduced it by half.

Five more were dropped when Bo and I decided that if we were hiring a hit man, we'd go farther afield than Colorado to find one. Eight more were chopped when Pops dragged out ledgers for the last two years and found their names repeated at least once. This effort took another hour. We now had three possibles.

The first was F. A. Wilson from Baker, Idaho, who could be reached at the Timberline. He was our prime suspect until Bo's call to his nephew confirmed that Wilson had been in the bar and mostly under the table since his arrival at two o'clock.

Next, G. Maggs, Dearborn, Michigan. He was staying at the Village Inn, but at the moment was having dinner with his wife in the hotel dining room. This, from the maître d'.

That left Roger Wessen of Winnipeg, Manitoba, Canada.

"He's staying in the Lighthouse Motel on the east side of town," said Bo, running his finger across the page. "It's not the kind of place I'd stay, if I could afford my own plane."

The door behind us opened. Pops Struble came in from his final round, wheezed his way over to the oil burner, where he warmed his hands without taking off his mitts. Bo joined him.

"Pops, have you ever heard of a guy called Roger Wessen? He's Canadian. The ledger shows he arrived here this morning, right after the storm."

"Wessen?" said the old man, his face reflecting the struggle to prod his memory. "Lemme see the ledger."

I carried it over to him and pointed out the name. Pops's eyes brightened. "Yep. Wessen. I wasn't here this morning, but I thought I knowed the name. He's the one who owns the plane we hauled into the hangar. Supposed to quit here this afternoon, but phoned instead, sayin' he'd pay me extra to get it outta the cold."

61

We found the Cessna's log under the pilot's seat. The registration, tucked inside, gave us his full name and address: Roger Wessen, c/o Marriott's Garage, 2420 Pembina Highway, Winnipeg, Manitoba. "Licensed Mechanic—Old Car Speciality."

Bo flipped through the log. "Lot of travelin' for a mechanic, Stoney. Look here, eight runs since January. Now Steamboat."

"Maybe he picks up parts for antique cars."

"Sure. On the other hand, maybe he's a flyin' hit man, using antique parts as a cover."

I looked around me as I sat in the pilot's seat. "None too tidy. Even the plane looks a little weary. Did you notice?"

Bo was buried in the log. "Yup. You'd wonder how it ever made it over the mountains. But it sure did. Listen to this. He left Winnipeg Thursday afternoon with an overnight stop at Rockglen, Saskatchewan. Friday he hops across the border to Great Falls, Montana, where he's checked out through customs, then on to Pocatello, Idaho, and Logan, Utah."

"Looking for parts, no doubt," I said dryly.

Bo grinned. "Naturally. He stayed overnight in Logan, waitin' for the storm to pass, then got in here this morning by ten."

"That'd give him lots of time to bump around to a few garages, spread the word what parts he's looking for. All the while, he's really working out how to set up the kill. And that probably included a trip to the jump to lay the pattern for this afternoon. Our friends from the Timberline obviously must have known exactly what number bib Samuels would be wearing."

Bo closed the log. "Stoney, you don't think we're takin' this a little too far, huh? Here's some poor bastard moving about minding his own business and we turned him into a killer."

I took the log from Bo and stuffed it back under the seat. "You may be right," I said, "but I've got a real feeling about this guy."

Bo pushed the door open, then peered at me over his shoulder. "Just don't forget where your last gut feelin' got us. You were ready to lynch the mayor's second cousin."

"On his mother's side," I added, chortling to myself.

Pops Struble had coffee steaming on a small hot plate. "Help yourselves," he said. We did, then joined him at the counter. Bo told him about finding Wessen's log. "Now we know where's he's been, Pops, how do we know where he's going?"

Struble gave us that toothless grin. "Easy. Foreigners gotta file flight plans. Y'know, where they're goin' next. Wessen filed

62

that he was headin' back to Canada. Manitoba, somewheres.''
Pops looked from Bo to me. "I coulda saved you the trip to the
hangar, but then you would have missed ganderin' at the plane
up close. Somethin' else, ain't she?"

Bo said, "What do you mean, Pops?"

Struble placed his cup slowly on the counter. "Yore not tellin'
me you went out t'see Wessen's plane and you missed noticin'
the engine? Carl Henry, you wouldn't see a tick if it were settin'
on the end of yer pecker."

"What about the engine, Mr. Struble?" I asked.

His eyes narrowed. "Just that Wessen's Cessna's got the
biggest friggin' engine you ever did see crammed in it. Nothin'
short of a Garrett three-thirty-one, turboprop. And it'd sure tear
the arse out of it if someone hadn't reinforced the whole thing,
like. A real fancy job."

Bo caught me smiling. "It doesn't prove a damn thing, Stoney."

"True," I replied, then asked Pops for the phone.

"You're out of your mind," was Bo's comment when my
finger stopped at the Lighthouse Motel listing. Then he shrugged.
"Go on. What have we got to lose?"

The phone at the motel end rang a dozen times before a tired
voice answered. I asked for Roger Wessen.

I waited. At last another voice came on the line. "Hello?" It
sounded clear, articulate.

"Wessen," I said abruptly, "it's me. Fleck."

Carl Henry watched me intently from across the counter. Out
of the corner of my eye I saw Struble shuffling back to the hot
plate. I listened for a moment, then hung up.

Bo looked at me, curious. "What did he say?"

"He called me an asshole—"

"Good for him. But it doesn't prove—"

"—then he jumped all over me for not working through the
agreed contact."

Bo's face split into a grin. "Godalmighty, Stoney, we're
really cookin'."

9

"Is that you, Stoney?"

The light went on. Sarah was sitting up in bed, her face in shadow. It was after two in the morning.

"Hi," I murmured from the depths of a leather chair on the other side of the room. "How are you feeling?"

"Lousy." She moved into the soft yellow glow of the bedside lamp. Even from here I could see her eyes were puffed and red. She slipped out of bed and started unsteadily toward me and knelt down beside the chair. She was wearing a brushed blue cotton nightgown with thin straps, leaving her shoulders and arms bare.

"The nightgown suits you," I said, touching her cheek.

"It should. It's mine. Monique insisted on driving over to the hotel and collecting a few of my things. She thought I would feel better."

"Did Carl Henry go with her?"

"He'd already gone, I guess, to meet you. He told me once we reached the ranch that Terry had been shot to death." She touched my hand with hers. "He thought it best I know right from the beginning."

I breathed in deeply. "Bo and I have traced the killer to a motel in town. He's a professional hit man, Sarah, tied in with Fleck and Corry. You know them, don't you?" She nodded, then looked away. I pulled her chin gently around until she was looking at me. "They're still in town, Sarah. All three of them."

She tried turning away again, but I jerked the chin back.

"They're waiting for us to surface. They've got a stake in us, Sarah, and they're working to protect their investment. Why do you think the kid was killed? Dammit, woman, he was blown out of the sky to scare the shit out of us. You *and* me." I let her go and stood up. She remained motionless, her eyes closed.

"And before you insist once again that it isn't my fight," I went on, "let me tell you something. I had a bank account back in New York with hardly enough in it to buy lunch. That is, till

64

someone started funneling money into it by forging my signature. A million dollars, Sarah. And it was Gerry."

She didn't look up. "How do you know that?"

"Because at Tremblant he gave me money to help find you. Ten thousand in traveler's checks. Already signed with¯ my name. The same forged signature." Sarah slumped against the chair. At last I was getting through to her. "So don't tell me I'm not involved."

Suddenly my anger was gone. I knelt down beside her and touched her face with my fingers. I felt such affection for her at that moment. And when she finally opened her eyes, I said, "Sarah, you have to start trusting me, Goddammit, or we aren't going to make it. I can't help us, without you. And I can't help unless you tell me everything. Now. Do you understand?"

Her eyes opened. She dredged up a smile from somewhere. "Okay, Stoney." It was little more than a whisper. "Just give me a minute to wash my face. Then we'll talk."

While she was gone, I walked around the room working the kinks out of my legs, then wandered out to the kitchen, where I'd left Bo earlier, brooding over a call we'd made to Bachman.

We had called him at home directly after my little chat with Wessen. Bachman had been less than enthusiastic about us tracking the killer to the Lighthouse Motel. In so many words he told Bo to lay off before we got ourselves killed, and hung up. We tried again, only to hear that if we persisted in bothering him, the sheriff would reinstitute the charge of obstruction. A curt g'night. Bo was furious. Back at the ranch, Calhoun was set free and we ate what Betty had kept warm for us in the oven. We also polished off what she and Monique had left of the bottle of Scotch. I had then checked on Monique, who was sleeping peacefully in one of the back bedrooms, before looking in on Sarah.

The house was quiet now, the kitchen empty. I switched off the light and returned to the bedroom. Sarah was sitting on the bed, hair brushed, face scrubbed. Her legs were drawn up, her chin rested on her knees. The change in her was also on an emotional level. I found myself sitting beside a different woman for the next few hours. If it was the whole story I wanted, then brother, I was going to get it.

She began by describing a world that to me sounded more like fiction than fact: treasures removed from ancient Roman tombs by thieves known as *tombaroli*, works of art stolen from museums, galleries, and churches and sold through the art under-

65

world. These same stolen pieces then shipped to the United States to pass legally through customs. The past? Yes, she said, the present too. About ninety-five percent of the ancient artifacts in this country had got here by some illegal means.

In 1970 the United Nations Educational, Scientific, and Cultural Organization, UNESCO, asked its member nations to ratify a document entitled "The Means of Prohibiting the Illicit Import, Export and Transfer of Ownership of Cultural Property." The UN hoped it might put an end to the international theft of antiquities, treasures, and art. When the UNESCO vote was taken, seventy-seven countries were in favor, one opposed the motion, and eight abstained. Among the eight was the United States. Sarah explained, "We abstained because powerful lobbies wanted to keep our museums and galleries growing. Compared to other nations, the U.S. has almost no antiquities of its own. They've got to get them from somewhere."

"But what if they know the stuff's been stolen?"

"They don't care. Let me give you an example. A few years ago a small gold statue of Siva was stolen from a temple in India. It was replaced by a copy. Now this priceless statue turned up first in Switzerland, then England, where it was openly offered for sale. It was actually *advertised,* Stoney, in a London newspaper. For one million dollars.

"An American collector bought it at about the same time that India discovered the fake. The Indian government was furious. It demanded that the American government send the Siva back, but the U.S. officials said it had been declared at customs here and legally there was nothing our government could do. What's more, the new owner admitted knowing it had been stolen and told reporters he spent millions annually on Asian art, his specialty. And much of it was stolen, too."

"Okay," I said, "but that's an individual. Surely to God our museums and galleries have more sense."

"Stoney, our museums and galleries are full of treasures taken from other countries. Of course we don't say we're harboring stolen goods. Heaven forbid. How many times have I argued this with my father-in-law, who uses the same old line. 'Look at Egypt. Its heritage goes back for thousands of years, and where does Egypt keep its antiquities? Rotting in dungeons because the country hasn't got enough imagination or desire or money or the hell knows what to catalog its artistic wealth.' Harold Warden has told me how their museums are a mess, and 'so what if some of those treasures are smuggled out of the country and end up in

Switzerland? They're then bought by people who place a value on the art, clean it up, and put it on display for everyone to see and appreciate.' That is Harold's argument, and when I tell him it is still stolen property, he turns around and tells me to put things into perspective. 'Take the Turks,' he says, 'whose treasures rival Italy's. Or Egypt's. Do the descendants of the Turks who drove the Greeks from Asia Minor have a right to art *made* by the ancestors of the Greeks? And what about those who destroyed the Mayan civilization and settled Mexico? Now their descendants lay claim to Mayan artifacts. Have they really more right to it than we do? It's a moral question,' he says. And that sort of thinking is prevalent among most of the curators and art collectors in this country. We base everything on bigger and better. Bigger museums need to grow, need to be filled, for bigger audiences to appreciate them.''

I cut in. ''Which in turn puts the pressure squarely on the curators.''

''Exactly. Now they must seek out works of art which will help to establish their museum or gallery. And more often than not they turn to Switzerland for their needs.''

''Ah yes,'' I said, ''good old Switzerland, the clearinghouse of the earth. And I suppose the Swiss wouldn't sign the UNESCO convention either.''

''That's true, Stoney. So art objects, paintings, anything of value pours into Switzerland from all over the world, then moves on to countries like the States, who don't recognize the UN statute. Let me give you another example. Hershel told me about being in Cairo one time.'' She stopped. ''I'm not boring you?''

''Not at all. It's fascinating. Go on.''

''Well, Hershel was looking for a certain Egyptian icon for a client of his. A rich New York collector. While there he bumped into a curator he knew from a small New York museum. Over lunch this curator told Hershel he had a meeting with a director of a state-owned museum and would Hershel like to come along. Hershel was delighted.

''Now, Egyptian authorities forbid the sale and export of artifacts they deem of value to the state. So after a tour of the public areas in this museum, the director took Hershel and the curator downstairs into the huge caverns.''

I listened as Sarah went on, saying how Hershel discovered shelf after shelf of dusty, untouched statues and carvings, tablets, lintels, and parts of ancient frescoes. At his feet were boxes of old coins and jewelry and tomb furnishings.

In the meantime, Hershel's friend, who had shown interest in buying a statue he'd seen on the first level, now saw a bronze statue here that he liked much better. The curator then turned to the director and told him this is what he'd come to Egypt for. The director was sorry, but that particular statue was restricted and therefore not for sale; it was "protected property." Even so, the American offered one hundred and fifty thousand dollars for it. Still, he was turned down.

It seemed a lot of money. I asked Sarah if it was worth it. She answered with a smile, "Hershel told me it was worth twice the price. However, there was no more talk of this statue. The three went back upstairs, where Hershel watched the curator's original purchase being wrapped in plastic and crated. He paid the eight-hundred-dollar sale price and was assured the purchase would be shipped immediately to such and such a customs shed in Zurich. Hershel was in the same shed several days later, passing his own goods through customs on the way to New York, when he bumped into the same curator. The man insisted on showing Hershel the crate shipped from the Egyptian museum. A tag on the outside listed the contents and price: eight hundred dollars. But the curator opened it, and inside was the *bronze* statue instead, and a bill for one hundred and fifty thousand dollars."

I shook my head. "You're kidding."

"I'm not. A couple of days later it passed through U.S. customs with proper papers and went on its way to the museum the curator represented."

"But what about the members of the museum's board? Wouldn't they see it was a scam?"

"Why would they say anything? Here's a valuable piece of sculpture for which they paid half the value, legally transshipped, duty-free. As for the curator, he and others like him build their reputations on coups like this. Besides, most men on boards of museums are usually avid collectors themselves, which brings up another point."

"Which is?"

"Say I was the curator with the bronze statue from Egypt. Maybe I'd go to one of my museum's wealthy patrons and ask him to donate this statue to the museum. However, it has already been paid for out of the museum's acquisition fund. It's just the patron's name we're after. The patron of course agrees, and I give him the original bill of sale plus a receipt for three hundred thousand dollars, the *real* value of the piece, which he uses as a tax write-off. So now everybody's happy. I have a 'front' for the

68

statue that protects the museum's good name, the donor has a windfall tax exemption, and my knack for attracting patrons doesn't go unnoticed.''

Something puzzled me. ''Who covers for the acquisition fund?''

''I've never figured that out for sure, but my guess is that they bury the original hundred-and-fifty-thousand-dollar expenditure in among the normal operating costs of the museum. Or maybe they pad the costs of other pieces they've bought out of the fund.''

''Where do the acquisition funds come from, anyway?''

''Donations, federal grants. Every museum has acquisition funds. And no country in the world is as generous to the arts as the United States. Our government allows one-hundred-percent tax exemptions on any gifts, monetary or otherwise, donated to museums by the public. In fact, you can deduct up to thirty percent of your gross income under the column of cultural donations. So wealthy collectors have a choice. Pay taxes or contribute to the artistic cause.''

''And the rest of us poor bastards pay the taxes.''

''Sad but true.''

''So are you telling me every art deal is illegal?''

''No, and I'm not trying to imply everyone in the business is crooked, either. But these things go on. And everyone has his price.''

''But surely this theft and smuggling isn't as widespread as you're making it sound.''

She leaned back against the headboard. ''Stoney, at the moment there is an Italian millionaire called Alfonso Baglio who owns a small fleet of fast boats. They're anchored in the Adriatic. Inland he has recruited an army of farmers and townsfolk who go about digging up ruins. After dark. These *tombaroli* use the most sophisticated equipment in tracing buried catacombs, graves, and tombs in search of treasures. Old Roman coins, icons, gold, silver. Carvings. Whatever they can find. Then they sell these to Baglio. It is people like this who have looted the country of more than four hundred million dollars' worth of treasures since the end of World War Two. Which works out roughly to losing a museumful annually.''

''So our little Italian friend with the fast boats takes his share. How does he get rid of the stuff?''

''He waits till dark, then slips across the Adriatic to Yugoslavia, where he ties up at some little outport. From there the goods are trucked to Switzerland and provided with provenance.''

"Provenance. You're referring to proof of ownership, I take it."

"That's pretty close to it. Some impoverished count with nothing but a family tree would happily say the gold statue came from the family collection—for a price. Or documents are made up for it. Forged maybe. Anyway, no one is worried. U.S. Customs don't really care about the background. If it's antique, more than a hundred years old, it comes in tax-free."

"And how do you get it here?"

"Different ways. You can have it shipped or you hire what they call a runner to bring it."

"Runners?"

"Yes. Airline pilots, for instance, make good runners. They command a certain respect. And they don't even need to try slipping it through customs, because as long as it's declared, everything is fine."

"Who make the best runners?"

Again the smile. "Diplomats, if you can talk one into working for you. Hershel says they're being used more and more today. Diplomatic pouches can't be searched. He thinks that's why so many diplomats these days are serious collectors. Once runners get the hang of it, they will pick up artifacts themselves. Gerry used to tell me that hardly a day goes by that some airline pilot isn't in one New York museum or another spreading out his wares for an eager curator.

"He also used to come home telling me what great deals he was into. Such and such a painting being sold to this gallery, that museum. He always spiced it up with behind-the-scenes intrigue. When I questioned the ethics, his pat phrase was, 'It's legal, perfectly legal.' The more I questioned him, the more he smiled and the less he'd say."

"And he was mainly involved in paintings."

Sarah breathed in deeply. "Yes. Paintings came first, and me further down the line. It was an addiction, his collection of works of art."

I yawned and glanced at my watch. It was after four A.M.

She yawned back. "Before we bring Gerry into this," she said, with her hand still at her mouth, "let me give you a little more background. Can you stay awake?"

"Sure, if you can," I answered.

"All right. I'm repeating myself, but during the last thirty years, art sales, paintings in particular, have skyrocketed. So much so, Stoney, that Wall Street lists this boom as a fifteen-billion-dollar market annually. And that's only in the United States. Over the past three decades stock values have gone up by about five times. The value of art? Thirty times. So you see, Van Gogh and Rembrandt are doing better than General Motors. And because of that, art theft in America is becoming a plague.''

"Do people realize it's that big?"

"They should. Every week the New York papers report something about an important painting being stolen. And somewhere I read that only one painting in twenty is ever recovered.''

I laughed. "But what the hell do you do with a stolen Rembrandt?''

"Lots of things. Some are held for ransom, though little is ever known about this, because insurance companies would rather pay the ransom than the full price of the painting. So the police aren't brought into it at all. Other stolen paintings end up in Swiss banks, in private safety-deposit vaults, and are left until the statute of limitations runs out on them. Still others end up in private collections, hidden away in secret.''

"But there can't be any value, Sarah, in owning a stolen work. And who's going to risk being caught with something so hot?''

"It sounds ridiculous, I know,'' she answered, "but it isn't.'' She thought for a moment. "Let's say someone steals a Rubens from a private collection. Or better still, from a museum. He then sells it to his 'fence,' who knows that although it's hot, this Rubens still has value. It has value because the longer it goes undiscovered, the less likely it is to be found. Now, he sells, the buyer buys, and the process begins again. With each successive sale, the price goes up. Hershel says it's like pork futures. Say you buy piglets today. Three months from now they'll be bigger, and so will their market value. Likewise, the Rubens increases in value the longer it sits. But in order to make a profit on futures, you have to know the market and when to sell. Prices are all based on what the traffic will bear. So you see, Stoney, Rubenses and piglets have lots in common. People dealing in stolen art must also know their market. And as long as they do, there'll be profit.''

The penny had dropped. "In other words, what we have here is an art underworld.''

"Exactly. Paintings are even stolen *to order*. You want a Gauguin, Matisse, maybe a Gainsborough? One of several art networks will get it for you, provided you can afford it. No matter whose wall it's on.''

"And you're going to tell me that this 'art underworld' is controlled by the Hercules Foundation."

"Yes." She hesitated. "That isn't quite fair. Let's say from within the foundation. There's a subtle difference. You see, on one level, Hercules is a legitimate organization, made up of 'old boys,' collectors, museum and gallery backers, and big business. They give the foundation its credibility as one of New York's most reputable private clubs. Then there's the inner circle, which virtually controls the flow of stolen art in this country. And abroad. Doing the things we've just been talking about."

"And everyone within the foundation knows what's going on?"

"No, the majority know nothing about it. But they're not entirely innocent, either. They don't ask questions. Just as long as they can pluck a few sweet deals for themselves—they don't want to know how it's done."

I thought about this, then said, "How would the actual mechanics of carrying out these deals be handled?"

"A number of little companies have been set up to front these transactions, Stoney. At least that's what I learned. You know, art-restoration houses, framing outlets."

I played a hunch. "Would Horizon Imports be one of them?"

She eyed me curiously. "Yes. How did you know about Horizon Imports?"

"I didn't," I said, "except that it's listed as Corry and Fleck's employer on their hotel registration. But now let's get back to you."

"Me," she answered, taking my hand. "I'm part of all this." She paused. "My life really started to come down around me when I discovered Gerry wasn't the upstanding citizen everyone took him to be. He was a prime mover within the inner circle."

"Huh. And what about Harold Warden?"

"Yes, he's there too. But from what I gather, reluctantly, somehow."

"He likes what it brings, but his conscience bothers him?" She nodded. "Did Hershel tell you all this?"

Again she hesitated. "Much of it, but not the real inside stuff. And certainly not until I'd known him for some time. Hershel didn't like Hercules. It shattered him enough to see what was happening to the art world, most of all the U.S. refusing to sign the UNESCO convention. Why he stayed in Hercules, I'll never know."

"Why did he join?"

"He didn't. Harold gave him a membership to repay a kindness. It's renewed each year by my father-in-law. For years Hershel did nothing about it, then a year ago he got involved, but only as a fringe member with no voting privileges."

"And the kindness?"

"Hershel took Gerry under his wing for five years after Harold persuaded Gerry to come into the art business instead of heading for Wall Street."

"Why the first five years with Hershel?"

"Because Hershel Nesbitt is probably the most knowledgeable art expert and appraiser in New York, if not in America."

"And Gerry, always one to back sure bets, jumped at it," I added needlessly. Didn't we both know him?

"Not at the beginning. In fact, it was the only time I can remember that we sat down as a couple and talked it over. I thought it was a wonderful opportunity. Finally Gerry told his father he'd give it a try. Harold marched him down to the Nesbitt Gallery and introduced him to Hershel. Gerry thought it was some kind of joke. This mild-mannered little man could help him? He could and he did. After five years Gerry had changed his opinion. But then, when Hershel one day said he'd taught him everything he knew, Gerry, being Gerry, thanked him and left the gallery. He never made an effort to see Hershel again."

I chuckled. "Some things never change."

"I'd felt bad for years about how Gerry treated Hershel. Then one day about two years ago I was shopping in New York and found myself down in Greenwich Village outside the Nesbitt Gallery. I'd never met Hershel, and five years had passed, maybe more, since Gerry stopped working with him. I collected my courage and went in, thinking I'd stay long enough to ease my conscience. Five minutes at the most. I stayed five hours."

I felt her head rest against my shoulder.

"You liked him?"

"Yes. Very much. We talked about many things and drank tea. We never once mentioned Gerry. I'm sure he sensed that I was at loose ends." She laughed to herself. "God, was I at loose ends. My life was coming down around my ears. We lived in a rambling old house in the snobbiest part of Old Greenwich, Connecticut. My neighbors were all bores. Gerry didn't want kids. Our sex life was nil. At least mine was. Not that I didn't feel sexy. I just couldn't express it to Gerry, not that he seemed to care. Then one morning the local plumber dropped by to fix a leaky bathroom faucet. I took one look at him and practically

73

raped him on the bathroom floor. My God, Stoney, I was in heat. We made love until four in the afternoon. He had trouble getting back out to his truck!''

"Did he ever get around to fixing the tap?" I asked, amused.

She was laughing quietly again. "No. And he never came back. Anyway, if my life was beginning to fall apart, this broke the dam wide open. I could hardly face Gerry for feelings of guilt. I never told him. Instead I made an appointment with a New York psychiatrist, and after pouring out my heart, plumber and all, in three long sessions, he told me my problem· was boredom. God, Stoney, I could have told him that much. What I wanted to hear was that everything was fine; oh, maybe I was suffering from a touch of premature mid-life crisis, but not to worry. Or maybe he should have helped me face the truth: that I was jealous of my husband. Gerry was doing things, I wasn't. Gerry was going places, I wasn't. His mind was constantly being stimulated, while mine vegetated. He'd come home late, bubbling over with the news that he'd outbid a roomful of buyers for a Cézanne or that he was off to Zurich to track down some ancient Egyptian baubles. And me? I was staying home and raping the plumber.''

"What happened to the psychiatrist?''

"The psychiatrist? Well, one day, after my umpteenth session, I decided I'd had enough and went shopping. That's when I found myself outside Hershel's. I was there the next week, and the next, and without fully realizing it, he was teaching me what he'd taught Gerry. Later, he'd take me on jobs with him. We enjoyed being with each other, and I guess with his wife dead, we filled a void in each other's lives. He was good fun and had such an impish sense of humor and a philosophy of life so different from the Wardens'. To him, art was mostly a profit-and-loss statement. To Hershel, it's a love affair.'' She squeezed my hand. "By the way, how is he?''

"Fine,'' I lied, then quickly changed the subject. "How did Hershel and Harold become friends? I take it they were, at one time.''

"From what I gather, it was one of those friendships that grow out of one person doing another a favor and the other spending a lifetime trying to repay it. At least that's the way it struck me, seeing it from both sides. It seems they were in World War Two, despite their ages, attached to something known as the Monuments, Fine Arts, and Archives unit under Eisenhower's expenditionary force. During the Normandy invasion.''

"Hold it, hold it," I said. "Before you go into that, tell me more about the connection between stolen art and the Hercules Foundation."

She glanced at me sideways. "Last autumn, three things happened that set me off again. The first happened during one of my usual Thursdays with Hershel.

"Hershel had taken me along while he appraised an oil painting owned by a prominent collector. After, as we did from time to time, we window-shopped at nearby galleries. We stopped at a nondescript little gallery on East Fifty-seventh street. There was a small oil painting in the window. Often Hershel would have me look at these closely, then describe their style, what era they were from, and any characteristics which made them appealing. This time, however, he bent down and studied it through the glass. Then he muttered something and dragged me off to the nearest pay phone.

"I have no idea who he called or what was said, but the conversation couldn't have lasted more than thirty seconds. When he hung up, I asked if anything was wrong. He shrugged it off. Later, at dinner in a Village restaurant, he was in a lousy mood. He drank too much. I kept asking him what was wrong. Finally he told me that the painting we'd seen in the gallery window was either a Corot or Bierstadt. It had been stolen from a museum in Dusseldorf in 1972, along with a Rembrandt, a Hals, and a del Mazo, and had never been recovered. He described to me the various stages it might have come through in order to reach the States. Then, it probably had disappeared into a private collection. Now the collector may have died, and his heirs, not knowing it was stolen, had put it up for sale. Or maybe the collector was broke and had sold it for ready cash. We went back to his gallery and talked for hours. Much of what he told me I've just told you now."

"Tell me, did Hershel ever mention Hercules in any of this?"

"No, he didn't."

"Another thing. Why would finding a stolen painting put him in a lousy mood? You'd think he would be delighted."

"I asked him that. He said it was pleasing to find it, but depressing to think that such a valuable painting could be stolen and later sold openly in a gallery window. Let me add, Stoney, that a few days later I saw a small news story in the New York *Times*. An anonymous tip had led to the seizure of a stolen painting found in a gallery on East Fifty-seventh Street."

"Hershel's."

"Of course. But there's more. I said to you a few minutes ago that three things happened to me. Well, the next two come fast. A few days after I was with Hershel, Gerry arrived home one night, late as usual. He had been with the Hercules executives in a meeting. Some collector was looking for a particular painting and did Hope-Warden know where he might find it for sale? It turned out that Gerry had been working on some sort of deal, and before the meeting was over, they had come to terms.

"Gerry and I never talked much about his business. That is, we never sat down and really *talked* about it. We nibbled at the edges. He was the expert. What could I add to keep such a conversation going? On this occasion I asked what painting he'd sold. A Cézanne, he told me, and bent down to kiss me good night. He had been drinking. As he started for the door, I asked again about the painting. He mumbled something that sounded like 'apples on a tablecloth' and wandered off to his bedroom.''

"*His* bedroom?" I asked without thinking.

She looked away, then went on. "I tried to sleep, but something was nagging me. I must have wakened a dozen times, Stoney. But it wasn't until Gerry had left for the city that it came to me. Cézanne's *Apples on a Tablecloth*. I could hear Gerry saying that the night before. Suddenly I was shivering all over. I was *sure* Hershel had mentioned it as being among the other paintings stolen in the last two years. And now Gerry had just sold it. I picked up the phone to call Hershel, then put it down. Instead I drove to New York.''

"To see Hershel?"

"No. To the New York *Times* clipping library. If the painting was stolen, I wanted to find out alone. After two hours, I was ready to give up when I found myself staring at a small news story dated Chicago, December 28, 1978. Three Cézanne oil paintings had been stolen from a locked storeroom in the Art Institute of Chicago.''

"Which paintings were they?"

"*Madame Cézanne in a Yellow Armchair, House on the River,* and *Apples on a Tablecloth.*" She rubbed her eyes.

"Several days later I asked Gerry as offhandly as possible if Hercules had sold any companion pieces to *Apples on a Tablecloth.* He said yes, two others, but didn't name them. Stoney, according to the article, they were valued at more than a million dollars each.

"I still couldn't believe Hercules was involved in handling stolen art. Maybe it was just that I didn't want to believe it. But I

76

couldn't ignore what I'd discovered, either. I started searching through libraries for any material related to art thefts. I became fascinated with it. Heavens, Stoney, I couldn't believe what I was reading. Illegal art traffic in the *billions* of dollars.''

"I don't suppose Hercules would be mentioned."

She shook her head. "No. Just references to a network of thieves' or 'the art underworld,' and yet here was Sarah Warden sitting on something that could blow the New York art scene sky-high and take her husband with it.''

"It obviously bothered you."

"That's putting it mildly. The old guilt feelings were back, nothing so simple as worrying about screwing the plumber. I felt I was deliberately undermining Gerry by asking him all sorts of unrelated questions about paintings, then matching what he said with the stuff I'd dug out of the books and articles I'd been reading, but I couldn't stop. I found myself challenging him about the ethics of collectors. It only underlined how far our marriage had deteriorated. I wanted to be loved so desperately. All this was tearing me apart. I started dropping things, or bursting into tears over absolutely nothing. I was alone for days on end. When he was at home, little things would start an argument and we would end up screaming at each other. He'd call me stupid, brainless, a lousy lay. How the hell would he know? He never touched me. He should have asked the plumber. I suppose it was just as much our lousy marriage that started me on the trail of proving that Hercules was behind the art thefts. If old Gerry could strike up a deal for the sale of *Apples on a Tablecloth*, why couldn't Hercules be in such a trade full-time?''

"All you had to do was prove it."

"True. And it came so unexpectedly. At a benefit ball sponsored annually by the foundation. For one charity or another. This was late last November. Everyone was there, Stoney. Gerry looked gorgeous in a velvet tuxedo. I wore one of those flimsy silk dresses that leave little to the imagination.''

"Your way of catching some of the attention that usually went to Gerry." I added, "It's called 'marital competing,' " and wished I hadn't.

But she smiled. "I'm sure you're right. I've never thought of it that way." She closed her eyes and reminisced. "Being Gerry's wife had its rewards. In public he was fun, gregarious, and surprisingly attentive. We came as a matched set.''

"I've followed you in the social pages. You were all of that," I replied, and again wished I hadn't.

She made a face and put her chin on my shoulder. "This might surprise you, but when I saw you and Monique together at the ski jumping, I felt . . . envious. I've never really thought of you with anyone, even when you were married. I didn't know Jane. Then, seeing you and Monique, I had this deliciously sexy thought of what you two were doing in bed."

I laughed. "Sarah Anne, you always did have an active imagination." Just as suddenly, the mood had changed. She was silent. "I'm sorry about Terry."

"How did you know I was thinking about him? God, the poor kid. And his family. Gerry first, then him. Will it never end?"

"Shall we call it quits for now?"

"No, it's good therapy." She sighed. "I knew I couldn't run from all this. If I'd only listened to you. When I looked in the mirror in the bathroom a moment ago, I was so frightened of being left alone. That's been the story of my life. When I found tenderness, I turned away from it, thinking it couldn't last."

"Maybe you thought of it as a weakness. You saw it first in your father. And when his marriage didn't last, tenderness became a false god."

The next words she spoke I could hardly hear. "Stoney, why didn't my shrink tell me that?"

"Maybe he did, but you weren't listening. It seems to me that Hershel was hitting the right notes, even if he didn't put them into words."

"And I picked up his cause to get back at Gerry because of his insensitivity?"

"Psychiatry scares the hell out of me," I said, easing her forward, then slipping my arm about her shoulders. "It digs too deeply into the psyche. Let's get back to the charity ball. It's safer."

It was Sarah's turn to laugh. "Maybe for *you*, Mr. Stone. You see, it was around midnight. Gerry was dancing with one of his many admirers. He had lots that night. He was in good form. He was the foundation's rising star and had been asked to be presenter of the yearly award to some outstanding member of the community. Of course, in presenting it he gave us one of his routines. Let's see . . . Boris Karloff . . ."

". . . ordering a Bloody Mary."

Another laugh. "You've heard that one." I nodded. "Anyway, he was a hit, and I loved him for it. He was in his element. So there he was dancing with one of his fans while I was getting pleasantly soused on champagne and talking to friends, when

78

this young guy came out of nowhere. He grabbed me by the arm and swung me out onto the dance floor. Before I knew what was happening, he'd clamped me hard to him, all the way down.

"Well, I was more annoyed than embarrassed. I tried to push him away, but I couldn't. He was too strong, so I decided to ignore him and pray for the music to end. That's when he started rambling on about me, how I was flaunting myself in a dress you could see everything through. And about Gerry, who thought of himself as God Almighty. I didn't need this. As it was, I was keeping myself afloat on Valium and booze. So I shouted in his ear, why was he taking out his aggression on me. In so many words he told me that he'd been rejected from joining the foundation's inner circle by one vote. My husband's.

"I told him I didn't know anything about an 'inner circle,' that Gerry was on the general executive. The kid laughed at me. He said not many people *did* know about it, not even most members, and if word ever got out . . . All at once, Stoney, I was listening. He was saying, 'And if they want to fight dirty, so can I.' You can imagine how fast I sobered up. We were in the huge, ornate ballroom of the Waldorf, and I worked him over to the farthest corner and listened. It helped that the kid was a little drunk and boastful. From the feel of him, I was also driving him nuts." She stopped. "Oh, God, I felt cheap. Dirty."

"Would you rather leave it till morning?"

She shook her head, then went on. He told her of having proof that this inner group was using the foundation as a cover for the importing and exporting of stolen art around the world. These paintings came through Hercules on consignment to collectors—members of Hercules—and were often obtained from lesser officials in such places as Greece, Turkey, and Egypt through bribes and blackmail. He explained how this group retained a number of pilots and diplomats, using them as runners because of their mobility. A few archeologists also smuggled artifacts from foreign digs. Especially from Turkey, where removing any artifacts is illegal. The same with Mayan treasures from Mexico.

Sarah was to find later that the guy was Allan Starkman, whose father was a member of the Met board of governors. Allan was in his late twenties, privately schooled, and known to be wild. And rich. In the meantime, Sarah had been sober enough to tell him he was being silly. If not, where was the proof?

"He laughed when I asked him that," she said. "So I bullied him a little, telling him he was drunk and when he sobered up he wouldn't even remember dancing with me. He then told me about having made photocopies of the transactions involving three Cezannes stolen from the Art Institute of Chicago in 1978, their storage in Swiss bank vaults while still hot, and the names of the three American collectors who later bought them here in the States."

"Did he tell you how he got the proof?"

"He would only say he had connections, but we're getting away from the point. When he mentioned the Cézannes, Stoney, my knees went weak. After all, I *knew* all about the Cézannes. Well, he took my slight swaying as a sign of his prowess with women and pulled me even closer. Then he went on. He had a list of the pilots and diplomats Hercules could depend on, as well as officials in foreign countries who could be bribed."

I sighed. "Hey, hold on. You're telling me that you learned all this from one dance?"

She paused. "No. After a few dances Gerry took me aside and politely told me I was making a spectacle of myself and to lay off Starkman. This was Gerry talking, the man who'd shown no real interest in me, sexual or otherwise, for years. I told him just as politely to go jump in the Hudson River and promptly asked Allan to dance. I was mad, really mad. For years I had put up with him being Mr. Expert on TV, put up with his sordid little affairs, one time I found lipstick on his *shorts*! But I loved him. Or hated him. Now I'm not sure which. And now too I was learning that this man, my husband, who was revered so highly in the art world, was actually using it to his own ends. My God, to think of the corrupt power he could wield behind that facade of respectability. Stoney, I was shattered. But I wanted proof. Gerry was breathing down my neck. So I ground this little bugger into me and asked when I could see him again. He named the day, I named the hotel."

We stopped for a while then. It was almost five A.M. Sarah went to the bathroom, giving me time to collect my thoughts.

She came back then and closed the door, the cotton nightgown clinging to her hips and breasts. It took me back to my little attic walkup in Cambridge, in those days at Harvard. On a Saturday night in winter she would pull on her cotton nightie and trundle off to the bathroom on the second floor. The beer bashes at the College Pub had that sort of effect on her.

"And what happened after the ball was over?" I asked as she crawled up beside me on the bed.

She made a face. "Gerry was in a rage. I remember wishing

80

all his little groupies could see him now. He swore at me, saying he and the Hercules executive committee were having enough trouble with the conniving, ambitious, treacherous little bastard Starkman without me fucking him on the floor of the Waldorf ballroom. His words, Stoney, not mine."

"A fit of jealousy?" I said, amused. "It doesn't sound like Gerry."

Sarah was actually blushing. "Gerry had his moments, believe me. Only one other person ever brought that much of his ugly side out."

"Who?"

The blush again. "You."

"*Me?*" It wasn't something I could believe. "Look, I hadn't seen old Gerry in fifteen years. Besides, I didn't run off with you. He—"

"Stoney, when he learned about the Algonquin, I'll swear he was ready to kill you. I have no idea how he found out. I don't want to know. But take it from me, you started many a dinner argument long before the Algonquin love-in. Remind me about it sometime."

For the moment I let it pass. "And Starkman?"

"I met him three times. At the Taft. I hated him, Stoney." She looked away and continued, her voice soft, "And yet I'd had so little physical contact with anyone over the past two years that I found myself doing things . . ."

"I understand," I said. "I hope you learned something for your trouble." She had.

Among other things, Starkman told her about an annual conference held by this inner group of Hercules members. It was usually in Switzerland, around this time of year, late February, early March, and attended by those who formed the special "executive" and some sixty to eighty others who had been voted into the inner circle. Strategy meetings, contracts signed with guys like Baglio for the next year, a preview of the art world in general, took place. According to Starkman, an auction was the highlight of the three-day meeting, from treasures, works of art, paintings held in Swiss vaults. So exclusive that even the rest of Hercules' twelve hundred members knew nothing about it. Much of Baglio's contraband would find a buyer here. What remained unsold would then be discreetly offered to collectors outside this charmed circle. Very chummy.

I was to learn something else from Sarah. From what she gathered, one man was the driving force behind the inner circle.

He was also the general manager of the Hercules Foundation itself. His name? Gerhard Hegler. Well, well. Good old Gerhard Hegler, I thought to myself, but for the moment let that pass too.

By the third tryst, Sarah found she had Allan Starkman where she wanted him. Whether he was obsessed with her or obsessed with being Gerry's wife's lover, she never knew. She didn't care. It was while showering together during the third meeting that Sarah insisted Starkman bring proof of what he had been telling her. She wanted the names of those people Starkman referred to as "Gerry's friends," the runners paid off by Hercules Two (Sarah's name for them), and lastly, photocopies of receipts concerning the Cézanne theft, storage of the paintings, and the names of the final buyers. By now the Taft Hotel was too familiar. Starkman insisted on a change of venue, to a motel called the Twilight Inn, near Harrison, New York. For what Sarah wanted, it would have to be a whole-nighter. She thought about it while she dried herself. If he'd throw in the date and place of the conference, it was a deal.

On the day she was to meet with Starkman, a Thursday night early last December, Gerry had phoned to say that he would be home for dinner, though he had to be back into New York for a nine-P.M. meeting. At eight-thirty, after he'd gone, Sarah went out to the garage to get in her car, only to find her keys missing; the electric lock on the garage doors was jammed as well.

"I was so scared. It was Gerry's subtle way of telling me he knew what was happening. Or at least that I was seeing someone else. He was home by midnight. We never spoke about it. The next Monday I was alone at home watching the late news. A body had been pulled from the water of Long Island Sound at a place called Milton Point. It had been identified as Allan Starkman, son of E. G. Starkman. I found Milton Point on the map. It was twenty miles from Harrison."

"Jesus Christ."

"I started drinking right then, Stoney, and thinking back to Thursday night. Gerry had said something about going to a Hercules meeting in town, so I knew if he'd killed Starkman he would have an alibi. I couldn't believe that I was thinking this way. I tried convincing myself that Allan's death was a coincidence. Then things got fuzzy and I was crying and when I woke up I was in a private hospital, drying out. Gerry was waiting for me. We drove home as if nothing had happened. The same day some police dropped by to question Gerry about Allan's death. I

82

hid in an upstairs closet with a bottle, knowing no one would believe me if I told them Gerry had something to do with it.''

"Do you think he did it?''

Sarah looked at me and shrugged. ''We'll never know. The next day when Gerry had gone to work, I dropped into my bank to withdraw money from my own account. By noon I was on a bus for Chicago.''

"And from Chicago?''

"I started west, keeping away from the airlines. I spent Christmas alone in a funny little motel in Reliance, South Dakota, waiting for the door to burst open and Gerry to walk in. He didn't. Three weeks later I found myself in the Denver bus station staring at a poster with 'Ski Steamboat' across it. I liked the sound of 'Steamboat,' so I caught a cab to the airport because if I had to ride in another bus, I would've screamed. I bumped into Monique there. She was alone too, and we hit it off. You know the rest.''

It was almost six o'clock in the morning. I slipped off the bed and went to the window, to stare out in darkness. It all sounded unreal, yet all too real at the same time. I couldn't quite believe that Gerry had killed Starkman. Stealing was one thing. Outright murder was something else. And yet the stakes were so high. Exposure of the whole operation would have been devastating to Gerry, this Hegler, and everyone connected to it. Which left us sitting here wondering what to do next. I had to reach Agostino. Otherwise, once the Timberline twins got us on their plane, God knows what would become of us.

Sarah called me from the bed. She was under the blankets and almost asleep. I bent down, and kissing her on the lips, told her not to worry. I had a friend back in New York with the FBI, and I'd be in touch with him. She wasn't to leave the ranch.

She looked up at me and smiled. "I won't, Stoney. And thanks." I held her hand until she was asleep. A few minutes later I was in the kitchen leaving Bo a note to say if he couldn't find me back at the hotel, I'd be camped out on Bachman's doorstep.

10

By nine o'clock that morning, Sunday, I was a new man; a tired one, admittedly, but fresh from a shower, shave, and breakfast. I had also pulled on my new prewashed jeans and denim shirt and cowboys boots, to find I looked more like the help than the guests. There were no calls for me from New York. I was about to phone again when *my* phone rang. Bo Jacobs was on the other end.

"I've got some lousy news for you," he said, clearing his throat. "Pops Struble just called here to say our friend Wessen is warming up the plane for takeoff."

I swore to myself. "Thanks, Bo, I'll get right onto the sheriff."

"Forget it, Stoney. I already have. That's the rest of the bad news. He says they couldn't get a warrant in time to search the plane. The sonofabitch just had all night. Now it's too late."

"Dammit," I muttered.

"He also warned me again that should you so much as stick your big toe anywheres near him or his deputies, he'll slap you into a cell so fast your head will spin. Same old charge. He can be an ornery old bugger when he wants to be."

"Let's look at the good side," I said, sitting down on the bed. "At least we don't have a hit man to worry about." I didn't bother to tell him the drive from the ranch a few hours ago had been anything but pleasant. What if he'd been after me next? I asked him instead about the pair at the Timberline.

"Little Max tells me they've just gone skiing. I watched them all the way to the first lift. Max has promised to phone the minute either of them so much as farts."

"How did I ever get along without you? By the way, tell Betty that apart from the odd cranky muscle, I'm feeling much better."

"You bet. Everyone here is still asleep. Kids and all. And while I'm on the line, mind tellin' me how come you were so fired up to leave here this morning?"

"Have you got a moment?" I answered, then told him briefly why Fleck and Corry, and their hitman, were hassling us. Now I

84

was trying to track down an agent with the FBI in New York, which was bound to take some time.

"I don't understand half what you're talking about . . ."

"Welcome to the club," I said. "Listen, keep a close eye on Sarah and Monique, will you? If those two guys are skiing, either they're on the prowl for Sarah and me or they're biding their time."

"Bidin' their time for what?"

"Further instructions? I don't know. Anyway, I'll phone you the moment I hear from the FBI."

"Good enough. And don't worry about the women. Betty hasn't had such good company for years."

"Fine." My mind was elsewhere. "Maybe I can get the Feds to light a fire under Bachman."

Bo snorted. "Just as long as the flames are high enough to singe his ass."

By four in the afternoon I was still nowhere, other than having cornered a couple of hours' sleep. During my fifteenth call to the FBI, the switchboard operator pleaded with me to be patient a little longer. It seemed Agostino had taken his family skiing for the weekend, no one knew quite where. She promised to do her best and said she would call me back. By six o'clock I gave up and phoned the ranch.

Betty answered. She sounded hesitant. Sarah had tried to reach me but the line to my room was busy. Carl Henry also wanted to talk to me earlier, but he'd been called out to Yampa airport to pick up passengers from a charter flight. She expected him back within the next half-hour, around the time she expected Sarah and Monique.

My breath caught in my throat. "Where the hell are they?" I asked. Just after Carl Henry left, Monique had suggested a soothing swim at the hot springs. "I didn't like it, Stoney, but I was outvoted. Sarah needed some sort of diversion. They're expecting you to join them. I lent them the Chrysler. I hope I didn't do anything wrong."

"Don't worry, Betty," I said, trying not to let on how scared I was. "But when Bo calls, tell him to meet us at the pool. We'll stay there till he arrives."

"I'll pass the message on. By the way, Stoney, if you should run into him first, tell him Little Max called. From Timberline."

I hardly remembered hanging up the phone, Bo's words echo-

ing through my head: "Max has promised to phone the minute
. . ." I knew damn well then that the bastards were on the
move.

Within fifteen minutes I was crowding the old jeep into the
parking lot of the pool complex. I braked it into a chest-high pile
of cleared snow and raced for the main door. A young woman
wearing a Speedo swimsuit glanced up from behind the counter
as I bolted by, then shouted after me, "Sir, street clothes aren't
permitted."

I yanked the far door open. Four strides farther down the
unheated corridor, on the left, was the entrance to the hot-springs
pool itself.

A rush of hot moist air enveloped me as I stepped inside. A
curtain of mist hung directly over the pool, so dense a cloud that
much of the room; from the surface of the water to the laminated
beams supporting the roof, was obscured. Behind me a door
opened. An annoyed voice said, "Sir, excuse me but . . ."
Ignoring it, I started forward, then crouched at the edge of the
pool.

Heads close to me bobbed about in the warm water. Several
women and a man. Another head was coming out of the mist. I
turned to get a better look. It was Monique. She saw me at once.
"Philippe!" Her dark hair was trailing behind her in the water.

I called out impatiently, "Where's Sarah?"

A second head glided out of the mist. "Right here." It was
Sarah, as blond as Monique was dark. I waved and stood up.
Another lifeguard had joined the young woman, the same guy
who had recommended the Gold Mine Restaurant the night I
came down here alone. I apologized for running right through,
saying I had been worried about my two friends; I wasn't sure if
they could swim. The girl's mouth relaxed into a smile. The pool
wouldn't close for another thirty minutes, if I cared to rent a
bathing suit. I thanked her. The kid was looking at me curiously.
Hadn't he seen me somewhere before? I told him about the Gold
Mine and how much I'd enjoyed it. He grinned at me, then
excused himself to continue his walks around the pool.

I was back soon wearing a pair of tan boxer swim shorts big
enough for a family of six. I found Monique bent over the pool
squeezing water out of her hair. Her rented one-piece outfit was
a damn sight more attractive than mine. We hadn't really seen
each other since Terry was killed, and I felt a sudden need to be
close to her again. I bent down beside her and said hello as I
slipped an arm across her shoulders.

86

She straightened so fast, she almost knocked both of us off balance. "Philippe," she whispered, "you startled me."

"I'm sorry. I guess the past twenty-four hours have been a strain on all of us," I said. I took a white towel from a peg on the wall and wrapped it around her shoulders.

"I will go to the locker room. My hair takes forever to dry with those funny little hot-wind machines in there." She was still shivering. "Will you tell Sarah where I am? She is waiting for you. At the deep end."

I found her there, holding on to the side of the pool, alone. She waved as I came out of the mist.

"You scared the living hell out of me, Mrs. Warden," I said, swimming up beside her and hooking my arm and elbow on the edge. "I thought after our talk you'd have more sense than to leave the ranch."

"Everything was closing in on me, Stoney, and with Monique suggesting a relaxed swim in the hot-springs pool, well . . ."

"No one can blame you," I said, staring down through the water at her bikini.

"It was foolish. I shouldn't need you to remind me." Her hand came up to pat the hair where it was pinned loosely on her head. She had missed a few strands. I pushed them into place, then touched the nape of her neck. Her eyes closed. She went on, "I stayed here, holding on to the side of the pool, watching Monique swim back and forth, back and forth, in and out of the mist. Then she didn't come back, and I started for the shallow end. And when I saw you standing there in your coat, I could have cried."

I found myself staring at the wall just beyond us, a wall of glass panels frosted with ice to the roof. "Carl Henry will meet us here," I said quietly, "so don't worry. I've put in calls to the FBI in New York. They're bound to arrange things here with the local police. It takes time." I stopped as the young lifeguard, clad in a towel and swimsuit, came by. He grinned, winked, and moved on, to disappear into the mist on the other side of the pool.

Both of us were silent. I watched her eyes open and fasten on mine. I discovered myself wondering what it would be like to make love to this woman again, here, now, in the pool, in this warm water. But when I opened my mouth to speak, it was to suggest something much more sensible. "Let's swim a bit," I said, pushing myself away from the side.

We were moving slowly now toward the shallow end. An elderly man came by doing the breaststroke. I'd been telling her that Monique had gone on ahead to the locker room. Sarah nodded, waiting for the old guy to be swallowed up by the mist, and said, "Stoney, I want to finish what I was talking about early this morning."

I stopped for a moment to tread water. "There'll be plenty of time later." She went on, I followed. "Relax," I said. "Bo will be here soon." He'd better be. With him around, there was less chance of Fleck and Corry trying much. My greatest worry was Monique, Sarah, and I stepping out into the parking lot alone.

We reached the shallow end, where a mother and her baby were playing in the water. A small ledge ran along the wall of the pool, at this end at least, several feet down from the surface. We sat on it and leaned back against the tiles, the water at our necks.

Sarah was restless. She said, "Did you know this is natural hot water coming from beneath the mountains at about three hundred gallons per minute? It's known officially as the world-famous Heart Springs."

"Why don't you finish what you were telling me this morning."

"You don't want to know the temperature? One hundred and three degrees. I read it in the women's locker room."

"I know what it is. It's very hot."

A hand touched mine under the water. "There is something in all this I haven't mentioned, Stoney, It's about Hershel Nesbitt. During the war, Hershel did my father-in-law a favor, as I've already told you. It happened after the Normandy invasion during the time they both had been recruited by the Monuments, Fine Arts, and Archives unit."

She began by saying that when the Nazis invaded much of the rest of Europe in 1939, they also plundered these countries for their valuable art. Some of this art was actually held for ransom and the money from it used to buy armaments. Other valuable pieces the Germans simply set aside because Hitler had a dream of building his "Fuhrermuseum" in Linz and filling it with the world's best art treasures, a dream he planned to dedicate to his mother. Many of his commanders, however, including Hermann Göring, the Nazi leader responsible for the Luftwaffe, Joseph Goebbels, minister in charge of propaganda, and Heinrich Himmler, of the Schutzstaffel, the SS, purloined huge collections for themselves. By the time the Allies hit the Normandy beaches, some five hundred million dollars' worth of captured art had reached Germany, or was still en route.

Sarah went on, "So with the invasion came the MFA&A, as Hershel called it. Its job was to find, identify, and salvage precious art as the Germans withdrew. The proudest moment for both Hershel and Harold came on the twenty-fifth of August 1944, after the six-day siege of Paris was smashed. They were among the first ones through the doors of the Louvre."

"I suppose the good stuff was missing," I said.

"Not really. Before France collapsed in 1939, the Louvre, many other galleries, and even private connoisseurs had crated up their collections and transported them south to places like the Dordogne, where they were hidden in lofts, barns, churches, and old châteaus. When the Germans took Paris and dropped into the Louvre, they found masterpieces like the *Mona Lisa* and *Venus de Milo* gone, along with thousands of others. The Nazi high command organized a special unit of soldiers whose only task during the war was to hunt down these hidden masterpieces."

By October of 1944, the Allied Fine Arts division felt safe enough to send batches of its people down into the Dordogne and other areas. The French resistance at the time was still digging up pockets of Germans, but most of the cleanup was done. According to Sarah, one such team was Harold, Hershel, plus a third man and a jeep full of provisions. Their assigned area was inland from Bordeaux. They moved from château to château, barn to barn, cataloging for later pickup the sculptures, the goblets of solid gold, the archival material, and the rare books which had been secreted away from the invaders. And paintings. Cézannes, Goyas, Van Goghs, Kandinskys, among many others.

There were some not-so-good days. They would come upon the remains of ransacked buildings where the Germans had already been. One morning, arriving at Souillac, the three heard rumors that five German trucks had passed through the town twenty-four hours earlier. The convoy was believed to be carrying paintings and rare objects removed from a château near Rastignac. This very château had been high on the team's list of priorities. They drove directly to it, only to find a smoldering ruin.

Sarah continued, "My father-in-law had been the driving force behind this little team. Harold organized the routes and made the reports back to Paris. He was working the three of them twenty hours a day. More if necessary, Stoney. To Harold it was a job and he'd managed to remain quite detached from the

89

horror of what war had done to the area and its people. But just before the episode at Rastignac, one incident changed him. They drove through a town, I can't remember the name offhand, where all the inhabitants had been annihilated by the Nazis. The sight stripped my father-in-law of his detachment. He began falling apart."

"How did he fall apart?" I asked. "He couldn't work any longer?"

"On the contrary. He drove himself even harder, lost his sense of humor, and worse, a sense of himself, so that by the time they reached Souillac, he was in bad shape. The charred shell of the château at Rastignac was the last straw. He told Hershel he was going after the German convoy alone. Hershel was to carry on as if he were still with them, filing the daily reports. Paris was not to know what Harold had done."

"But that's ridiculous, Sarah," I said. "How could he have stopped it on his own?" My attention was on the old man with the breaststroke, who had come back to sit on the submerged steps vacated by the mother and her baby. He was swirling his feet in the water.

"Hershel thinks Harold Warden was unhinged at the time. He told Hershel he would use the local French resistance, the Maquis, to cut off the convoy, or he'd die trying." Her words trailed off. Then, in a whisper: "That old guy's listening, Stoney."

I'd had the same feeling. "With both ears. He's just nosy, but let's go." We started swimming slowly back toward the deep end. I learned then how Harold had taken their vehicle and an abandoned pistol they had found along the way, leaving Hershel and the other guy to scrounge for their own transportation.

We reached the deep end. I hitched my elbows on the edge of the pool, listening.

Hershel had carried on, making daily reports, planning where to go next. In the confusion at the Paris headquarters, no one was aware of the change. I pointed out that Warden obviously had come out of it alive.

"Yes," she said, "but not by much. He disappeared for a month. Poor Hershel was sick with worry. He felt guilty for not having reported that Harold had gone. But he had promised Harold he wouldn't. Then one morning in late fall, my father-in-law appeared. He was bearded, clothed in rags, and barely alive. He couldn't even speak. How he ever found them remains a mystery, because they were constantly on the move. Anyway,

Hershel stuck by him, nursing him back to health. Many times he added his own rations to Harold's, to build up his strength."

"What was Harold's explanation?"

"He never gave one."

"What does Hershel think happened?"

"He suspects that Harold might have been caught in a crossfire between the Maquis and the retreating Germans. Or maybe he became one of the resistance fighters himself."

"Where would this have taken place?"

"According to Hershel, the Germans, trapped in . . . well, middle France, were trying to reach northern Italy. They were going by way of Grenoble, then using the passes through the Alps. East of Gap. And up as far as Chamonix, taking them into Italy or even Switzerland." She paused. "The Marquis stopped many of them."

"And what of Harold, Hershel, and the third guy?"

"They were later returned to Paris and assigned to General Patton's—I think Hershel said—the 347th Infantry division. At least Hershel and Harold stuck together. They had several third partners. Hershel was very proud to have been on hand when seven thousand paintings were discovered hidden in a salt mine at Alt Aussee, near Salzburg. They were heading for Hitler's museum."

"That's all very interesting, but . . . ."

"But what does it have to with us?" she said, drawing herself up beside me. Below the water our hips touched. "It is this. Hershel and my father-in-law were asked to remain with the MFA&A after the war. For a year only. During that time they met a German art expert released by Allied troops from a German prison. The story goes that this man had refused to be recruited by Goebbels to help organize and transport paintings exclusively for Hitler's Linz project. Goebbels had him dumped in jail, where the Americans found him four years later. And do you know who he was? Gerhard Hegler."

"You're kidding," I said.

"No. And I think that is where the problem lies. Hershel has admitted to me that he dislikes Hegler. I have a feeling it goes back a long way. And I'm sure Hershel hasn't told me everything. But one night at a party I overheard Gerry arguing with his father, saying that Hershel Nesbitt had to be ousted from Hercules. And it would have happened a long time ago—by Hegler—if Harold hadn't stuck by his friend. So it isn't only us I'm worried about, Stoney, it's Hershel too."

91

"You may be right. He was beaten up while I was in New York." Sarah made a noise in her throat and pressed her cheek against my arm. "I had a feeling at the time that it happened because he talked to me. Somebody was worrying about what he said, since he was loaded. But don't worry, he's all right." She lifted her head to say something. Our faces came together.

I was pressing my lips to her forehead when a voice said, "Uh, excuse me."

The lifeguard was hunched down beside us. "Sorry to bother you, but it's two minutes to closing. He looked at Sarah, then back at me. "Are you Mr. Stone, by the way?"

I hesitated. "Yes."

"You got a call. From Mr. Jacobs. He described you and I told him I thought you were still in the pool with"—he glanced at Sarah and blushed—"with the blond lady. He wants you to wait for him here." The long-legged kid was having trouble taking his eyes off Sarah. I was having the same problem.

"Thanks," I said. I might as well have been talking to the moon. "Thanks."

"You're welcome, sir." He blushed some more and straightened up. "You two don't have to hurry. You've got a few minutes more. I'll do my rounds, slowly like."

Sarah's eyes hadn't left mine. As the bare feet padded away, she touched my cheek, then brushed her lips against mine. "You look so much better than the last time we met."

I grunted. "It wasn't until the divorce went through last spring that I decided to start taking care of myself. Someone had to."

"You've lost weight."

"Twenty pounds. The divorce did that. I didn't want to become too fit. I just wanted to slow down the aging process. I jogged. I even dug out my old army training manual and brushed up on self-defense." She giggled and touched my nose with her finger. "What's so funny?"

"A lot of good it did you. Didn't Fleck and Corry rough you up behind the . . . ?"

"The hotel. It was two against one. Besides, they fought dirty."

Another giggle.

"I even began a Tae-kwan-do course. That's Korean karate. Just for the exercise, not self-defense. I gave it up after eight lessons."

She kissed me lightly on the lips. "Why?"

92

"I got tired of guys jumping up and kicking their feet in my face. And yelling. God, how they yelled."

Sarah pulled away from me. "Karate? Did they teach you how to break boards with your bare fists?"

"Hell, no," I said. "I only had eight lessons. Even so, I worked my way up to splitting day-old buns. With one chop." Her face beamed, then went serious as she slipped a hand up behind my head. Pulling me close, she murmured, "That's the Stoney I remember. I feel I don't deserve it, but this is my first real laugh in so long . . ."

Our bodies came solidly together. Our mouths touched, then pressed harder as I eased my knee forward. I felt her legs begin to part. We were clinging now to each other, clinging to the edge of the pool. I could smell her skin, feel its softness under my touch. I worked my fingers under her bikini top to feel her nipples harden. She moaned, then whispered, "Monique . . . is waiting for me . . . in the changing room . . . oh . . . Stoney . . ." Her hand dropped down my chest to slip under the elastic of my trunks. My groin burned as her fingers encircled my penis and pressed it against my stomach. I moved my hand then from her breast, found the flimsy waistband of her bikini, and gently pulled it back to brush my fingertips along the fluffy softness of her pubic hair.

Something was wrong. I could feel it.

Sarah must have sensed it too, because she stiffened. I jerked back from her just as a knee pinned my arm supporting us to the side of the pool. At the same instant a clothed forearm locked around my neck and jerked upward, cutting off my breath. Sarah's eyes went wide. She began clawing silently at the arm about my neck. A hand came out of the water and clamped over her mouth. With one savage yank she was pulled from me. The guy behind her in a bathing suit was Fleck. Helpless, I watched her disappear, struggling, into the mist.

I was having my own problems. Jammed firmly against the side of the pool, I felt my body being twisted outward, freeing the arm pinned by the knee. Corry's knee, of course. I couldn't see him; I didn't have to. He was also on dry land, giving him leverage to do whatever he wanted with me. At the moment he wanted me under, and to do it he merely put his free hand on my head and pushed down.

The water rose up past my mouth. I flailed back at him with my arms. He laughed and in a deep, harsh voice said, "You are

93

about to drown, Mr. Stone. It's no use struggling. You will drown, then poof! you will also disappear. Good-bye, Mr. Stone."

I was sinking, though the arm was still around my neck. Leverage. Jesus, I needed leverage. In desperation I fought to get a foothold against the side of the pool. It wasn't possible. I was facing away from it. Then I must turn around.

Water trickled down the back of my throat. I was having difficulty keeping my mind from drifting off. Strangely enough, I knew I was about to die, but little by little I cared less and less. But, goddamn it, I did care. Then turn around, I told myself.

I grabbed the arm about my neck with both hands and kicked and jerked and struggled. The soaked cloth of Corry's coat and my wet neck acted somewhat as a lubricant, and I was turning. Now my knees hit something. The side. It had to be. Blinded by the pressure of the arm, I pulled my legs up until my feet struck something solid. Then I pushed back with all my strength.

At first I couldn't budge the bastard. In my choking, half-delirious state I wasn't even sure I was pushing. Then something gave. The arm loosened and now the whole damn body came crashing into the water on top of me.

In the struggle beneath the surface I saw Corry's twisted face. He was fully clothed, though this didn't hinder him from wrapping his powerful arms around me. We were rolling over slowly until at last my back struck what I took to be the bottom of the pool. Corry pinned me there, and pulling one hand free, began pounding my head on the concrete.

A weird feeling of euphoria swept over me. Through blurring vision my eyes settled on his unprotected crotch. I drove my knee straight up at it.

Bubbles broke from his mouth. As he doubled up, I tore myself from his grip and pushed away. My only hope now was to lose myself in the mist and reach the shallow end of the pool. But somewhere along the way, darkness closed over me.

11

Everything was swirling around me, and when it stopped, I opened my eyes.

Carl Henry Jacobs was beside me, looking a little fuzzy around the edges. I blinked a couple of times; he was still fuzzy.. My throat felt raw and sore.

"Hullo," I croaked. "Where am I this time?"

He was frowning.

"Routt County Memorial Hospital. Emergency. He paused. "But you could just as easy've waked up dead."

I didn't understand.

"According to the sheriff, you came the thickness of a cow pat away from drowning. Lucky you ain't so good at it. Wait here, I'll fetch the nurse."

Bo had to be joking. I wasn't going anywhere, strapped on one of those high, narrow stretchers and covered with a sheet.

Then I heard voices. But when I tried to move my head, shock waves of pain riddled my neck. So I lay still and started piecing things together.

Nothing made sense. The last thing I remembered was sitting in my hotel room waiting. Waiting for what? My memory started trickling back. Waiting for a phone call. Then what? I'd taken the jeep into town and stopped at . . . Oh, my God.

"Bo!" I yelled hoarsely.

His head came around the curtain. "The nurse is busy—"

"Bo, they've got her," I said, struggling against the straps. "Fleck and Corry got Sarah. Corry damn near drowned me." I couldn't move. "I have an eerie feeling I was supposed to disappear as well. *Poof*, as Corry put it."

Bo glanced at me sideways. "I told the sheriff somebody tried to nail you, but he said you just got careless. Exhausted yourself swimming too many lengths of the pool. You were alone when the kids fished you off the bottom. And if they hadn't given you mouth-to-mouth whatchacallit, you'd be practicin' on a harp right now." He came close and stared at my neck while I sought out the buckles. I couldn't reach them.

"What's the matter?" I asked.

"From the looks of it, you not only got careless, you were also out to strangle yourself. Corry, huh?"

"Exactly. I exhausted myself trying to stay alive." I told him my version, then asked about Bachman.

"His cruiser was parked alongside the ambulance when I got to the pool." He looked at me and shrugged his shoulders. "Dammit, Stoney, I couldn't get there any sooner. Those yahoos on the charter were bombed. I practically had to carry them out to the limo. You got my message?"

I nodded, then started pulling at the straps again. "Look, get these things off me. Surely to God we can convince Bachman that Sarah's been kidnapped. Ten to one they've taken her to the plane." But he didn't move. "Bo, for Christ's sake!"

"Stoney, I . . . I can't. The nurse told me there might be complications. They have to run some tests."

"Fuck the tests," I said, straining to sit up. "It's the plane—"

Bo cut me off. "Don't worry about the plane. With no night-light facilities at Yampa, nothing flies out of there after dark."

I gave one last yank at the strap across my chest and gave up. Why couldn't Sarah have stayed at the ranch? Then I thought about Monique. I asked Bo if he saw her at the pool.

"She sure wasn't around when I got there. In fact, I thought Sarah and her must've gone back to the ranch. You too, till the door to the pool opened and damn me if it wasn't you they were wheelin' out on the stretcher."

I didn't like the sound of it. What if they'd dragged Monique off too? But surely the kids, the lifeguards, would have seen something was wrong. I lay back then and stared at the ceiling. "Bo," I said, "would you do me a favor? Check the Village Inn to make sure Monique is okay." It struck me she might have got tired of waiting for Sarah and me. "And the kids. It's probably late, but could you track them down? Maybe they saw more than Bachman says."

He sighed. "Okay, but it'll take time. It's after eleven." He grinned. "Don't go away."

It's a mystery how long I remained in that curtained-off cubicle. It seemed like hours. No one came near me. I shouted many times, which did my throat no good at all. Finally I must have dozed off, because the next thing I knew, Carl Henry was standing at the end of the stretcher, scowling.

"Stoney, Corry and Fleck had help at the pool. From Monique."

Stunned, I tried to sit up. "Oh, shit."

"It's true. I'm sorry."

"How do you know?"

"The hotel clerk. He told me she checked out around eight-thirty tonight."

"So?"

"She also checked out Sarah Warden, paying both accounts. The clerk showed me her signatures on the bills."

Monique. Jesus, what a fool I'd been. She must have been sent to keep tabs on Sarah. The casual meeting in the Denver airport, the friendship. And when Monique and I met at the Cave Inn. The surprise when I told her my name. No wonder! Goddamnit, I thought, what was I doing here? I was way over my head in a game where people were getting killed.

"Stoney?" Bo was leaning over me. "There's more. You remember my nephew read Fleck and Corry's registration cards at the Timberline? They were both marked Horizon Imports? Well, Horizon Imports showed up on Monique's card too. At the Village Inn."

I closed my eyes. When I opened them, Bo had turned away.

"Y'know, Stoney, it fits. She talked Sarah into going to the hot springs. But how could she have possibly set it up with Fleck and Corry?"

"By insisting Sarah would feel better having a few of her own things when staying overnight at the ranch. Like a nightgown. So who drives back to the hotel for them? Alone."

Bo swung around and came back to the stretcher. He was excited. "And I'll bet you she was Wessen's contact."

"Right. Which makes Monique an accessory to the kid's murder."

"Sweet Jesus."

I felt hurt, betrayed. Monique, always there in the right place at the right time. Monique, part of the Hercules Foundation. I could have kicked myself for not seeing it sooner.

"Stoney, I tracked down the lifeguard. He told me what he'd told the sheriff. Bud, that's the kid's name, says he came around to give you and Sarah the two-minute warning. He left you, ah, sort of snuggling, and walked around to the shallow end. There was a guy in the water he hadn't seen earlier. He told him the pool was closing as well. The guy, I guess it was Fleck, said fine, got out, and started drying himself off. So Bud wandered back to the main area to help his partner clean up for the night."

"And that's when Fleck stopped toweling himself."

"You've got it. Next, Bud looks up from sorting rental swimsuits to see the blond, Sarah, heading into the women's changing room. A moment later the guy who was drying himself paraded by to the men's changing room. Bud looked for you, figured you passed while he was counting the swimsuits, so continues on. In a little while the blond and a brunette, let's say it's Monique, come out and head for the exit. The guy with the towel is already waiting for them."

"By now I'm floating around on the bottom of the pool."

"Or getting strangled by Corry," said Bo. "Anyways, Bud started wondering about you. He looked in the changing room, and when you weren't there, he called Jenny to come along to the pool. Bud said everything was quiet, like. So they did the usual check. Jenny walked around the edge, leaving Bud to swim up the middle. That's when he stepped on you."

"Thank God for that."

"He yelled for Jenny to help. They got you onto the terrazzo floor and took turns giving you the mouth-to-mouth business till you showed signs of pullin' through. Then they called for an ambulance and the sheriff."

"I can understand calling for an ambulance, but why the sheriff?"

"Because they discovered one of the glass doors opposite the deep end of the pool had been forced open. There were footprints leading in and out. That, plus the fingerprints they found around your neck."

"Exit Corry," I said, "nursing a sore pair of nuts. Bachman of course wouldn't come and ask me for my side of it. Hell, no. On the other hand, why wouldn't he?"

"Beats me, but something is goin' on around here. There's a part-time deputy sitting out in the waiting room picking his nose. I asked what he was waitin' on and he said, just passing the time keeping an eye on a patient down the hall. Well, Stoney, you're down the hall."

"So Bachman's put me on hold," I said.

Bo glanced at the straps. "Looks that way, friend. You've been meddling, and he doesn't like it. Maybe he's just carrying on the investigation into the kid's murder his way."

"And while all that bullshit goes on, Sarah's been abducted," I added bitterly.

"That's the part that rubs me the wrong way," said Bo, striding to the curtain and back.

"Good, then loosen these straps and we'll go do something about it." I wasn't quite sure what.

Bo held up his hands. "Uh-uh. Not me. We gotta get you out of here legal or Bachman'll be breathing fire down our necks before we've cleared the building. You sit tight."

He returned within ten minutes looking pleased with himself. "Now, listen, Stoney, just do as you're told. I'll meet you out in the parking lot." With that he was gone.

A minute hadn't gone by when the curtain was thrust aside and a skinny guy breezed in wearing jeans, a white hospital jacket, and a stethoscope. He peered at me through eyes enlarged by the thick lenses of his glasses. "Christ Almighty," he muttered, and disappeared.

He was back in a few moments carrying a clipboard under his arm. A distraught nurse with bleached blond hair came running along beside him. She looked as if she was digging in for a fight. "But Dr. Lewis, you can't," she wailed. "I have been authorized by my supervisor—"

"Nurse, I'm the authority around here," he barked, "and you should know better than to leave a conscious patient trussed up like that. Unstrap him." She did, without looking at me, then stepped aside. He dismissed her, holding back a grin of satisfaction until she was gone.

"That little bitch," he said, nodding toward the curtain. "She knows every trick in the book. You can bet she's playing one side against the other to boot." He pulled the clipboard out from under his arm and dropped it on the stretcher. "Often as not she gets away with it, and that's what hurts." He stopped and flipped through the few pages attached to the clipboard. He glanced at me from time to time. "Rumor has it she's been screwing the night supervisor, a woman who's built along the lines of a Sumo wrestler." His face broke into a grin. "In the supply cupboard. God, what a sight."

The examination was routine. When he'd finished, Lewis said, "You're fine, Mr. Stone. Your throat's raw as fresh liver. Swallowing will bring on some discomfort for a day or two, like you've been chewing broken glass." He turned back to his clipboard and finished writing before he looked up. "In your interest, I've noted officially the obvious fingermarks on your throat. That bastard must've been trying to break your neck." He pointed to a locker against the wall. "Your clothes."

Wearing nothing but the sheet, I pushed the stretcher aside and reached for the locker door. "I hope I'm not getting you into trouble."

"No reason to worry. Medically you're fit. Better than average for your age. Keeping you longer would only burden the taxpayer." He talked as I got dressed. "There's another amusing rumor that old Gretchen, the supe, promised that patient P. A. Stone would remain in Emergency overnight. Someone had enough tests listed opposite your name to choke a horse. That's Bachman for you. He works the angles, and it pisses me off. Especially where the hospital is concerned. So when I find I can do him a disfavor, it makes my day." He smiled. "Or night. By the way, you might drop by the cashier tomorrow. Admin would appreciate it." He picked up the clipboard and stuck it back under his arm. "A door down the corridor to the right leads to the parking lot. Otherwise you'll have to tiptoe through the waiting room.

"Thanks a lot," I said, picking up my coat. "If you ever need a favor . . ."

He pulled back the curtain, then stopped. "Sure, tell Bo to show up at our next poker game. Give me a chance to recoup my losses."

"I'll tell him," I said as the curtain closed behind him.

Bo was waiting with the engine running. He had Bessy the limousine. We sounded like the entire Seventh Motor Brigade as we shot across the snow-covered parking lot and bounced down onto Deer Foot Avenue.

"Where to?" he shouted.

"Yampa airport."

You could almost touch the mounting tension as we left the limo in a remote corner of the airport parking lot. It got even worse when the dark shadow ahead turned out to be an empty car with a battered left-front fender. A few steps farther and we found the padlock had been broken on the chain-link gate. We slipped through the darkness and circled around behind the main building, then took off to our left, where we'd both seen the plane parked.

A dozen paces along, I hauled us both to a stop. Something was burning. A sharp, acrid smell. Unable to place it, we agreed to let it go until we'd found the Horizon jet.

I had taken a few more steps when I found myself alone. Bo's voice came out of the darkness. "Stoney, over here." Angling off to the right, I bumped into the tail section of a small plane. He was cursing just ahead of me.

"Look at this," he grumbled. A match flared and I was staring at a bulky orange something on wheels.

"What the hell is that for?" I asked.

100

"It's a goddamn electrical booster for starting jet engines, that's what it is. They must have broken it out of the hangar."

Suddenly my chest constricted. I whirled around and peered out into the night. Then I began running across the field. The smell of smoke was getting stronger. I had it in my mind that somewhere out there a small executive jet was waiting for enough light to take off. I hit a snowbank, tumbled, and rolled. As I picked myself up, I thought I saw something glowing ahead of me. I stumbled forward, reached it, and bent down. I was staring at the dying embers of a spent emergency flare. Farther on was another; beyond that, another and another.

I stood up, gazing into the night. Bo was beside me now. "Me and my big mouth," he said quietly. "Who'd ever think the bastards would line both sides of a runway with flares? Jesus, Stoney, I'm sorry."

We found the night watchman lying trussed up in the hangar. We left him screaming excitedly into the phone for the sheriff. Bo's only comment came as we climbed back into the limo. "I sure hope that poor sonofabitch has better luck with Bachman than we're havin'." They were the last words to pass between us until we reached Steamboat. It was three A.M.

The main street was empty. I expected Carl Henry to drop me off at the parking lot next to the pool, where I'd left the jeep. But instead he stopped outside the Harbor Hotel, unraveled himself from behind the steering wheel, and went inside. He was back in five minutes, fuming.

"What's the matter?"

"Plenty," he said, closing the door. He sat for a moment staring through the windshield. When he spoke, his voice was hardly audible. "Something's been bugging me, Stoney, and it's Bachman. But not the way you think. We've been heaping a lot of blame on him, not that he isn't a shifty, ornery sonofabitch. But there's one thing no one can accuse him of. That's Bachman not taking his job seriously. Now, with all this screwing around, the kid's death, on-again, off-again charges against you, it got me thinking. The sheriff's either being paid through the back door for a cover-up, or someone is pressing down on him from a very great height. Knowing him, I'd say it could only be this last one."

"And you've just phoned a friend."

"Yes," he said, without taking his eyes off the windshield. "Herb Hofstetter, the deputy, and I go way back. I just woke him up and asked outright why the sheriff is pissing all over one

101

Philip Stone. He clammed up first off, saying he could get fired on the spot for just opening his mouth. After a bit of cursin' back and forth he told me that even the sheriff was disgusted with hassling you, but he was just following orders."

"What orders? Who from?"

"Well, Herb says it was really more of a request, telling the sheriff that no matter what happened, he wasn't to take Philip Stone too serious. And that request came straight down from the same goddamn bunch you keep assuring me *and* yourself will come to your rescue. The FBI. New York City."

"Christ, no," I whispered.

Bo's head came around. "Christ, yes."

I couldn't sleep.

Instead, I watched the early-morning light filter down through the log-pole pines and spruce scattered across the upper reaches of Mt. Werner.

I couldn't think, either.

At eight A.M. I phoned Carl Henry Jacobs.

The single-engine chartered Beechcraft squatted on the packed snow warming up for the flight that would take me over the mountains to Denver. My gear was on board. Walking out to the plane, I slipped Bo two envelopes, one with enough cash to float a gala dinner for two young lifeguards who had saved my life, enough to include a few friends. The second contained a countersigned traveler's check to cover my hospital bill from the previous evening.

We stopped short of the Beechcraft. "Life's going to be kinda dull without you, Stoney." Bo squinted at me from under his battered stetson. We shook hands. I started to say something totally inane, but he cut me off. "Keep in touch, you hear?"

I promised.

Taxiing out to the runway, I was suddenly gripped by an overwhelming sense of loneliness. I was on my own again, without Bo to fill in the gaps. It wasn't a very pleasant thought.

12

By midafternoon my scheduled flight from Chicago had landed at Kennedy. I brooded in my seat while those who make a career of being first off an aircraft thundered down the aisles. The rest of us followed quietly in their wake. I had reached the covered ramp leading from the plane when a voice said, "Mr. Stone? Philip A. Stone?" My stomach turned over.

He was a big guy, broad across the shoulders rather than tall, with shortish hair.

I nodded and kept walking. He matched my stride, flashing a small leather folder under my nose. It held a metallic crest and an identification card bearing his stamp-sized portrait with "Federal Bureau of Investigation" printed on it in bold black letters. I never thought I'd be relieved to see the FBI.

"Coggan," he muttered, slipping it back into an inside pocket. He was watching me with that irritatingly bored look of someone who doesn't have to rely on giving good first impressions to make a living. "We'll have to hurry or you'll miss your flight."

"Now, just a minute, dammit," I said, shaking off his hand as it touched my elbow. "I want to see Agostino." A second man, cloned with the same short hair, same expression, moved in on the other side of me.

"No problem," they said.

If it hadn't been for the mop of curly black hair and the lopsided nose, I never would have recognized Agostino as the man I'd shared breakfast with in the Algonquin Rose Room. He was wearing faded jeans, boots, a dashing wool sweater-coat, and talking to a woman behind the ticket counter of American Airlines. We pulled up three abreast just as he turned, clutching a ticket envelope in his hand.

I opened my mouth to begin the tirade I'd stored up since Steamboat, when Agostino shoved the airline envelope at Coggan and abruptly walked away.

I bellowed after him, "Hey, goddammit, where do you think you're going?" Heads turn.

"Home," came the crisp reply over his shoulder.

I started to follow, only to have Coggan and friend each take an arm. So I whipped around to shake free. "Coggan," I barked, "go let your hair grow, why don't you?" and promptly bolted after Agostino.

I caught up with him in the crowded open concourse and grabbed a handful of sweater-coat. The other pair weren't far behind.

"You sonofabitch," I screamed at him, mindful that we'd stopped traffic. "You could have saved the kid if you had returned my call. But you wouldn't. You knew what was going on and you let it be, Agostino, you let it be."

By this time Coggan had me in a half-Nelson, or in one of the related Nelson family strangleholds, while his chum was prying my fingers from the sweater-coat. Agostino remained motionless, his deep-set eyes fixed on mine as I peppered him with more abuse. "Wanton bloody butchery, that's what it was. And you're to blame, Agostino."

I guess it was this last remark that triggered it, because suddenly the agent jerked loose and jammed a finger damn near up my nose. "Now, you listen to me, Stone. I warned you to stay away, but you, you knew better. So look at your own part in all this. The kid would probably still be alive if you hadn't screwed up."

"Why didn't you call when I needed you?" I countered. "And don't tell me you were off skiing. Do you really know what's going on? They've abducted her, goddammit, while you bastards . . ." I hesitated and glanced around at the faces peering at us, listening, watching.

A voice among the onlookers said, "Someone should get the police." Then another said, "I think they *are* the police."

Agostino, flushed, stepped back. He told Coggan to let me go, told the crowd to move off, and took me by the arm. "Jesus Christ, Stone," he muttered as we started to a small mobile snack stand, "you bring out the worst in me." He bought the coffee. I took mine black. We walked back to the concourse and I told him I knew stories that would curl his hair.

"And I suppose you got it all from Mrs. Warden?" he said, sipping from the paper cup. When I said yes, he nodded. "Well, that's part of the problem right there. She's had psychiatric help."

"And you're about to tell me it's all a figment of her imagination?"

"You said it, not me."

"That's not what I mean, dammit."

He looked at me over his paper cup. "Easy, Stone." He paused. "Look, I'm sorry about the kid. From what I hear, there's some involvement with narcotics."

I stopped. "And you believe that? Because if you do, we're in real trouble, Agostino." We started walking again. "Have you heard the name Wessen? He's the hit man who shot Terence Samuels."

"And who told you that?"

"No one. We . . . I found his plane. I told your friend Bachman, but he let him fly off." I sighed. "Under your orders, no doubt."

Agostino tossed his cup into a litter can as we passed. "The name doesn't ring a bell."

I was on the verge of exploding, but held on. "What about two guys named Fleck and Corry?"

"Ya, they work for somebody called Horizon Imports. From what I've heard, they were out in Steamboat to escort Mrs. Warden back to New York. There were certain business dealings concerning her husband's estate."

"Agostino, dammit, they abducted her! Can't you get that through your thick skull? And they came close to drowning me. Doesn't that mean anything to you? As for Horizon . . ."

We had come around ·a corner and were heading for the flight-gate section, with Coggan and the other guy following behind. Agostino had me by the arm. "Had I been there, Stone, I probably would've helped them. You're such a pain in the ass."

"Very funny. She's still been abducted. What are you going to do about it?"

"Nothing, because your imagination is running away with you. She's in New York, staying with her father-in-law. Harold Warden." His grip tightened. "And she's fine."

"Bullshit. If you'd only listen to what I have to say. She's a frightened woman who needs help."

"I couldn't agree with you more," he said, reaching back to take the airline envelope from Coggan. He went on, "According to her shrink, Mrs. Warden has paranoid schizophrenic tendencies abetted by two things. First, an overworked imagination, and second, an unsympathetic husband who dealt with her as he did with everybody else, dishonestly."

Coggan interrupted, telling him we would have to go down the corridor to the right.

"Stress also had her doing many, ah, strange things," he said as we continued on, "like peddling her butt around New York and Old Greenwich. Bedding younger guys, drinking to excess. So you'd have to be an idiot to believe what she says."

"You've got it wrong," I said, "and if anything should happen to that woman, Agostino, I'll haunt you for the rest of your miserable life."

He ignored me. We were approaching a barrier where bags were being checked electronically. We stopped short of it. Agostino made a little speech, saying I was being sent back to Canada against his better judgment.

"We have reason to believe you might have been working on a scheme with Hope-Warden to funnel certain profits into bank accounts"—there he waved his hand—"but the IRS hasn't made any recommendations."

"Look," I said, "I can explain that."

"Take my advice, don't incriminate yourself." He looked at me for a moment. "There is one other thing, the possibility that you've been used." His look was almost paternal.

I felt as if a load had been lifted from my shoulders. I said, "At least that's something."

"That's the only reason we're letting you go. My idea was to have you stick around for a couple of days, but my superiors think you've done enough damage."

"Fair enough, but there are things going on."

His face reddened. "Knock it off, Stone. What do you take the Bureau for, a bunch of idiots? You're the one who's driving us nuts. Amateur detectives, Christ!"

"Okay, okay, but promise me something. You'll talk to Sarah. Somehow get her alone and no matter how farfetched it sounds, listen to her. Please. She's in something up to her neck."

Agostino patted me on the back, easing me toward the barrier. "You go peacefully back to the Laurentians and I promise we'll have a chat with her. If it seems necessary, we'll give her protection. How's that?"

It was crap, but the choice was hardly mine. "May I make one phone call?"

Agostino peered at his watch, then shook his head before glancing up at me. "No time," he said. "Sorry. These two friends of mine will just make sure you get on the right jet." He walked away without so much as a good-bye."

Montreal. Dorval Airport.

Someone had been thoughtful enough to have my ski gear and

106

single piece of luggage rerouted to Montreal, so after clearing customs I dropped them on a chair in the open waiting area on the main level and went to a nearby pay phone. Besides making a call through to Hershel Nesbitt, the one I'd wanted to make at Kennedy, I would retrieve my stuff that arrived at Dorval six days ago, probably by now to be found in the lost-baggage department. Also I'd pick up the Canadian work permit which Agostino had assured me—the first time around—would be with the airport's immigration office.

The pay phone. I dialed the long-distance operator and gave her Hershel's gallery address while I fumbled out enough loose change to pay for it. It struck me as the call was being made that he might still be in the hospital.

But it was Nesbitt, all right. I asked how he was feeling. His reply was a short "Fine, fine, son." I told him where I was and how I'd come by way of Colorado. Leaving out the whys and wherefores, I explained that Sarah was back in New York. "Only, the circumstances seem somewhat bizarre, Hershel. Now, listen, is there some way you can slip her over to FBI headquarters, on the sly? I've already talked to an agent about her. His name is Jim Agostino."

"Agostino?"

"Yes, Jim Agostino. I can't explain, but it deals with what she's mentioned to you. You understand?" As I waited for an answer, something bumped against my leg. I glanced over my shoulder to find a cleaning buggy with canvas sides and wheels parked behind me. A guy in gray coveralls stamped with "Airport Cleaning Inc." seemed to be waiting for the people ahead of him to move on. Meanwhile, Hershel had said something I missed. I asked him to repeat it.

"I have had dealings with your Mr. Agostino, son," I heard him say.

I felt relieved. "That's good, but the difficulty is getting Sarah away from her father-in-law. This I can't explain either. You'll have to take my word for it."

"I do take your word for it, but something puzzles me. If you say she is with her father-in-law, it wouldn't be in New York. Harold hasn't been here since the funeral."

A sudden chill went down my spine. "What do you mean?"

A third voice cut in. "Your three minutes are up, sir."

"It's okay, operator," I said, jamming the slots with fresh coins and talking to Hershel at the same time. "Where is he, then?"

107

The clanging of the coins stopped. Nesbitt's voice came clear. "He's in France, preparing for the annual Hercules conference, which started yesterday. Sunday. Do you know Hercules?"

"Yes, yes," I said quickly, but my mind was elsewhere. Agostino, that lying bastard. Why would he say Sarah was in New York. Well, maybe she was and Hershel was wrong. I hurriedly switched the receiver to the other hand, and in doing so, bumped the same buggy. The guy, fairly big, blond, was leaning on the other end, casually looking about him.

"Hershel," I said into the receiver, "this is very important. Can you find out for sure if Sarah is in New York? At Warden's?" Yes, he said. "Then please find out. I'll phone back. Is five minutes enough?" It was. I hung up. Turning, I found the cart was still blocking me in. "Excuse me," I said politely, but the guy was too busy trying to attract someone's attention. Following his line of view, I found myself staring at a second, older man with dark hair and glasses and wearing the same natty gray outfit. Judging from where he stood, he was either trampling on my baggage or damn close to it. At that moment he spotted the guy nearest me, who in turn jerked his head back in my direction.

It must have been the timing, or maybe the look of accomplishment on the older man's face, but suddenly I knew that the gesture was aimed at me. Hair bristling on the back of my neck, I quickly reached down with both hands and gave the cart a hard push forward. It skittered away, slamming into those milling about us. There were a few curses, and somebody yelled, "Hey, buddy, watch what you're doing with that thing." I slipped into the crowd and shouldered my way up the open corridor. Any feeling that I had overreacted faded when I glanced behind me a second or two later. The guy was coming after me, cart and all.

Walking faster, I realized I'd lost sight of his partner. But not for long. I spotted the second set of coveralls running a broken field pattern between the couches and chairs on a course that would bring him to this open corridor, but some distance ahead of me. In other words, I'd soon be trapped. On my left was a wall with doors scattered down its length, the first marked with the sign of a baby's bottle. Ahead of me, the guy with the glasses had reached this open corridor. I could see him searching among the passing faces for mine. I stopped and whirled around. His friend was closing in. I walked on slowly, wondering if I should bolt into the waiting area, then thought better of it. They'd have me in the open.

A few steps farther and I was passing a door marked with the

108

familiar silhouette. The little figure wore a skirt. Too late, I crouched down and ducked inside.

Six feet farther inside was another door. I shoved it open and went in.

A woman, fiftyish, in a fur coat, was rouging her lips when she saw my reflection in the mirror. She gasped. As she spun around, her lipstick clattered to the floor.

"Lady, please," I said, walking toward her, "I won't hurt you. I need help." Clutching her purse and whimpering, she backed off, bumping into the sanitary-napkin dispenser. Her eyes went wide and she started crying. "Get out of here, lady, and get the police," I whispered, trying not to frighten her. "Get the police." I'd worked myself around by the row of washbasins, hoping to force her away from me and toward the door. At last she pulled free of the dispenser and shuffled silently past the three cubicles opposite the basins. Then she lunged for the door, only to burst into tears of frustration as she pushed repeatedly at it.

"Pull, lady," I pleaded with her. "Dammit, pull." And she was gone.

The washroom was empty. I leaned against the wall and closed my eyes, fighting off the panic rising in my chest. Slowly thoughts began taking shape. First, I reasoned, only one would actually come into the washroom, the other remaining by the outer door so his partner inside wouldn't be disturbed. Fine, but what could I do with him here? Surprise the hell out of him. How? Then I thought of something. I felt better already.

Quickly I hurried down to the third cubicle, the one farthest from the washroom entrance, slipped inside, and locked the small door behind me. Next, I removed my snowboots and placed them facing outwards. Anyone bending over couldn't miss seeing the lower half of them. With luck, he might even think my feet were still in them.

This done, I dropped to the floor and wriggled under the partition into the middle cubicle.

My plan, put together as I went along, was pretty amateurish, but I was stalling desperately to give the woman an extra minute to collect her wits, and hopefully fetch the police.

Time was short. I left the middle cubicle with its door open enough so it looked unoccupied and scrambled into the first one, nearest the entrance. This door I set slightly ajar to show it wasn't locked, yet closed enough; I didn't want to be seen behind it.

The sound of banging doors, presumably from the men's washroom next door, filtered through the wall. They'd be here next. My heart pounding in my ears, I climbed up backward onto the rim of the toilet, steadied myself, and waited.

A door opened. Then the inner door next to me. Shoes clicked on the washroom floor. One pair? With luck.

The shoes hesitated.

I held my breath.

They moved on. I counted the clicking of the heels. Six, maybe seven.

Cold sweat ran down my nose from my forehead. Some reached the corner of my eyes. I couldn't move. Dammit, where were the police?

Down the way, a door rattled. The locked cubicle door. It had to be. A voice said, "Come out, Stone."

Silence. Then shuffling.

I saw him. Dark hair, glasses. Through the crack in my door. He'd moved back now, toward the washbasins. He was holding something in his hand. I couldn't see it clearly.

Soon he'd find only my boots there, then come looking for the rest of me.

I saw the foot come up, then brace itself against the wall behind it. Suddenly the guy disappeared. A resounding crash echoed round the small washroom, followed by a loud grunt.

In that split second I dropped to the floor and lunged for the far cubicle, praying that whatever else might go wrong, I'd at least catch the bastard off-guard.

I found its door barely hanging from the hinges. Beneath it, legs jammed between the wall and toilet bowl. Old Coveralls, it seemed, had been counting on me to take the full force of the door buckling inward. It hadn't worked.

But what next? Looking around, I could see nothing to defend myself with, short of hitting him over the head with the napkin dispenser bolted to the wall. Nor would I get any farther than the outside door. I swore and glanced back. A leg was loose. Now a hand reached down to pry something loose from under the other leg. What came free was a gun that popped out and slithered to a stop below the door. I leaped for it, missed. The hand had snapped it up. Numbed, I stepped back to the wall, watching the fingers curl around the handle grip, then tilt the long-nosed barrel upward.

I moved, driving my body forward. I hit the sagging door, felt it tear free from the broken hinges and smash headlong into the

110

kneeling man in its path. Swept along by its weight and my own momentum, I plunged on in a flurry of arms and legs to bounce off the back wall and onto the toilet, pinning Old Coveralls under me and the green metal door.

Hurrying now, I tossed it aside and propped the guy up against the toilet. He was in bad shape. Out cold. His glasses were gone, his face was cut, and his busted nose was pumping blood down onto his chest.

I began round two with more confidence. After hauling on my boots, I retrieved the pistol from behind the toilet. Basic training hadn't done much to endear me to weaponry, but crossing the washroom, I balanced the gun in my hand, knowing I had to get the feel of it.

According to the inscription on the side, this nasty little piece of goods was a .223-caliber Walther PPKS. Its own barrel of blue steel had been extended another four or five inches by what I took for a type of silencer, a metal sheath slightly wider than the Walther barrel but with the same bore and snugged into place by a small set screw found on the underside.

By now I'd passed through the inner door, pausing long enough to get a firm grip on the weapon. A few steps farther brought me to the outer door. A deep breath, and I opened it. The gray outfit filled the doorway. I jammed the barrel hard into its owner's back where the flesh was soft, just below the ribs.

Neither of us spoke as I eased him back into the washroom. He eyed his bloodied partner, stretched out on the cubicle floor, then leaned obediently on the washbasin counter while I flushed a revolver out from the belt inside his coveralls. Only then did I ask who had hired him, what they had planned to do with me. His hesitation lasted the time it took for me to slide his own heavier gun into the soft flesh, then jerk it up under the back of the rib cage.

What I found out was enough to make my skin crawl. It was also enough to get me out of there. I nudged the sullen bastard over to the far cubicle, telling him to do what he could for his pal before he bled to death. As he bent down over Old Coveralls, I raised his revolver and brought it down butt-first.

I still couldn't believe this was actually happening to me.

But I was learning fast. The blow landed squarely behind the right ear, dropping him without a sound.

Next came a hasty cleaning up. Fearing any further gunplay, I wedged open the top corner of the napkin-dispenser door with the barrel of the revolver, dumped both guns inside, and snapped it closed. Then I left the boys to themselves.

The cleaning cart was still blocking the washroom entrance when I reappeared moments later. I gave it a wide berth—I'd learned from Number Two that it was to be used to smuggle my body off airport property—and hurried away to collect my gear. I managed to get it and myself into a waiting taxi before the shock of what had happened turned me to jelly.

I kept my head during the thirty-minute ride to Mirabel, the sister airport handling overseas flights. I desperately needed that half-hour to get things back into perspective. I looked at what I'd learned from Number Two.

He and Old Coveralls held a contract on my life. One-half of it would see me dead before reaching the Laurentians. The other half would have my body disappear without a trace—shades of Corry and Fleck. Why me? He didn't know. How? Through a deal struck with a local disposal firm that incinerated refuse on a large scale. My God! Who put out the contract? Pressure on the gun gave me the answer. Horizon Imports. How much was I worth dead? Twenty-five grand.

Twenty-five thousand dollars to see me dead, I marveled, watching the snow-swept countryside blur by. Dead and incinerated. We might have been talking about the weather. It was then in the washroom that I knew returning to the Laurentians wasn't possible. An armed garrison couldn't protect me there. For that kind of money the pair wouldn't give up so easily. If they did, there would always be someone else to take their place. Like Roger Wessen. Besides, I'd be endangering the lives of those around me, subjecting them to a couple of itinerant hit men. No, the Laurentians was out of bounds. Then where? Back to New York? Not likely. I had a growing distaste for Jim Agostino. Why couldn't he have set me up for what happened in Dorval washroom? With his hands-off attitude in Colorado, he was running pretty good interference on Hercules' behalf. My distrust for people in general these days had just hit an all-time low. I remembered Monique.

Which left Sarah. She was the key. She could expose what was going on within the inner core of Hercules. Unless someone got her away from that bunch, her life wasn't worth any more than mine. So far, I'd been lucky. It couldn't last.

I was heading for Mirabel on a hunch that Sarah was already in France. Somewhere. I was depending on Hershel to have the

112

answer. I called him back the moment I reached Mirabel. He sounded less than enthusiastic on hearing my voice. He confirmed my suspicion. Sarah was indeed there. When I asked where in France, he said, "Son, for your own safety, I cannot tell you. I'm sorry, believe me."

"My own safety?" I bellowed over the line. "Jesus, Hershel, that's funny. In the past two days I've survived a drowning and a fiery furnace and you're worried about my safety." I tried to speak slowly. "Hershel, you have to understand this. There's a contract out on me. Two guys just tried to kill me. I got away, but not by much. I have to find Sarah, goddammit. Together we might survive. She means a great deal to me, Hershel. Where the hell is she?"

A pause. I counted the seconds. Then his weary voice said, "Hercules is meeting in the French Alps. Near Chamonix. The place is called Les Pins. She is there now, with Harold. Be careful, son."

I sighed. "I will. And thanks."

Within five minutes of that call I had the last available seat on a Swissair overnight flight to Zurich with a connecting flight to Geneva, leaving in an hour.

It was a long hour. I haunted the cavernous building, fearing I would turn a corner and bump into a pair of battered cleaners pushing a cart.

I didn't. I found a small kiosk and bought several postcards. On the backs, I scribbled a note to Bo Jacobs. At least someone besides Hershel Nesbitt would know where I was going.

In a postscript I mentioned the skirmish in the Dorval washroom. Bo deserved to know how well I was defending myself. I mailed these enclosed in an envelope begged from the woman operating the kiosk, then went in search of my flight.

13

Geneva, Tuesday noon. We dropped down through the thick cloud cover, struck the runway with a deliberate thump, and taxied to a halt in front of the modern concrete and pinkish glass of Cointrin Airport's main terminal. We were deplaned with the precision of a Swiss watch. By two o'clock local time we were on a bus making slow progress down through the main part of the city, its narrow streets suddenly giving way to broad avenues and its snub-nosed, narrow-gauge electric streetcars blocking traffic with every frequent stop. Soon we were skirting the sparkling water of Lake Geneva, caught in the only burst of sunlight we would see that day. And then we began the gradual climb toward Annamasse and the French frontier. Though apprehensive of what lay ahead, I leaned back against the seat and congratulated myself on having made it this far. I promised myself I'd keep a very low profile.

Snow was falling heavily when we pulled off the autoroute at Le Fayet and started up the narrow twisting road carrying us into the mountains. On one side I could see nothing beyond the guardrail, on the other just the chunky grayness of a blasted cliff wall. Ice and hard-packed snow kept building up on the windshield, forcing the grizzled old driver to have to stop twice and free the wipers. Finding traction again had been difficult. The ancient bus would slip backward, stop, then inch slowly forward to the applause of the passengers.

At last the climb ended, the bus picked up speed, and we shot along the valley floor with a visibility of practically nil.

Soon Chamonix came out of the swirling snow, a cluster of low buildings huddling against the storm. Here we slithered along streets and around corners, swaying first to one side, then the other, before the bus suddenly lurched one last time and shuddered to a halt. The driver's broad grin appeared in his rearview mirror. "Chamonix, mes enfants." He pushed a handle that opened the doors. A blast of wind rattled its way clear to the back of the bus.

I followed everyone else, thinking my first move would be to find the tourist bureau about accommodation. The others were grouped near the luggage-compartment door arguing among themselves. As I approached, one of the passengers said, "Sure there's someone else. How about him?"

Heads turned. People shifted to one side, and I found myself staring at a woman in a yellow ski outfit. Sarah!

"Stoney," she cried, stumbling toward me. I grabbed her and held on. "Stoney," she whispered, "I thought you were dead."

"They're still working on it," I replied. I looked at her. Her hair clung to her face. Her makeup was gone. "Are you all right?" I asked.

"Fine," she said, gripping my arms. "How are you?"

"Lousy. I've just missed being killed twice in the past twenty-four hours. Once in a hot pool, once in a women's washroom. I'm tired, I'm frustrated, I'm goddamn mad, and I wish to hell I knew what was going on.''

"I know, Stoney. I'm the same. But I'm awfully glad you're here."

"How did you know I was coming?" I asked.

"I didn't. But someone must have. They brought me down here saying I would be meeting an old friend of Gerry's. I never thought it would be you."

Just then two swarthy gents dressed in expensive skiwear materialized out of nowhere. So did a very long gray Mercedes-Benz, from behind the bus. Corry was at the wheel, Fleck beside him.

From its matching white stucco-and-concrete exterior to the high ceiling and crystal chandeliers of its lobby, the Majestic was obviously a hotel steeped in old-world elegance. We'd come here directly, a drive that seemed no longer than a few hundred yards.

Dropped off under the portico at the main entrance, Fleck guided us swiftly through the lobby to a plush reading room and hurried away. We waited a moment, then slipped over to the door. The two heavies were right there, hovering in the lobby. Our only exit was blocked, leaving us with nothing to do but wait.

The reading room was empty. We moved to a far corner and sat down. "Now, tell me," I said, "where exactly have they got you?"

"Up in the mountains. A place called Les Pins."

"That's where the conference is."

"How did you know?" she asked.

"I talked to Hershel. Is Monique here too?"

"Yes." She paused. "Stoney, she's one of them."

"I know. What's going on up there?"

"I don't know. They don't tell me anything. But they're all up there. Harold, Gerhard Hegler, the lot. And the conference is on, just as Allan Starkman said it would be. But I haven't seen any of the horse-trading. We only arrived yesterday afternoon. Last night I was paraded around as the pretty widow." She bowed her head and twisted the plain gold wedding band on her finger. "The rest of the time I was confined to my room."

"That ring," I said. "I don't remember it in Colorado."

"I . . . didn't have it on. Hegler makes me wear it here."

For a moment neither of us spoke. Then I asked what had happened in the hot-springs pool.

"They told me they'd kill you if I didn't cooperate. Monique was in on it. She'd packed my bags and everything. The bitch." Silence again.

"How is she?"

"I don't know and I don't care. Anyway, I don't see much of her. We seem to have traded roles since Steamboat. Now she's the life of the party. I heard a bunch of the members came down to the casino last night by helicopter. She was with them. From what I gather, Monique is quite a mover."

"Don't I know it." Sarah was distracted, "What's the matter?"

"Gerhard Hegler's here."

My, my.

I shook hands with a balding, energetic man in his late sixties, maybe younger, with shrewd gray eyes and old-school charm. I remembered him slightly from Gerry's funeral, leading the pall-bearers into the chapel. Up close he appeared heavier and shorter, though his full-length fur coat may have given me that impression.

The first hint that we were to play games came when he apologized for not being with Mrs. Warden when I arrived. He continued in his clipped, precise manner saying that he hoped the flight from Montreal hadn't been too exhausting. Listening to this bullshit, I had an urge to reach over and choke him. Instead I simply let him go on.

The snowstorm had cut off the valley, he explained, from Les Houches at one end to Argentière at the other. And of course the two helicopters owned by Les Pins had been grounded. Accommodation had been made available here at the Majestic, for us and other late arrivals caught in the storm. He hoped we would be comfortable. Then, with a quick smile, a parting handshake, Gerhard Hegler was gone.

But not so the two guys in the lobby.

It was the manager himself, a gentle, gracious man, who insisted on showing us to our rooms. The old open-grilled elevator carried us to the fifth floor with all the dignity of a dowager queen. M'sieu Gratien stopped at a set of neighboring doors. I asked for my key. He hesitated, but handed it over anyway and then turned his attention to the right-hand door and Sarah. I unlocked mine and went in.

I was in a room fit for a visiting potentate, with its high frescoed ceiling, tall, shuttered windows, and a carpet deep

116

enough to get lost in. The bed was king-sized and canopied, the wallpaper embossed with lively old winter scenes of the local citizenry sliding and climbing among the mountain icefields. Music played softly from a stereo I had yet to find, a basket of fresh fruit was on the table, and beside it a bottle of white wine chilling in a silver bucket. So much for spur-of-the-moment accommodation.

But nothing came as more of a surprise than what I found when I opened the doors of the walk-in closet. It was filled with clothes. Ski outfits; half a dozen sport jackets; slacks; jeans; a knee-length sheepskin coat; a second, shorter version; two tailored mohair tuxedos in midnight blue. I was obviously in the wrong room.

I started for the door, thinking I might catch Monsieur Gratien, when I noticed my own ski bag, boots, and suitcase in the alcove next to the bathroom. Baffled, I detoured to the dresser and yanked the top drawer open.

Lightning had struck twice.

There were sweaters in this one, mostly cashmeres; the middle drawer held shirts; and the third, socks, Jockey shorts, and pajamas.

The pajamas, if you could believe the label, were pure silk. Like everything else, expensive. Like everything else, brand-new. Reaching down, I lifted up the pajama top and let it unfold. I caught myself wondering how it would look on Monique . . . then dismissed the fantasy as quickly as she had dismissed me. Besides, I was too busy being amazed by the monogram on the pocket. PAS. Unless I was mistaken, these were my initials. And this was my wardrobe. I couldn't help thinking I should be planning for a long stay, when the connecting door between our rooms burst open.

Like me, Sarah had found a whole new wardrobe. "And look," she said, " this note came with some yellow roses."

I opened it to find our agenda for the next eighteen hours, beginning with cocktails in the hotel bar at eight o'clock, dinner reservations for two at Le Royal, the restaurant in the Casino de Chamonix. A footnote suggested we dress formally. A footnote to the footnote said the keys for the Mercedes could be picked up at the hotel reception desk anytime after nine o'clock, for the drive to the casino. I looked for a catch. There wasn't one. I read on: Wednesday. Eleven o'clock. Departure for Les Pins, weather permitting.

A neat handwritten note on the back explained that the wardrobes came with the compliments of the Hercules Foundation. It was signed "G. Hegler." Postscript: Would we join him at the casino after our dinner there. I read it again. You'd have thought we were almost guests.

Sarah was standing by the dresser looking at one of my monogrammed shirts. She wasn't smiling. Neither was I. "What are you thinking?" I asked.

"That it's scary." She came over and touched my hand. "But we're right about one thing . . ." She broke off.

"What?"

"We mustn't let our guard down, Stoney. If we do, we're finished."

"Fair enough," I said. "And we go at the first opportunity. Tonight, if possible."

I had just dropped into my chair after dancing up a storm with the mayor's wife when Gerhard Hegler sat down beside me, looking immaculate in his tailored black tux and bow tie set off against a white pleated shirt. He watched the couples swirling by us, then turned and clapped me brusquely on the shoulder. "Your Mrs. Warden is absolutely captivating, Mr. Stone," he shouted over the music and laughter around us, "absolutely captivating. Our friend Joachim Smith must think so too. This is his fifth dance with her."

Seventh, I could have said, but didn't.

Smith, introduced as the boisterous industrialist and art collector from Pittsburgh, hadn't kept his eyes off Sarah all evening. And Gerhard Hegler, of course, was right. She was absolutely stunning with her blond hair piled on her head, the black silk evening dress slit to the thigh and clinging to her everywhere else. She had taken my breath away earlier when, wrestling with my bow tie, two bare arms slipped down over my shoulders and I saw this vision reflected in the mirror.

"You are enjoying yourself, Mr. Stone?" Hegler again.

"Yes, very much," I lied. "Admittedly, we weren't expecting such a reception."

Little wonder. We had arrived late to be greeted by the maître d', who smiled at us broadly when we told him our names and led us directly to a table of twenty hosted by Gerhard Hegler. Sarah and I were introduced as the guests of honor to those assembled, including the mayor of Chamonix, his wife, numerous members of the town council, their wives, and several others classified, like Joachim Smith and I, as "late arrivals" to Les Pins.

118

Guests of honor? Baffling as it seemed, we went along with the charade. Who among these townsfolk would believe that the guests of honor were actually prisoners? Nor could we risk telling them. It would only endanger their lives.

The evening was one continuous round of drinks, innumerable toasts to the lasting friendship between the United States and France, and eating. Eating when we weren't dancing or making frequent trips to the gambling rooms above. But reality was never any farther away than Corry and Fleck, whose presence cast a shadow on our every move.

The final cabaret show of the night brought us back to the main room, and more dancing. The mayor's wife, a robust, jolly woman in her mid-fifties, had taken a fancy to my fractured French and had hauled me out on the floor many times during the evening. But the last polka had sent her reeling to the nearest washroom and me back to the table. I'd just sat down when Hegler pulled up a chair beside me.

The conversation about Sarah's beauty had begun here, followed by Hegler asking if I was enjoying myself and me replying that I hadn't quite expected this.

"I'm sure you didn't, Mr. Stone." Hegler's gray eyes were twinkling. "However, I thought it a splendid opportunity of introducing you to the local hierarchy and at the same time honoring you both. Mrs. Warden for her unaffected charm, and you"—his face broadened into a smile—"for your talent for staying alive."

So it was cards-on-the-table time. I pretended to be surprised. "And what's that supposed to mean?"

He looked at me benignly. "Come, now, Mr. Stone, we are both aware that you have been a nuisance to Hercules and that I have been trying to get rid of you. It is that simple." He leaned forward, resting his forearm on the table. "Unfortunately, things haven't worked out the way I'd hoped. I've been most distressed at the way my people have handled the matter, first in Colorado, then in Montreal. The airport, wasn't it? Of course, it never would have been my choice. But then, I'm not in that line of work."

A waiter began clearing away the last of the dishes. I watched him absently for a moment, until Hegler ordered him to fetch two cognacs. "Tell me," I said, fighting to keep the emotion out of my voice, "why are you doing this to me?"

Hegler's expression didn't change. "Personally, Mr. Stone, I have nothing against you. But we have too much at stake to let you interfere."

"We, meaning Hercules?"

He hesitated. "Yes. You see, we consider ourselves guardians of the past. It is people like me who will ensure that the world has a past to look back to through art, paintings. Treasures. We work, how should I put it, on a very delicate balance. When this balance is disturbed, we run the risk of becoming . . . well, ineffective. Do I make myself clear, Mr. Stone?"

"Precisely." I took a deep breath. "You steal from others, be they foreign countries or people like yourself. You cheat private individuals and governments. If you have to, you'll even kill people to get your way. God knows what else you do in the name of art."

Hegler was obviously enjoying this encounter. "Mr. Stone, apart from being too harsh and unrealistic, you are terribly naive, something few of us can afford these days. We are actually liberating treasures committed to dungeons for centuries. I could go on, but this is hardly the time or place. Let me say, however, that in accomplishing our goals, it admittedly means bending a few rules."

I snorted. "Bending a few rules?"

Hegler held up his hand. "Today, bending rules is a way of life. Look around you, Mr. Stone. Respected aircraft corporations think nothing of bribing officials in foreign countries to buy their product, all in the name of profit. Members of a local town council are paid under the table to enable the construction of an amusement park on prime agricultural land, solely in order to attract tourist dollars. Here you have a few greased palms, but the benefit to the community is worth tenfold. Summer jobs for students, tax revenue." Hegler sat back while the waiter set two snifters on the table before us. Then he cupped the large glass in his hands. "Forgive me, I'm digressing. But now at least we understand each other."

I felt myself coming to a boil. "The only thing I understand, Mr. Hegler, is that you are nothing more than a—"

"Hi." Sarah was standing beside my chair. "Like to dance?"

I got up, leaving my cognac untouched.

Those demoralizing few minutes with Hegler had shaken me. Sarah must have sensed it, because her arm tightened around my shoulders. "Stoney, you just can't let him get to you."

"Does it show that much?"

"Not really, but I could see it coming. Remember, this is only

120

the beginning. I've known Gerhard Hegler for years. He's a bastard. He'll pick away at your weaknesses until there's nothing left. And then he'll toss you aside."

"Or kill you," I grunted. "I wonder what Gerry did wrong?"

We swayed together, and when the music stopped, we found ourselves alone on the dance floor, staring at each other.

Joachim Smith suddenly appeared beside me, slightly drunk. He asked if he might cut in.

"Sorry, Joachim," I said, unwilling to take my eyes off Sarah. "Mrs. Warden and I are on our way back to the hotel."

The headlights of the Mercedes swept across the drifting snow as I swung the big car into the lane leading to the hotel.

Sarah was beside me, her head resting on my shoulder. "They're still with us, aren't they?" she said.

I glanced in the rearview mirror. A set of amber running lights glowed through the falling snow. A second car coming in from the other direction slowed and disappeared behind the hotel.

"Yes." We'd had the same escorts for the earlier trip down to the casino.

Sarah sat up, pulled the coat around her, and looked back. "It's ridiculous," she muttered. "What do they think we'll do, drive off into the night on an empty tank of gas?"

It was true. There had only been enough fuel to get to the casino and back. The gauge was now on empty.

"Stoney, what are we going to do?"

"We're going to hold on," I replied. "That's all we can do."

I closed the shutters and wandered across the room, loosening my bow tie, wondering what was keeping her. The silver bucket was full of fresh ice packed around a bottle. I lifted it and read the label: Canard-Duchène 1959. Nothing but the best for Hercules, I mused. They owed us that much, at least.

Still no Sarah. I carried the bucket to the night table and began twirling the bottle gently in the ice, when I heard something behind me.

Sarah was coming toward me, barefoot and naked beneath the same flimsy gown. Her hair, swept up earlier to give a certain sophistication to the evening, now tumbled about her shoulders. Gone too was most of her makeup, with only a trace of lipstick accentuating her deep rich tan.

I reached out and touched her bare shoulders, letting my fingers drift slowly down until I could feel her full warm swell

121

beneath the silk. Her nipples rose hard against my palm and I felt myself stiffen as I pushed my body forward. Our arms went around each other, our mouths brushed, lingered, then came together.

I was tasting her now as I once had, filling my lungs with fragrance I'd never forgotten as we fell onto the bed.

She stretched out, the material of her dress pulled taut over her thighs, outlining the hump of her pubis. I cupped her breasts, then ran my hands lightly down her body. She was stroking my leg, her arm brushing against my groin. As the musky aroma of her body filled my senses, I brought my mouth down fully on her crotch and exhaled through the fabric, feeling the heat of my breath penetrate the skin below.

We made love then, a desperate, frantic kind of love, still clothed, our bodies thrusting, grinding slowly against one another, our passions rising higher until at last Sarah's body trembled uncontrollably, then stiffened. Driving her hips upward, she suddenly cried out even as I exploded deep inside her.

Later we lay stripped and warm beneath the feather duvet, sipping champagne, touching. We talked about the past, the first time, as teenagers, we had made love. We were drifting off to sleep when I murmured half-jokingly that the last time we went to bed together, I'd awakened in the morning to find her gone.

She laughed and reached down, fondled me under the duvet. "You mean at the Algonquin? I have the feeling you will never let me forget it."

"I won't," I said, kissing her bare neck.

She let me go, and sitting up, looked me in the eye. "In that case, let's settle it right now. Sure I walked out on you then, but were you ready to commit yourself, by leaving Jane and the kids? No way. And rough though my life was, I wasn't prepared to give it up for you. The difference was, Stoney, I admitted it. You wouldn't. You hedged, just like you did years ago at Harvard." She looked away.

I pulled her gently down onto my chest. "It's true. I wanted that night at the Algonquin to go on forever. When I found you gone . . ."

Sarah moved her head, kissing me along the line of my chin. She stopped at my ear and looked up. "Strange how little things change our lives. Forever."

"Our meeting on the street? It didn't change—"

"I wasn't thinking of that. It was a weekend during exams. I'd finished mine and I wanted to go away with you, just overnight. But you had an important exam on Monday and swore you wouldn't be leaving your room for forty-eight hours. I stormed off and ended up with some of my girlfriends at the pub. Gerry was there. I told him about you. He laughed and said he'd studied all he was going to for that exam and what the hell let's sneak off for a dirty weekend."

"And you did."

"Not at first. But he persisted. I guess I got a little drunk." She lifted her head. "I must tell you this, Stoney."

"Go on."

"He borrowed a cottage from a friend. At Prouts Neck. In Maine. We were alone. I remember feeling so aroused I could hardly swallow. I kept thinking of you, but wanting him. We drank wine by the fire. Lots of it. We started making love. It came in waves, washing over me, carrying me up and up, and I was crying and yelling at the same time. Then something snapped inside me. Stoney, I was crying your name. Gerry was screaming at me, shaking me. Then he hauled on his clothes, grabbed a bottle, and stormed outside.

"He came back a few hours later. I tried to explain that you and I had been together so long, it was natural to call your name. He wouldn't believe me, and I was so shaken. We drove home in the middle of the night. We never spoke. I didn't see him for three weeks. I took it out on you. Then the letter came. It was from Gerry, asking me to marry him."

"I could never understand."

"Why I married him?"

"No, what happened to us."

"It wasn't you. It was Gerry. He was bursting to go places. I wanted to be with him. And we did go places and do things. But you always popped up somewhere. In arguments, mostly. Little squabbles that ended up with both of us screaming at each other. He'd finally drag out you, saying that I was still in love with you. It was . . . something he couldn't forget. Prouts Neck. And he could never accept that I loved him better. I wanted us to see a marriage counselor. Of course he wouldn't."

"Feelings of guilt. A natural phenomenon. Man steals best friend's girl and he carries it around as guilt."

Sarah smiled. "You'd make a lousy psychologist," she said.

"Why so?"

"Because, Philip Stone, any psychologist worth his shingle would say Gerry was using you, in this sense, as a convenient

123

crutch. How better could he end an argument, especially one he was losing?"

"You win."

She giggled. "You're no fun, you give up too easily."

"That's because I'd rather fuck than fight."

Her eyes went big. "Mr. Stone," she exclaimed, sliding her body onto mine. "Okay, who's on top?"

We took turns.

Twice during the night I'd gone to the window to find the black car still parked below. One look down the corridor showed a guy lounging by the elevator and stairs. I thought of alerting the hotel management, but Hegler had already gone to the trouble of having our phones cut off.

At precisely ten o'clock we were wakened by a knock on the door. Almost immediately, a note appeared under it. Gerhard Hegler was wishing us a good morning and hoped we hadn't overlooked the agenda. Per the instructions, we would be leaving the hotel at eleven sharp, along with Joachim Smith and the others. The wind had died during the night, but it was still snowing too heavily for the helicopters. Part of the trip would be by télépherique to an upper ski station called Lognan. From there, private transportation had been arranged.

14

The cable car swayed as we clattered over the support arm of yet another pylon and continued silently upward in the dense cloud.

Somewhere above us would be La Croix de Lognan. At sixty-five hundred feet it was the first station on the cable run to Les Grands Montets, a series of peaks in the Mont Blanc chain.

Of the fifty or sixty crammed aboard, perhaps a dozen were Hegler's crowd, including Joachim Smith and his small band of rowdies, who were still carrying on much as they had at the casino last night. The rest were skiers, French mostly, clutching their skis and poles and staring gloomily out at nothing, undoubtedly wondering if the cost of this trip was worth it.

Sarah and I stood near the front window, racking our brains

for a way out of this mess. But it was damn near impossible. For one thing, we had no skis, which ruled out the possibility of making a break for it once we hit La Croix. Besides, Fleck and his sidekicks were sticking to us like glue.

Worst of all, this trip was taking us inexorably farther and farther away from any hope of escape.

I was longing to be one of these skiers, with only the weather to worry about, when Sarah tugged at my arm. "Look," she said, nodding toward the window.

A wave of excitement rippled through the car. The cloud hadn't seemed as thick anymore, but I wasn't ready for it to suddenly drop away, leaving in its place a breathtaking panorama of sunlit snowcapped mountains spread out beneath the bluest sky I'd ever seen.

Cheers broke out around us.

Meanwhile, we were climbing even steeper as the car cleared the last pylon and made its final sweep into the dark entrance of the Lognan station.

We stopped. The doors on one side rattled open and the crowd of eager skiers surged out, taking Hegler, Smith, and the rest with them. Fleck and Corry, however, held us back until the car was empty, then led us down a flight of narrow steps nearby and outside.

We were on a wide wood belvedere packed with healthy, tan-faced skiers soaking up the warmth of the sun, their lunches and bottles of wine spread out on picnic tables.

With Fleck leading and Corry behind, we threaded our way between the tables to the far railing. Joined by the other two guys, they positioned themselves nearby.

Ignoring them, I turned to Sarah. She looked as good as the view. She was wearing a light blue ski outfit picked from her new wardrobe and a pair of fluffy fur snow boots. Her hair was loose about her shoulders. She'd removed her ski gloves, and taking a small paisley scarf from her pocket, tied it around her head. She caught me watching her and smiled.

"Listen," I said quietly, "I want to know exactly where we are." A loud clanking noise from behind us turned out to be a cable car similar to ours, red with yellow trim, emerging from the opposite end of the building. Well above the treeline here, it glided out over the vast unbroken snowfield that stretched for miles in either direction as it swept steadily toward the peaks beyond. I tried following the cables, but soon lost them.

"That's the car to the Montets," she said. "You can't really see the station from here."

"And where's Les Pins?"

She turned me around to face down the valley. "See those very high peaks off to our left?" She was pointing to a spot on our side of the valley. "And the white dome of snow up behind them?"

I nodded.

"That's Mont Blanc."

"Highest mountain in the Alps," I muttered. "Geography. Sixth grade. But it's round. I thought it would be pointed."

"It fooled me, too," she replied, pulling on her gloves. "Anyway, Les Pins is between here and Mont Blanc. So is a glacier, on the other side of Les Pins. It's called the Mer de Glace. Above it, the Vallée Blanche. Together they'll give you fourteen miles of the best skiing you'll ever see."

"It'll have to wait," I said, looking directly across the valley at the mountains opposite. "What's over there?"

"The Aiguilles. 'Needles,' in English. A cable car runs from Chamonix up to several good ski stations. Plan Praz and Brévent. Another to Flégère."

Satisfied, I glanced back down our side. "Now, there's a tunnel here connecting France and Italy."

Again she pointed to Mont Blanc, then traced a line straight down. "Right under there. Your bus would have passed the road leading up to it yesterday when you came up from St. Gervais. You see, you would've passed Les Houches and the Mont Blanc tunnel before arriving in Chamonix. A distance of about ten miles. Argentière is at this end of the valley."

"Good," I said, trying to put everything into perspective. "I think I've got it."

"Then there is just one more thing," she said, aiming a finger out across the snowfield. "See those little black dots? Our transportation."

The black dots became two large, fully tracked vehicles—the sort often found at Arctic exploration sites. Dark gray, built high off the snow, they looked powerful enough to tackle anything but the energy shortage.

Sarah and I were ushered aboard the one loaded with boxes of supplies brought up by cable car from an earlier run. These were lashed down in the center of the passenger compartment, leaving barely enough room us. We sat with our backs to the porthole windows. Corry sat across from us, his boxer's body jammed

126

into a bronze ski suit. As always, his metallic blue eyes told us nothing. I'd have sworn the man never blinked.

Hegler occupied the small jump seat next to the driver, a slack-jawed character wearing an old army-surplus coat and tuque pulled down to his eyebrows.

For the better part of two hours the snow machine bobbed and weaved through unbroken snow, scooting around drifts too high or valleys too deep for it to handle. At last Hegler pointed to a ridge above us. "Les Pins, Mr. Stone."

At first I saw nothing but another outcropping of rock; then, as we climbed, a portion of this rock took shape, molding itself into an extraordinary building of hewn logs, carved balustrades, and tinted windows set against a backdrop of raw, bare peaks and glistening snow.

Within half an hour we found ourselves at an entrance beneath a wide wood deck extending along the front of the building. Hegler led us inside and down a narrow corridor, telling our party, which now included Smith and the others, how the lodge, once a hotel, had been built from forest pine, or "daille," as the local Savoyards called it, around the turn of the century. He and Harold Warden had bought it in 1947 from a count who had fallen on bad times. "We have made extensive alterations since," Hegler was saying as we filed up a nearby staircase. "The lodge was abominably cold, forcing us to install a new heating system. Then we added the huge windows to do justice to the view, as you will see."

We were in the foyer now, with its high beamed ceiling supporting two enormous antique lamps suspended on chains. A wide circular staircase swept up along one wall to the floor above. Directly below it was the main entrance with a pair of the largest paneled doors I have ever seen.

Behind these was an enormous room, complete with a ceiling several stories high, chandeliers, and a massive stone fireplace big enough to walk into. It reminded me of a baronial banquet hall from out of the Middle Ages. Impressive and decidedly not from the Middle Ages was the far wall, made up entirely of sections of glass. Beyond it lay the mountains, cut by valleys and glaciers, ringed with pinnacles of rock, and bounded by snow.

Thirty or forty people were gathered by the fireplace, some wearing business suits and ties, others in sport coats and turtlenecks. A blazing fire crackled behind them.

Then Hegler introduced us all, without missing a name. I

127

found myself shaking hands with a commonwealth of nations, and to my surprise, at least a dozen of them told me how happy they'd been to hear I was coming and congratulated me for my generous support of Hercules and the arts in general. Sarah, who had been watching from the sidelines, thought it quite funny.

"*You,*" she whispered when attention was diverted to others, "a patron of the arts? I can't quite believe my late husband had such a sense of humor."

"I don't think Gerry's sense of humor had anything to do with this," I said. As we talked, she steered me away from the others.

"While you were meeting everybody, I overheard someone tell Joachim Smith that a list of paintings to be auctioned was circulated among the members this morning. To quote him, it was 'dynamite.' Our friend Joachim got very excited and said he would pick up a copy from Gerhard right away. I'm sure I could get my hands on one, maybe even Joachim's."

We stopped at the windows.

I watched her remove the scarf and fluff up her hair. "Look," I said, "I don't think we can worry about the paintings. I just want to get us out of here. Alive." I envisioned the headlines: "ESTABLISHED MEMBER WORLDWIDE ART ORGANIZATION, YOUNG WIDOW, PERISH IN SKI MISHAP." "And that means tonight. Before we're found dead down some crevasse."

"I've got news for you," she said, stuffing the scarf in her pocket. "From what I've learned on previous visits here, you're not found dead down a crevasse. You're not found at all. Give me time to get my hands on the list or find the paintings. Gerry once told me something about a subbasement . . ."

"Sarah, for Christ's sake, who cares about the paintings?"

She frowned. "Listen, the list is important. Without it we have no proof that these people are crooks. I've gone through a lot, Stoney, and I'm not prepared to let them get away with it."

Sudden laughter. We turned as a handful of skiers spilled through the far door.

Taking Sarah by the arm, I had started back to join the others when she nudged me. "Look who's with the noisemakers."

My head came around. Monique! She had lifted her hand, probably to wave at Sarah, when our eyes met. For a moment she looked incredulous, but she recovered quickly. "Philippe," she cried, running toward us. "Mon Dieu, Philippe Stone."

I glanced at Sarah. She had stepped back, her face taut with anger.

Monique threw herself at me. I grabbed for her and staggered,

128

fighting to keep my balance. She wrapped her arms tightly around my neck, and before I was fully aware of what was happening, she was whispering hysterically in my ear, "Philippe, please, you must hit me. Hard. Trust me, Philippe. Now!"

At once she thrust herself from me with such force it could only have looked as if I'd done the pushing. I caught the desperation in her eyes. I drew my right arm back and drove it forward.

My fist caught her high on the cheekbone, spinning her savagely back into a chair. She clawed at it, trying to keep herself upright, but it was too late. Her legs were already buckling and she pitched forward onto the floor.

No one moved. I stared at the crumpled figure, hardly aware of the sharp pain in my hand.

Then the room exploded.

Hands grabbed me, pinning my arms back, bending me forward. Legs crowded around. I heard someone say, "She's okay. Stand back. Give her room to breathe." Bodies shifted and I could see her sitting on the floor with her back against a chair. Another voice said, "You may let Mr. Stone go." It was Hegler's. I straightened, rubbing my wrist where someone had gripped it. Those closest to me scoffed openly. I didn't blame them.

Gerhard Hegler looked around at the others for a moment, then raised his hands. "I'm afraid our Mr. Stone here has an embarrassing way of expressing himself, even to old friends. Please let me apologize for his behavior. And now, if we might—" He didn't get any further.

"It is for me to apologize to Mr. Stone." Monique was coming through the crowd. She stopped next to me and looked at the faces around us. "Lately I have caused Mr. Stone much anguish. I am ashamed of myself. When I saw him now, I was hoping perhaps he had put aside our personal differences." She paused and lightly touched her swollen cheekbone. "Unfortunately for me, he hadn't." Somebody laughed softly; others joined in. Encouraged, Monique reached up and kissed me, first on one cheek, then the other.

What the hell is this? I thought to myself.

Hegler suggested cocktails, then turned to Monique, insisting on taking a closer look at her bruised face. Knitting his brow as he did so, he recommended an ice pack to keep down the swelling and was about to call for one when he was summoned away to the phone. It struck me that Monique seemed relieved to see him go.

With Hegler gone, the party broke up. I looked around for Sarah. She was talking to Joachim Smith.

I was conscious now of Monique still standing beside me. My bitterness was coming back. I started to move away, when her words stopped me. "Philippe, I must talk to you. While M'sieu Hegler is gone. Please, just very quietly walk me out onto the deck. I don't want to attract attention, but we haven't much time."

Again her eyes had that faint look of desperation I'd seen earlier. This had better be good, I thought as we slowly headed for the door.

A light breeze was blowing diagonally across the wide deck. Indifferent to the view, I pushed through the deep snow and reached the far railing. "Okay, Monique," I said, "let's hear it."

She moved in close, and looking off toward the mountains, said, "I am distressed, Philippe, because I have deceived both you and Sarah. When I saw you here, now, I couldn't believe it. In Colorado I learned at the last minute that you might be killed. And I couldn't do anything about it. I was under orders . . . to do nothing."

"Orders from Hercules," snapped a voice behind us.

Monique turned. "No, Sarah," she answered softly, "from the International Police. I am working for Interpol."

My mouth dropped open. "Good God."

"Oh, Monique," Sarah whispered. "Why didn't you tell us in Colorado?"

"I couldn't. It was too risky. You might have done something, without even knowing, that would have given everything away."

"Like saving Terry Samuels' life, for instance?" I said without thinking.

She gazed at me steadily. "Philippe, no one expected anything like that to happen. We were all as shocked as you."

"Who's 'we'?" I waited for an answer.

"In this case, the FBI."

I was struck dumb. "Agostino! You're working for Agostino?"

Monique's eyes darted toward the lodge, then back at me. "Careful, Philippe. Someone is sure to be watching. We cannot remain here long."

While we were talking, Sarah had wrapped some snow in her

130

scarf. "Agostino," she said, pressing it now against Monique's injured cheek. "Isn't that your friend, Stoney?"

"That's the guy."

Sarah readjusted the snow. "But, Monique, you're working for Hegler."

She closed her eyes. "Yes. I am what you call a 'plant.' I'm here to find out as much as possible about M'sieu Hegler and the Hercules organization."

By now being out here was making me nervous, but I couldn't see anyone watching us from inside. And I had so many questions. "Have you any idea, Monique, how Hegler knew I was coming?"

She opened her eyes. "No, Philippe. Many things happen that I know nothing about. I do not know, for example, why I was sent to Colorado to keep eyes on Sarah. Gerhard Hegler gave me orders and M'sieu Agostino told me to follow them to the letter."

Sarah was filling the scarf with fresh snow. She said, "Monique, you mentioned getting information about the organization. It's the auction you're interested in, isn't it?"

She looked at me, then back to Sarah. "Yes. How do you know?"

I cut in. "It's a long story. Now, Monique, the police. Where are they?"

"Chamonix. James also."

"James?"

"M'sieu Agostino," she said quickly, touching the cheek lightly with her fingers.

It was badly discolored and swollen, but the skin wasn't broken. Sarah, putting the ice pack back in place, remarked, "Surely he doesn't expect you to work up here alone?"

She hesitated. "Yes. The first thing the police wanted was a list of the people here. I was to pass it to a contact at the casino without delay. So I surrounded myself with a few of the more wild gentlemen here and coaxed them into persuading one of the helicopter pilots to fly us down for some gambling." She smiled to herself. "I met my contact and gave her the list."

"Next?" I asked.

"I was then supposed to discover what paintings would be auctioned. I would be contacted while skiing."

Sarah interrupted. "Do you have the list yet?"

Monique shook her head.

131

I glanced back anxiously at the lodge once more. "Did you make contact?"

"Yes. On the téléphérique to Les Grands Montets. I told him I was having difficulty getting the list. He assured me that soon I would have help at Les Pins."

"Who?" I asked. She didn't know.

Sarah removed the ice pack and looked closely at the cheek, saying at the same time, "Stoney, maybe it's you."

"Me?" I said.

"Why not? Gerhard wouldn't give you a second thought. Besides, who else could your friend Agostino send?"

"How the hell should I know?" I said. "Believe me, though, he didn't send me."

She smiled. "No, but he didn't stop you, either. Isn't that the same thing?"

15

Before leaving the deck, we all agreed Sarah and I should escape that evening. With the list of the paintings. Sarah would work extra hard on Joachim. I suggested Monique should come with us, but she turned this down flat. Someone, as she put it, had to keep an eye on the store.

We entered the lounge to find the cocktail hour indeed in full swing. A bar had been set up in a corner, and Hegler, seeing us, waved us over.

"And how was the view?" he asked when we had finally reached him through the crowd. Without waiting for an answer, he turned to Monique and said, "My dear, you do not look very well. Should you not lie down and rest before dinner?" It struck me as a curious sort of request. Almost a command. And unnecessary. The fresh air and Sarah's ice pack had done her good. Much of the swelling had gone.

"Yes," she answered quite deliberately, and turned away.

Sarah, ignoring Hegler, said to me, "I'll go with her, but wait for me. I won't be a moment."

Hegler abruptly motioned to a young man wearing a greenish outfit similar to the bartender's. "Erich will show you to your

132

quarters, Mr. Stone," said Hegler, without addressing me directly. "I am sure you will find them comfortable."

By now I was pretty indifferent to Hercules' chic. This was a room of soft tans and rich browns, of two Salvador Dalis and a Picasso—stolen, no doubt—and lighting so indirect I had difficulty finding even the bathroom switch. My clothes, as I'd come to expect, were neatly in place.

Dinner. Black tie.

For the occasion, Gerhard Hegler produced guests from Chamonix ferried up by the two helicopters, which included the mayor's party. A nice touch of public relations, this, having the locals meet members of Hercules en masse. It was also a good omen: the snowstorm had obviously cleared the valley.

Monique was missing from our little predinner gèt-together. I was worried but could do little, as Hegler insisted on introducing me to everyone I hadn't met. This included some Americans wintering in the valley, a clutch of foreign diplomats, and two aging former U.S. senators who arrived in such a state of wheezing and coughing, you'd have thought they'd walked up. However, these same two old codgers cornered Hegler long enough after introductions were made to let me slip away.

I found Sarah with a cherubic, happy little guy from Arizona whom she promptly sent off for refills. Tonight she was dressed in emerald green.

"Have you seen Monique?" I asked.

"No," she answered, "but she said she'd meet us here before dinner."

"This is before dinner."

She guided me away from the main group. "Listen. I was about to tackle Joachim Smith to see what I could get out of him when the Arizona Kid showed up. We started talking about paintings, so I mentioned the auction list as if I owned one. And, Stoney, his eyes lit up. He began babbling excitedly about it. I'm sure he has a copy on him. He keeps putting his hand in his pocket."

"Maybe he has an itch."

She scowled. "Not that pocket. His breast pocket. Now, if I can get him a little tippled . . ."

I grunted. "He's probably planning the same diversion, but for a different reason." We laughed. "Don't forget Monique, huh?"

"I won't."

I started walking off, then stopped. "By the way, I've been wondering about your father-in-law. Where is he?"

The smile on her face faded. "I hear he always shows up bombed . . ." Something behind me caught her attention. "Oh, no."

I turned to see Harold Warden, his face a pasty white, standing in the doorway; tall, elegant, and very drunk. He was swaying from side to side and had reached out a hand to steady himself.

"He's been like that ever since he got here. He spends much of his time in his room. I'd better go to him. I'll drop in on Monique as well." She had barely left me when Warden missed a step and started to teeter. Sarah rushed forward, but it was Fleck and Corry, stuffed into matching dinner jackets, who emerged to grab Warden and smartly wheel him back out the door so smoothly that I doubted whether more than a few saw what happened.

Sarah followed them, so I quietly moved to the bar. While waiting for the busy bartender to take my order, I found myself chatting idly with a mild-mannered guy, perhaps in his late thirties. He was a skiing buff and had spent much of the winter traveling to resorts in Colorado, Vermont, the Laurentians, and Europe. He mentioned Leysin, in Switzerland, his favorite place to get away. It must have reminded him of something amusing, because the corners of his mouth turned up. He had just begun to describe the village when we both noticed Sarah pushing toward us through the crowd. He excused himself.

"Corry and Fleck wouldn't let me near him," she said, resting her elbows on the bar. She was visibly upset. "Despite everything, I love him and I hate to see him this way. It isn't like him."

"I feel sorry for him too," I said, "for your sake." I waved to the bartender. He nodded back. "What about Monique?"

"Her door was locked. When I called out, I'm sure I heard her moving around inside, but she wouldn't answer. I want you to come back with me."

"Okay, but let's order a couple of drinks so it looks like you're giving me a guided tour."

I caught the bartender's eye again. This time he took pity on me. I ordered a Tom Collins for Sarah and a beer for myself. While waiting, I asked if she'd seen the guy I'd been talking to.

134

"He's one of the few I missed when Hegler was introducing me around." No, she hadn't. Was he here now?

The drinks arrived. I looked around as I poured my beer into a glass. "Yes," I said, "the guy by the pillar."

"With the dark hair?"

"And the purplish tux."

"Yes, I've met him. He's a friend of Gerhard's. His name is Roger Wessen."

Somehow I got the glass back onto the bar top. Roger Wessen. Jesus Christ! It was all I could do to exchange my beer for a martini, on the rocks, very dry, very double.

Walking along the third-floor corridor with Sarah a few minutes later, I couldn't get Wessen off my mind. As we'd left the lounge, casually carrying our drinks, I'd had an urge to drop my glass and strangle the bastard with my bare hands, as coolly as he must have pulled the trigger to kill young Samuels. This same guy who stood next to me at the bar, quietly describing a little Swiss village, might just as easily have walked me out onto the deck and splattered my brains across the snow.

Sarah was talking. I missed it.

"I asked what the matter was. It's Wessen who's bothering you, isn't it? You went as pale as a sheet when I mentioned his name. Who is he?"

"I don't know. I mistook him for someone else. Now, where is Monique's room?"

"On the left. I don't believe you. About Wessen."

"It's not important," I said, stopping at the next room. We left our glasses on a hallway table nearby, then pounded on the door until it opened.

Standing before us was a large woman in a crisp white uniform who told us in broken English to go away. We wouldn't. She finally told us that Miss Brosseau had complained of dizziness and a severe headache and had called for her, the lodge nurse. She wasn't about to let us into the room, either, but we had something she didn't. Two of us. So while Sarah distracted the woman with much arm-waving, I slipped over to the bed and clicked on the nearby lamp.

Monique was there, all right, her dark hair spread on the bolster, the blankets pulled up around her shoulders. Her face was turned away from me, and as I bent over her, the nurse found her best weapon; she threatened to scream very loud. We backed out the door and closed it behind us.

It wasn't until we reached the first-floor landing that I told Sarah our friend had been beaten. "Badly," I said.

She stiffened. "How badly?"

"I only saw her face. Both eyes have been blackened. Her lips are cut. Hegler must be on to her. Maybe he's got a line on the police, who knows? Whatever, we have to get out of here tonight. *With* her." We continued down the stairs.

"And what if she isn't well enough to ski?"

"There must be one of those toboggans in case of a ski injury around somewhere. Especially away up here."

"Yes. It would be stored in one of the sheds behind the helicopter pad." She sniffed, and when I looked, there were tears in her eyes.

We could hear voices and laughter filtering through the lounge doors. "Okay, Sarah," I said, keeping my voice down. "When we go back in, I want you to see what you can do about the auction list. If you can find out where the paintings are, so much the better. But we're leaving tonight, whether you get anything or not. Now, what's on the agenda after dinner?"

"Someone told me a five-piece orchestra is coming up from the valley. They'll play in the lounge."

"Good. Now, where are the skis kept?"

"Down off the basement hallway, where we came in today. First door on the right."

It was midnight.

Sarah was dancing with the little guy from Arizona. I cut in. She was excited because she had almost got her fingers on the list. I told her the moment the band quit and the evening ended she was to change and meet me under the deck. "I don't care how you do it, but be there. We'll use the confusion of the guests being flown out in relays to cover us. Can you do it?"

"Yes, there's a fire escape down the hall from me. Or I can use the back stairs. Don't worry. What about our seeing-eye dogs?"

"Fleck and Corry have been spending most of their time around the bar. I just hope they stay there. The other two are just floating around. I . . ." Joachim Smith was weaving toward us. I gave Sarah up without a fight.

I slipped out of the lounge during a raucous, hand-clapping, foot-stomping number, the kind where everyone joins in, and headed directly to the ski room.

The door was unlocked. I paused long enough to see if anyone

136

had followed me, and ducked inside. I closed the door, felt for the light switch, and turned it on.

The room was full of skis, with racks down either wall, along the back, and two up the middle. I started down the right side, scanning the rack for the familiar red-and-white ski bag or my Rossignols with the Steamboat decal. I found the skis and poles midway; the empty bag had been tossed onto an overhead shelf.

Sarah's Dynastars were on the far rack and easily identified by the same decals. I bundled them all out the nearby exit below the decking and dumped them into the deep snow at the corner of the building before racing back inside.

The toboggan was next, so I walked cautiously down the corridor, past the stairs leading to the foyer, and continued along the dimly lit passage until I came to another staircase and the back door leading onto the courtyard.

Outside again, I ran across the hard-packed snow of the courtyard, dodging the two large helicopters, only to plunge into deep snow as I headed for the three sheds fifty yards farther on.

From the first came the drone of a generator. I passed it up in favor of the second, where through one of the small panes making up the window I saw the shadowy outline of a snow-tracked vehicle. Shivering from the cold—I was still dressed only in my tuxedo—I took off one of my light shoes and smashed the glass with the heel, then reached in and unlocked the door.

I found the toboggan, more by feel than sight, leaning against what might have been a workbench. I wrestled it outside and dropped it into the snow. It was the standard rescue toboggan of molded fiberglass, with ribs on the underside designed to act as runners and covered by several layers of heavy canvas. A handle, U-shaped like one found on a baby's pram, was folded back along the length of the toboggan when not in use. This I now swung forward, and hooking my arm through it, started back for the lodge.

Ten minutes later I stumbled back inside. Though half-frozen and soaked to the skin, I managed to stow the toboggan in a snowdrift not far from our skis.

Now for Monique.

Using the back stairs, I went directly to the third floor and into the corridor. Music and laughter drifted up from below as I ducked into my own room. By the light of the bedside lamp I yanked my ski suit on over my tuxedo, then stuffed a pillowcase with every bit of warm clothing I could fit in, plus my ski boots. This done, I eased the door open and peered out.

The corridor was empty. Taking a deep breath, I grabbed the pillowcase and hurried along the hall to the far end.

A tray of empty dishes outside Monique's room suggested the strong-armed nurse might still be keeping her company. I tried the door. It was locked. Needing something to pry it open, I rummaged through the dishes until I found a knife. Wedging it between the door frame and the molding, I poked around till I felt the catch. Then I jabbed it forward while putting slight pressure on the door with my shoulder. It worked the third time, and I breathed easier.

Slipping inside, I closed the door and stood still, waiting for my eyes to adjust to the dull orange glow of the night-light on the far wall.

Beside it was a chair. In it was nursie, head bowed forward, arms folded across her thick chest. She was asleep, bless her. Taking pains not to disturb her, I stepped over to the bed.

Monique was lying on her side, like before, facing the wall. Putting down the knife, I eased back the comforter to see she was wearing the same pajama top I remembered from Colorado. I touched the cloth, feeling it between my fingers, then leaned forward.

Her breathing was steady, so I brought my mouth close to her ear and whispered her name. She didn't move. I felt a chill go through me. What if they'd given her something stronger than a mild sedative? Not wanting to think about it, I put a hand under her shoulder and eased her onto her back. She moaned. I quickly clamped my other hand over her mouth and held on. The nurse stirred, then settled down.

I tried again, whispering my name, when suddenly her head jerked sideways and pulled free of my hand. Even as I tried stifling the second groan, it was too late. It broke across the room.

Dropping Monique back on the bolster, I swung around to see the wide-eyed nurse lurching out of the chair. For a moment I couldn't be sure if she'd seen me. Then the look of surprise gave way to a grunt of satisfaction which told me one thing: she was going to deal with this on her own, before calling in the reserves.

It was then I remembered the knife. For a second I couldn't think what the hell I'd done with it. On the bed. I'd dropped it on the comforter. I swung around, feeling for it. I couldn't even see the damn thing.

I turned back. She was smiling, beckoning me away from the bed. She was a big woman. Big and thick. Carrot-colored hair and tiny eyes.

In desperation I glanced around for something to even up the match. At the moment there was no contest. Carrot Top knew it. I could see it in those little eyes. She stood now in the middle of room, coaxing me to leave the protection of the bed. Without taking my eyes off hers, I moved slowly along the bed, groping behind me for that goddamn knife until I bumped into the bedside table, nearly upsetting the lamp. The lamp! From what I could see of it, it was tall, solid.

Without wasting a second, I whirled around, grabbed it with both hands, and jerked it free of the plug. The loose wire snapped back at me as I tore away the flimsy shade and clutched the lamp just below the bulb and socket.

I turned back none too soon. Carrot Top's charge was a blur of white uniform.

I counted to three, then swung the bloody thing like a baseball bat.

The blow caught her in full stride, smashing solidly into her midsection. An expulsion of stale breath and spittle hit me full in the face as bits of the heavy clay lamp flew in all directions. With one prolonged groan the nurse sank to her knees, then slowly began to slump forward. Taking no chances, I lifted what was left of the lamp and brought it down hard across her neck and shoulders, driving her onto the floor. She bounced once and lay still.

Breathing heavily, I stepped back to the bed and had one arm under Monique's shoulder, pleading with her to wake up, when the room suddenly went very bright. I didn't move. A voice chided me, "To use an old cliché, Mr. Stone, that is no way to treat a lady." The man behind the voice needed no introduction. It was Gerhard Hegler.

I remained where I was, holding Monique. Her eyes were closed, her breathing regular. I closed mine, cursing myself for not having been more careful. To be caught before we began . . .

Gerhard Hegler moved around me and sat on the edge of the bed. He was all black tie, black tux, and smiles. He wagged a finger at me. "Now, now, Mr. Stone, don't take your failure to heart. Surely you must accept by now that you are always under surveillance. And yet you intrigue me. Knowing this, you doggedly persist in playing your little games. Hiding skis at the corners of buildings, dragging out our rescue toboggans. As for your astounding propensity for abusing women . . ." He nodded to the figure on the floor. "Poor Fräulein Schmidt. I wouldn't want to be around when she gains consciousness if I were you, Mr. Stone." His eyes came back to me. "But then, you won't be."

I wanted to scream at him, wipe the bloody grin off his face, but I bit my lip. I thought of Sarah telling me to hold on, just hold on.

"And do not worry about Miss Brosseau," he went on. "We will take good care of her. Good night, Mr. Stone." The quick smile, a nod.

Hands grabbed me. I struggled but felt my body rise up, then drop down across Monique. She moaned, and I screamed. The struggling and shouting probably lasted all of a few seconds; then something suddenly jabbed sharply into my buttock and I felt myself drifting off into the sunset.

16

I had wakened not knowing where I was. Nor did I care. I remembered lying in the dark and calling out because I was incredibly thirsty. But I couldn't move, I couldn't think, and when no one came, I cried myself back to sleep.

It was morning. The room was full of sunlight. I was still very thirsty, I still couldn't move. I couldn't even lift my head off the bolster. Besides, my brain was hardly ticking over. So I lay there pretending to be drinking, and when I couldn't stand this any longer, I slowly pushed the covers aside and eased myself down onto the floor, then crawled to the bathroom. Somehow I managed to drag myself up the side of the tub and turn on the tap. When I couldn't drink any more, I leaned back against the tub and closed my eyes. And slept.

Now I was awake again. Someone was calling me from far away. When I opened my eyes, I found myself still on the bathroom floor, still wearing my rumpled tuxedo. I took stock to find most of last night was missing. So were my shoes and watch. Though feeling pretty thick between the ears, I got up and was drinking from the basin tap when I heard the same voice calling me again. This time it didn't seem so far away.

"Mr. Stone, come to your balcony."

That voice suddenly filled in all the missing pieces. Monique, Carrot Top, the broken lamp. And Hegler.

I crossed the room, opened the glass panel, and stepped in my stocking feet onto the snow-covered balcony.

"Mr. Stone!" came a chorus of voices now from down below. Squinting against the sunlight, I peered over the railing to find Hegler, Joachim Smith, the Arizona Kid, and several others whose names I couldn't remember, smiling up at me from the main deck. They were all dressed for skiing.

"Good morning," I said testily, looking out beyond them to the mountains, then back again.

Hegler was grinning. "It is hardly morning, Mr. Stone. It is almost one o'clock, Thursday. We have been waiting for you." He paused. "We thought you might enjoy a few runs from the Grands Montets while the weather holds. Besides, the fresh air will do you good. We've asked Mrs. Warden to come along."

"How thoughtful of you," I said, then added, "By the way, Mr. Hegler, how is Monique today?"

His expression didn't change. "Much better, Mr. Stone, much better. The swelling has gone down, though the cheek is still slightly discolored. She was up for breakfast this morning and took part in several of our discussions." He turned to Smith. "Wasn't she with you, Joachim?" Smith couldn't remember. Hegler shrugged and looked up. "How is half an hour, then? Grab yourself a bite to eat, then meet us in the courtyard."

It was Joachim Smith who had the last word before the little group trudged back inside. He bellowed up, "And don't forget your ski outfit, Stone. It's one hell of a lot more practical than the tuxedo you're wearing." His remark was greeted with loud guffaws.

I remained on the balcony for a few minutes, worrying about Monique. Hegler was lying, of course. She had been too badly beaten to show up today. I was in no shape for skiing either, but I wanted to stay close to Sarah.

My feet, with nothing between them and the snow but thin socks, were beginning to tingle. I took one more look at the mountains, then stepped back into the room to find Corry lounging in one of the large chairs, his expression, as ever, inscrutable. I sighed and crossed to the bathroom, thinking that Hegler was right. I must be a slow learner.

141

"Welcome aboard, Mr. Stone," was Hegler's greeting forty-five minutes later, shouted over the roar of the helicopter engine. He was standing in the wide side door dressed in a one-piece tan ski outfit, his gray hair flattened against his skull by the terrific downdraft from the revolving blades. I grabbed the hand he pushed out to me and got one leg up, but with ski boots on, it wasn't easy.

From behind, Corry gave me a boost, and in I went. The door clanged shut, the floor trembled, and suddenly we left the ground. I found myself standing on a mass of skis.

Having come from the bright sunlit courtyard to the dim interior of the chopper, I couldn't see a damn thing. It was Joachim Smith who took pity on me and got me seated with my back against the padded fuselage.

I settled back, waiting for my eyes to adjust to the lack of light. From what I could see, there were no windows or seats. I blinked several times. Bodies and faces were taking shape. One of them was Sarah, with the familiar scarf about her head. She was directly across from me, next to the narrow door that probably lead to the cockpit. She was talking to her friend from Arizona. She glanced across at me. Her eyes seemed to ask if I was fine. I nodded. She relaxed, and putting her head back against the fuselage, closed her eyes. Including Sarah, there were about ten of us aboard, two of them the "heavies" from our meeting at the bus.

Hegler sat down next to me and said, "This may not be the most comfortable way to climb a mountain, but it certainly beats the lineups, no?" When I didn't answer, he went on, "I quite understand why you aren't at your best, Mr. Stone. Nurse Schmidt assures me you will feel like new with fresh air in your lungs. At the moment, you are still suffering the aftereffects."

"Aftereffects from what?" I asked.

"Tuinol. Withdrawal brings on a slight lapse of memory, confusion, a slight tendency toward aggressiveness."

"Don't forget thirst," I said, looking to see if Smith was listening. He wasn't. His chief preoccupation these days seemed to be watching Sarah. I turned back to Hegler. "Thirst and a very great desire to break your neck."

Hegler exploded with laughter and for a second or two rocked back and forth. "There," he said at last, "aggressiveness. Nurse Schmidt was right, though I will credit you with a vivid sense of humor despite the relaxant. I have been assured by the nurse, to repeat myself, that the best method of clearing the drug from your system is strenuous exercise. And, Mr. Stone," he said with a twinkle in his eye, "exercise is something we will all experience very soon."

The helicopter dropped us off on a small plateau just below the station at Les Grands Montets. A long flight of wood steps brought skiers down from the cable car, depositing them on this plateau where the actual run to Lognan began.

Oblivious of the stares of those watching us from the steps, Hegler quickly marshaled us into unloading the ski equipment, then inadvertently waved the chopper pilot off before most of us were clear. A frenzy of snow and particles of ice whipped up by the rotating blades sent us scurrying in every direction, much to the delight of those not affected. Seconds later the machine was a mere speck disappearing over a ridge, its high-pitched whine still ringing in our ears.

I had hurried into my gear, hoping to find a moment with Sarah, but it wasn't to be. Flanked by—what must have seemed innocent enough—the two bodyguards, Sarah and I were kept well within the group as Hegler, eager to get started, whisked us off, not in the direction used by the skiers from the cable car, but the other way. I didn't like it, but having no choice, I adjusted my sunglasses and tuque and pushed off with the rest.

Here the plateau soon narrowed, caught dramatically between a rising wall of rock on one side and a vertical drop of several hundred feet on the other. It wasn't long, however, before we veered through an opening in the rock and dropped headlong down into a wide valley.

As for me, it was some time before I found my ski legs. I tumbled again and again, usually as the result of crossed skis or bad balance. Nurse Schmidt should have told her friend Hegler that another aftereffect of an obviously excessive dose of a sodium pentobarbital was a crippling lack of coordination. It became so bad that during one of the few stops forced on us all by shortnesses of breath, Sarah slid around one of our bodyguards and pulled up beside me. I could tell that she was desperately worried about me.

In the few minutes we had together, I explained what had happened last night, why I hadn't shown—and as she could see, the drug was still having its effect on me. I learned from her that she had waited out by the corner of the building for an hour, then, realizing something had gone wrong, had slipped back to her room without being seen. When I told her she undoubtedly had been watched, she wasn't surprised; the odds had been stacked against us, though to her it was worth a try. And the list, I asked. She had only time to nod and smile before we were on the move again. It would be the last time we'd get close enough to talk until we reached the bottom.

Keeping up to the others became less of a problem. The more I skied, the better I fared. Strength returned to my legs, my head cleared, and if it hadn't been for the gnawing fear that Sarah and I weren't here just for pleasure, I would have thoroughly enjoyed myself.

For what seemed hours we plunged down through a series of small valleys, one moment battling snow that boiled around our thighs, the next clattering over wind-packed drifts, all this surrounded by mountains stretching on forever beneath a sky so blue, so close, you could almost reach out and touch it.

At last the rugged terrain exhausted itself. Again we were skiing a limitless snowfield, each trailing a plume of snow crystals behind him.

Ahead, Hegler had veered sharply to the left and promptly disappeared. We followed, cleared the same ridge, and found him waiting on a promontory overlooking a glacier of magnificent proportions. Beyond and far below lay the Chamonix Valley.

This glacier was the Mer de Glace, quite literally a sea of ice, spawned in the uppermost reaches of Mont Blanc, where pressure, he told us, transformed snow into ice. Then, drawn by gravity, the glacier starts its imperceptible descent, carrying with it a surface deeply scarred by crevasses, pockmarked with twisted columns and mounds of frozen blue ice.

We listened while Hegler named the peaks and needles surrounding the domed summit of Mont Blanc, then watched while he traced the routes taken by such famous climbers as Balmat, Saussure, Félicité Carrel. He pointed to one of the highest aerial cable cars spanning the glacier, but hardly visible from where we stood. When asked about a building far across the Mer de Glace, seemingly dropped in the middle of nowhere, he explained it had once been a hotel but was now used strictly as a summer attraction for tourists wanting a closer look at the glacier. It was served by a cog railway from Chamonix and called Montenvers.

Hegler now turned his attention to outcroppings well back from the ridge and far below us. If we had good eyesight, we were told, we could pick out Les Pins among them, though it bordered the snowfield. Relieved that we had almost made it

144

back without incident, I glanced at Sarah. She was standing beside Joachim Smith. She pushed up her goggles and sighed.

The run down to the lodge was the highlight of the day. With our host once more in the lead, we all picked our own line of fresh powder and let go. I slipped in behind Sarah to match her zig with my zag, thus leaving in our wake a snakelike pattern of figure eights.

Too soon we slithered to a halt in the courtyard, ten snow-clad figures whooping with delight. Sarah drew up beside me to give me a silent hug, as I stuffed my tuque back in my pocket. Amid the clamor, Hegler bellowed that since it was only three-thirty, there was time enough for another run. He pointed to the helicopters behind us. "The pilot is still on board, everybody. Joachim?" Smith, obviously tired, shook his head and bent down to release his skis. Hegler worked his way along to everyone, even Sarah, who also refused, then turned to me. "Now, Mr. Stone, surely you can't resist."

"Thanks, but no," I answered. "I couldn't make it." I jabbed a ski pole at the release behind my boot, missed, and tried again. Hegler was persistent. "Then we will ski this lower portion only. Just the two of us. Unless Mrs. Warden . . ."

Sarah, watching the rest move off toward the back door of the lodge, shook her head, then glanced at me. Hegler saw the exchange and became his jolly old self. "Yes, of course, fatigue can ruin a good run." He looked at us both. "Drinks, then, in the lounge." He bent down and removed his skis. As I shouldered mine, he thrust his at me good-naturedly. "Hold these and my poles, Mr. Stone, while I tell the pilot we won't be needing him after all." Before I could answer, he'd clomped off toward the helicopters.

"I don't trust him, Stoney." Sarah whispered.

"Neither do I," I said. I had a thought. "Look, while I keep him occupied, track down Monique. I don't believe she's up and around, as he says."

"Neither do I."

"Then let's take—"

"He's coming back." She hesitated, then quickly kissed me on the lips, stepped back, and swung her skis over her shoulder. Her eyes softened. "Be careful, Stoney." I was watching the door close behind her when I heard the sound of Hegler's boots crunching on the snow behind me.

"I'm sorry to resort to such persuasion, Mr. Stone . . ."

My head came round.

145

He was a few feet away, holding a revolver aimed at my midsection.

A sick feeling swept over me. "Isn't this taking things a little too far, just to have someone to ski with?" I asked dryly, while I kicked myself for being such a stupid asshole. Surely to God I could've seen what was happening. But not me!

Hegler flashed me a smile. "Not under the present circumstances. Tell me, out of curiosity, why did Mrs. Warden leave in such a hurry?"

"Why—" The racket of the helicopter engine firing up cut me off, so I started again. "Why don't you ask her?" As I waited for an answer, I noticed that he was keeping me between the gun and the lodge. It prompted me to think not everyone knew what the sonofabitch was up to. At the moment, neither did I.

"It does not matter, really, why the hurry," he went on. "It saves me having her dragged back to the lodge. Now, if you will carry our gear over to the second helicopter, as if maybe you have changed your mind about a last run . . ." I didn't move. His smile broadened. "It makes little difference to me, Mr. Stone, whether you climb into the helicopter alive or we bundle you in dead. The choice is yours."

A moment later I found myself sprawled across a tangle of poles and skis with a knee, Corry's, planted firmly in the middle of my back. As the door closed, I caught a glimpse of Sarah stumbling blindly toward us, her face twisted into a scream.

I lay still, feeling the edge of a ski digging into my face. We were rising fast. Straight up. The compartment was dark. I sensed rather than saw Hegler move away from the closed door. He told Corry to toss me in a corner. My head struck a metal ribbing between the pads. As I slowly pulled myself up on my elbows, I saw Monique.

Dressed in her ski outfit and boots, she was wedged in a corner, her head resting on her knees. She was having trouble breathing.

We leveled off. Corry, his face bland as ever, sat next to me. Hegler had stopped in the narrow doorway heading to the pilot's compartment, but now started toward us, balancing himself against the swaying motion of the helicopter. He was holding the same revolver he'd used on me in the courtyard. Handing it to Corry, who tucked it under a leg, Hegler moved away to sit on the floor directly opposite the main door.

Monique was moaning. It wasn't until she raised her head that

146

I realized her mouth and part of her nose were covered by a thick gag. I watched her for several agonizing minutes, then closed my eyes, as if it would stop me from hearing her retch. Unable to stand it any longer, I shouted, "For God's sake, man, at least let her breathe!" When Hegler made no effort to move, I did.

Corry grabbed for me and missed. As I scrambled over the skis, Hegler screamed, "If he touches her, Corry, kill him!"

From behind came the metallic click of the revolver's hammer dropping into place. Monique's head jerked up. She gave a muffled cry and rocketed her body forward.

I stopped short and whirled around. "Don't be stupid, Corry," I yelled, jabbing my finger at the wall behind Monique. "The fuel tank for this goddamn thing is between you and the pilot." It was a wild guess, but I didn't care. "Or why don't you just shoot in our direction, it's the same thing. You might get lucky and hit the pilot or cripple the fucking engine. Then we'll all go down." I turned back to Monique and tore off the gag. Flushed with rage, Hegler stormed into the pilot's compartment.

Sturdy ropes bound Monique's hands and feet, but I wisely let them be. Instead I pushed the hair away from her face.

She had been badly beaten. Apart from the black and swollen eyes, her lips were puffed and cut, her nostrils plugged with dried blood. She was also having difficulty focusing on me, and when she tried to speak, she did so haltingly.

The helicopter began buffeting.

Hegler appeared in the small doorway. I missed the signal between them because Corry suddenly stood up and leveled the revolver at us.

The shaking got worse.

Hegler didn't move from the doorway until several rows of small bulbs along the ceiling of the fuselage blinked. Only then did he close the door, and holding on to the ribbing, work his way around to Corry. I was trying to figure out what they were up to when Hegler barked, "Come over here, Stone." Before I could move, he had snatched the revolver from Corry and shoved it out in front of him. "Get over here, Stone, or I will kill you!"

Monique groaned, pleading with her eyes that I would do as Hegler said. For her sake, I crawled over the skis and pulled myself up beside him. For my trouble, I got the revolver in my ribs. A nod to Corry. It wasn't until he'd reached the door that I fully realized what they had in mind.

Corry dragged it open. A blizzard of snow and frigid air

ripped into the compartment. Against the shattering roar the helicopter pitched wildly, shifting the skis close to the opening. Overhead a voice barked, "Gerhard, it's time. For Christ's sake, make it fast." It was Fleck.

Corry was on the move. The copter bucked as he scrambled over the skis. He landed on Monique, which sent them crashing back against the wall. I was screaming obscenities when the barrel of the revolver was shoved hard against my teeth, forcing my mouth open. I felt the muzzle tearing flesh from the inside of my cheek before it stopped at the back of my throat. Hegler then twisted it, which brought my eyes in line with Monique.

She was struggling in vain to kick Corry away. Grabbing her by the hair, he yanked her head back. One short, sharp blow from his free hand caught Monique squarely on the chin. As she slumped forward, Corry scooped her up and with one motion turned and threw her out the door.

I was gagging now, spewing blood out the corners of my mouth. Hegler pulled the gun free and jammed it back into my ribs. Gasping for breath, I watched Corry rub his hands down his brown nylon jacket as he started back for me. Behind him the curtain of snow was blowing across the open door. I remembered how at the Montets, we'd scrambled away as the rotating blades of this same helicopter created a blizzard just like this one. So at the moment we couldn't have been far off the ground.

Then I knew it! Monique and I were going to be left to die of *natural causes*. No bullet holes. Animals and birds of prey would do the rest. And there would be no chance of surviving without . . .

The skis! Sweet Jesus. I had to take them with me!

The compartment shook violently. Above our heads the row of bulbs started flashing continuously. Hegler's eyes went wide. "Get him out of here," he bellowed, but Corry was thrown against the fuselage. Like Hegler, I was holding on to the ribbing. Now he swung the revolver up to my head and screamed, "You get out or I will blast you."

It was my chance. I shuffled backward, feeling for the skis with my feet. In the middle of the compartment I hesitated, then turned toward the door. Corry, driven by Hegler's ranting, lunged forward, inadvertently putting himself between me and the door. This was what I'd been waiting for.

In that second I lashed out at the skis, kicking them toward the open door. Some shot out and disappeared; others stopped short of the door. Arms circled my chest, crushing me, and I kept kicking, kicking, again and again. Behind us Hegler was screaming to Corry to let me go and step aside, but the goddamn gorilla held on, forcing me toward the opening.

The wind and snow were tearing at me now. All at once I had a giddy feeling we were going straight up. Monique! I had to get out. As I jerked my body forward, something picked me up and blew me into the mist.

I was turning over and over. The tightness around my chest was gone, and I felt as if I'd fall forever when something light and fluffy closed in and sucked me under.

Everything was still. I was on my back and I couldn't breathe. My legs were heavy and I wondered if that's how they felt when they were broken. I got ahold of myself then and began sweeping the snow away from my face. More took its place. I tried to move my legs so I could roll over on my stomach, but I couldn't move them. My lungs were bursting and I kept sweeping at the snow until something different touched my face. It was a breeze, and I opened my eyes to see blue sky, and mountains very close.

I also heard the thwump-thwump of rotary blades..I lay still. The sound came closer, then went away. But I knew it would be back.

Sitting up, I called out for Monique. Her name echoed back to me several times. We were on a plateau not much bigger than a ledge. I wanted to find Monique, but my legs were numb. I dug furiously at the snow over them, when I came to something brown. Nylon. It was part of a jacket.

It was Corry's. He was still in it. Dead.

I found Monique fifteen feet away, where the surface of the snow was broken, and two feet down. Thanks to Corry's handiwork, she was still unconscious. I dug her out, untied the ropes, and made her as comfortable as I could before scrambling about on my belly gathering up the skis and poles protruding from the snow. Of the four pairs, a ski and pole were missing. I had found mine last. Both of them. I dragged them all back to Corry, then dropped in on Monique.

Her eyes were open. I put my arms under her. Despite the puffed eyes and assorted cuts, her face brightened.

"Philippe," she whispered, "where are we?"

I kissed her on the nose. "That's a good question. How do you feel?"

"Thirsty."

God damn them.

Her eyes were watching mine. "They left us here to die, didn't they, Philippe? I heard them talking about it."

"Who?"

"The nurse. Corry and Fleck. They were getting me into my ski clothes and boots. The nurse told me what they had in mind. Left to die, with no way out."

"You're right," I said, "but we're not going to die. We've got skis." I told her what happened.

She frowned. "Then they will be back."

"I know."

It wouldn't be easy. We were in the middle of nowhere. With no way of getting down from here—the drop was several thousand feet—we would have to climb the nearby rock face to the next level, wherever that might take us. How Monique could handle it in her condition was the key.

"Philippe, they will come back because they cannot leave us with the skis." She looked away. "They will bring Roger Wessen. I was his contact in Steamboat. I had no idea—"

"Forget it," I said. "It wasn't your fault. As you say, they'll be back." I helped her sit up. "We have to get out of here. Now, listen. You've been given a drug which knocked you out. You feel lousy, but believe me, it will pass." I didn't mention the beating.

"And Corry. He is here, then?"

"Yes, over there. I take it Hegler shot him while trying to hit me. He went berserk seeing the skis go out the door. It wasn't part of his plan."

She looked around her, then back at me. "We will need Corry's clothes," is all she said.

It took us less than twenty minutes to get moving. While I retrieved the ropes and hunted down the errant ski, Monique stripped Corry down to his long underwear, which I'd insisted she put on under her red warm-ups. We shared the rest, from tuque to socks.

Corry had stopped a number of bullets, high in his back and one in the neck,. with enough power to drive us out the door. A combination of kick from the gun and turbulence kept the bullets high, or I too might have been lying dead next to him. We buried him, naked, in the snow. It was probably one of Hegler's skis I used to smooth out our tracks leading to the rocks.

We were climbing steadily among the rocks, perhaps several hundred feet up from the plateau, when we first heard the steady drone of a helicopter. We'd hoped to reach the ridge above us before their return, but it obviously wasn't to be.

Taking no chances, we dropped our skis and poles between two bare rocks and covered them with snow dug from hollows that the wind couldn't reach.

The sound was getting closer. I crawled among the slabs of rock and boulders searching for somewhere to hide. I had rejected one gap between a boulder and the rock face as being too narrow, but changed my mind a second later when Monique shouted, "Philippe, look!" She was pointing far down beyond the plateau.

I saw it, all right, the same copter that had been parked beside its larger brother in the courtyard. Silver instead of dull green, this version was sleek, smaller, and at the moment rising quickly toward us.

Monique, her face drawn, anxious, joined me. Our refuge would be a tight squeeze. I helped her out of Corry's jacket, worn despite its blood and bullet holes, and along with his padded ski pants knotted about my waist, tossed it inside. Without a word, she dropped down and slowly wedged her body in sideways. I followed.

We'd made it, almost. The space was cramped, forcing our backs against the rock face and legs up tight to our chests.

Feeling better now, I leaned out to see the helicopter pirouetting wildly over the plateau, moving from one broken patch of snow to another, probably trying to clear away the surface with the rotary blades and find us hiding. Or dead. Neither was that to be. Whoever was flying the thing must have thought so too, because he gave up and tried landing. For some reason, this failed too; maybe the plateau wasn't wide enough, or the air currents were too unpredictable.

But this wasn't the end of it, as I knew it wouldn't be. They were coming after us.

I watched the helicopter position itself above the plateau, then begin a slow swing back and forth across the rocks, each turn bringing it closer. In the next few frantic moments Monique and I crushed ourselves deeper into the crevice. It did little good. Unable to move, we waited for the worst.

The worst came with a sudden rush of wind and a rollicking, thunderous explosion of noise as the copter hovered into view from behind us. I found myself staring up at its silver underbelly, at the sole of a boot protruding from the open passenger door, at

151

the barrel of a rifle resting across a knee. . I froze, struck by visions of a head peering down; it would take no more to spot me.

As quickly as it came, it was gone. Twice the sound faded, then grew loud again as the search continued.

Silence.

Monique stirred beside me.

"They'll be back," I said.

Five minutes. Nothing. That bastard Hegler. I thought I knew him by now. I looked out. Something caught my eye. Following a line down between the rocks, I saw light reflecting off a metal surface. The bindings! The downdraft from the copter had blown the snow clear off the skis.

Fearful that if I could see the reflection others could too, I cautioned Monique to stay put and yanked myself free. My legs cramped and stiff, I stumbled from rock to rock and dropped onto the skis. I'd just managed to cover up the bindings when the sound of the copter broke the stillness.

I dropped to my stomach and hugged the ground.

It came down from the ridge in one long uninterrupted sweep over the rocks. When I finally lifted my head, I saw it hovering over the small plateau. At last it turned to spin off down the valley, leaving us to our own fate.

A blast of cold air greeted us as we finally pulled ourselves onto the ridge. We scurried for shelter behind some nearby rocks. Now hunched down out of the wind, I insisted we rest, something Monique dearly needed. I had pushed hard to get this far, wanting to put as much distance as possible between us and the plateau, in case Hegler tried something else. At each stop Monique had taken longer to catch her breath, and the sooner we could ski, the better.

I could almost hear myself reciting the course I'd given at Tremblant while I explained the first rule of survival to Monique. Conserve as much energy as possible. Time is the least of our worries. Rest frequently. Your natural body fat will sustain you for days, along with drinking water. Eating snow causes dehydration. So melt it in your hand. Overexertion leads to fatigue, fatigue to a feeling of hopelessness. Great theory. Now I'd have to put it into practice. With Monique's head against my shoulder, I untied the sling I'd used to carry the skis and poles on my back. It came from the rope which had bound her. This done, I tried to decide which direction we should take.

152

For one thing, I was certain we had been dumped in a remote area somewhere on the Mont Blanc side of the Chamonix Valley. Nor could we have been airborne more than a half-hour at most.

Next, direction.

I thought back to the times I'd seen the sun during my short stay here—at Lognan, Les Pins at sunset, skiing down from the Montets—and came to the conclusion that the Chamonix Valley ran roughly east and west. Then, God willing, we should head north.

Finding north wouldn't be a problem. From my Tremblant survival course came the answer for finding directions without a compass. Since we weren't likely to find moss growing on the north side of a tree, I borrowed Monique's watch, which was still in good working order, and turning it like a compass, aimed the hour hand at the sun. Then I drew an imaginary line bisecting this hour hand and twelve o'clock, which became the north-south axis.

I got up and stretched. Knowing our direction made us both feel better. Monique looked almost cheerful as we climbed into our skis.

We pushed away from our shelter to see stormclouds rolling over the mountains behind us. It was five o'clock by Monique's watch, leaving us with no more than an hour of light. I wanted to be away from here.

The snowstorm caught up to us as darkness closed in. It struck with such force that it almost tore us out of our skis. Somehow we held on, battling the next hundred yards, then the next and the next. We lost each other several times, then finally tied ourselves together using the two pieces of rope knotted, to give some length between us, to the legs of Corry's warm-ups.

Our progress slowed, stops were more frequent. The thin air stripped our throats dry, making breathing not only painful but at times impossible. Huddled together during our rests, we fought off the urge to gorge on snow and instead eked out drops of water by melting the snow first with our bare hands. For a while then we would hold one another to share the warmth, the comfort, of another body, before pulling apart reluctantly and going on.

Soon other ridges were left behind, gullies cautiously probed for and skirted. We were conscious every moment of keeping the storm at our backs. It had come out of the south, and we could only hope it was constant enough to help us keep moving in the right direction.

Hours passed. Our muscles ached so pitifully that resting didn't ease the pain.

The storm grew worse. Stopping now meant digging into snowdrifts to seek momentary comfort from the driving wind. During these times I insisted we try to sleep, which bothered Monique. She was sure we would never wake up again. I assured her that so long as we weren't totally exhausted, discomfort from the cold would arouse us. At first, then, we slept fitfully. As the night wore on, this changed: it came too easily.

We were fighting our way out of a gully. I had tried to keep the rope between us taut, and when we finally collapsed on the ridge above it, our lungs were on fire and our tongues so thick that swallowing was sheer agony.

I lay still, listening to the harsh rasping sounds of my own breathing, when it struck me that I should also be hearing the storm. I twisted over on my back and peered upward through eyes partially closed by ice and frozen sweat. But I didn't see the storm. In its place were stars filling the empty sky.

I was watching those stars now, unable to move, unable to think, when I felt something warm against my cheek. I tore off my glove to find they were my own tears.

"Monique?" She was lying in the snow, not moving. *"Monique!"* I was shaking her, feeling my self-control slipping away as I watched her eyes roll back, the eyelids closing over them. "Goddammit, Monique," I screamed, then suddenly gathered her in my arms and crushed her against me. "Monique, oh, God, Monique, don't sleep. Now now. Not yet."

Her cheek was cold. I closed my eyes and felt my body floating upward. I was clutching Monique, taking her with me, up, up. . . .

"Philippe?"

My eyes snapped open. Her eyes were showing beneath Corry's tuque. "Come," I said, "we have to go."

"No, Philippe. First it is important that you listen to me. Why I am here. So you will understand."

I started to protest, then saw the exhaustion in her eyes. "We have time," I said softly.

She began, haltingly at first, to tell me about her birthplace in France, Oradour-sur-Glane—she had mentioned it before, in Steamboat—of her father's small but respected art gallery in nearby Limoges, of World War Two, when the Germans were

154

looting France of its art treasures. Her father, fearing his collection might be taken, had brought it home, thinking it would be safer in the small village. He'd turned down an offer at the time from a close associate named Lussier to remove the collection to Lussier's château in the Dordogne, where other works had been stored. But in spite of the danger, her father couldn't bear to part with it.

Monique was two when the German troops appeared in Oradoursur-Glane. Saturday afternoon, June 10, 1944. She would learn with horror years later how the entire population had been ordered into the village square. Her mother, fearful of what might happen, wrapped Monique in a tablecloth and joined the others. There were six hundred and fifty-two in all.

The men were routed into several barns, the women and children into the church. Monique was too young to recall the bursts of machine-gun fire that slaughtered the men, or the crackle of flames as the same barns were put to the torch. Neither would she remember the first staccato of bullets within the church when her mother dropped to the floor and covered Monique with her own body.

As she spoke, Monique's eyes brightened, her hands began moving to emphasize her words. Adrenaline was pumping energy into her body. I encouraged her to go on.

She was back at the church again, describing how her mother, with her and a farming neighbor, Madame Rouffange, crawled between the bodies and reached the side door, unnoticed, even as the church was set on fire.

Monique's mother died from her wounds in the grass beyond the church, leaving her daughter and Madame Rouffange among the ten survivors. Almost half of those who perished were children.

The massacre had been in reprisal for a German officer killed by guerrillas near Oradour-sur-Vayres, twenty kilometers away. The avenging S.S. detachment had mistaken one village for another.

Much of what Monique told me had come from her foster parents, the Lussiers. She grew up in Paris with them, and it was Georges Lussier whose love and knowledge of paintings had filled Monique's life. Then, after so many years of shutting out the tragic events of Oradour-sur-Glane, Monique went back.

"Madame Rouffange lived alone, off the new square. I was told she talked to no one. I was the exception. She told me what I have told you. She told me more. I vowed I would track down

155

the man who ordered the murder of those poor innocent people. If he were dead, I would not rest until I spat on his grave.

"I found his name listed among the war criminals. But he had been killed on the Russian front."

"So you never found his grave," I said.

"Yes, I did. At a place called Furstenwalde. He had died on the twenty-third of April 1945. His name was Major Otto Dickmann.

"That might have ended it," she went on, "had I not come across an article that said twenty percent of French works of art were still missing. I wondered, rather naively, if my father's collection had survived. During my search for Dickmann, another name kept cropping up. Major Heinrich Steiner. He was listed as a protégé of Martin Bormann, himself a close friend of Hitler. From what I learned, Steiner had been there during the killings, though he didn't seem directly connected."

"Monique."

She stopped. "You want to go on, don't you?" I nodded. "Please, a few minutes more."

"The Lussiers had both died by this time, leaving the bulk of their estate to me. The Dordogne château had long been disposed of, and I was living alone in the Paris apartment. I read a great deal. Everything. Again I came across the name of Steiner. This time he was described as a *gruppen meister,* a group leader, one of many employed by the German high command to collect works of art. Such a man wouldn't be in Oradour-sur-Glane unless he knew about my father's collection."

"You traced him?"

"Yes."

"He was alive?"

"He was reported missing. His file in Bonn has never been closed, like so many others. I had a feeling about him. Do not ask me why. For two years I searched libraries, records, anything. Steiner had been busy during the war, shipping tons of valuable art back to Germany. I began to know him so well. Then, about a year ago, something extraordinary happened. I was at a gallery opening in Paris, when I overheard someone mention his name. I almost died. I turned quickly to the man and asked if he knew Steiner personally. He laughed and quite calmly said yes, he was living in both New York and Paris. Paris at the moment. But the man must have seen the look in my eyes. It scared him off. He excused himself and left. I tried to catch up

156

to him, but he got away. In a taxi. I went back inside. Now at last I had something to go on. I began in earnest to find Steiner.

"About six months ago a man knocked at my apartment door. He was in his sixties. He introduced himself as Inspector Gaudet of Interpol, then asked if I would mind accompanying him to headquarters. When I asked what he wanted, he told me he couldn't say, but would appreciate my coming along. I agreed. We drove to the Interpol headquarters, in St.-Cloud, a suburb of Paris.

"There I found myself in a small office with seven others, one a woman. I was barely seated when they asked why I was interested in a man named Steiner. Before I could answer, the woman—her name was Jeanine Gobeil—began listing my movements over the past six months, dates, times, places. She asked the same question again. I told them everything. I saw no reason not to. By the time I finished, I was in tears. One of the men, an American, came around the table and sat on the corner of it. He said it was just as well I hadn't found Steiner, because quite possibly I wouldn't be alive to talk about it. He also told me I was going about things the wrong way and maybe Interpol could help. I burst into tears again. I had worked so hard. The man put his arms around me. I will never forget it. He was so kind. It was James Agostino."

"Of course," I whispered.

"He told me all of them in the room were worried about me. Interpol had been informed that Steiner knew someone was sifting through his past. He didn't think it amusing. According to James, Steiner didn't know my name yet, but he was getting close. I was amazed, telling them that I had really made so little progress in finding the man. James Agostino said I was wrong. I knew Steiner, he told me, but probably better by his other name. Gerhard Hegler."

"Oh, my God."

"Yes, Philippe, they are one and the same. I knew Hegler. At least I knew of him. I'd seen him at gallery openings, receptions. Of course I wanted to hear more. The others were hesitant, but James convinced them I could be trusted.

"So they told me about Hegler. He was in Oradour-sur-Glane the day of the slaughter. It is believed he had come to confiscate paintings owned by an Henri Brosseau. He had left his friend Major Dickmann the following day and gone south, gathering up as much art as he could find before continuing on to Germany."

"And your father's paintings?"

157

Monique looked at me. "They were certain he got them all. About sixty. Mostly impressionists. But it seemed likely the paintings and trucks had been destroyed by the Maquis, possibly between Grenoble and Chamonix.

"You see, the Germans occupied the Chamonix area for two years, until the middle of 1944. By then pockets of the Maquis were killing everything in a German uniform. The local Savoyards here took no pity on the retreating convoys escaping through to northern Italy or Switzerland."

"The Maquis saw nothing of the paintings?"

She smiled. "The Maquis were interested in revenge, Philippe, not works of art. What went on around Chamonix was never really documented, not even after the war. The Savoyards are a quiet, tough people. Stubborn, too. Whatever they did with the Germans was their business. But it is told that one group of Germans took refuge in an old hotel outside Chamonix. They lasted three days until the Maquis wiped them out."

"But what about Steiner? He obviously got away."

"Yes. According to what Interpol learned, he showed up during the Allies' drive into Germany. And that's when he met Harold Warden. 'Hegler' claimed he was jailed because he refused to help the Nazis collect art. Can you believe it?"

"Then Warden only knew him as Hegler."

Monique nodded.

"Ironic, isn't it? It's obvious that Warden also introduced him to the Hercules Foundation."

"Yes. James told me then about Hercules, and how the new Hercules was the centre of the stolen art trade. He asked if I thought I could get close enough to join. Well, I certainly had the background, and there was a small branch operating in Paris. With my help Interpol could break Hercules and I could help ruin the man who stole my father's art collection and possibly watched him die.

"I accepted James's offer without a second thought. I gained Hercules' confidence by dropping a hint one day to M'sieu Hegler that I had a couple of original oils I couldn't display. A Picasso and a Bonnard, supplied by Interpol. M'sieu Hegler checked them out and indeed found them stolen. He decided then to trust me. Later I was sent off to make friends with a woman traveling to Colorado. It was Sarah, of course. I was not told why I should make friends."

During the stopover in New York Monique had contacted Jim Agostino, who told her to carry on with Hegler's orders to the letter; otherwise, as she explained, "I would be risking not only my own life but also Sarah's.

"James gave me a telephone number where he could be reached at all times, Philippe. I was to keep him informed on everything that was happening." Her voice wavered. "There were times when I felt so ashamed of myself, so very ashamed . . ."

"You had no choice," I said, pushing myself up on an elbow. "Besides, here we are. Hegler will abort the auction, obviously, by flying the paintings back to Switzerland. Agostino will wonder what the hell happened to us, hold out till the last minute, then hit the bloody place for nothing."

Monique seemed to be smiling. "No, Philippe, you have it wrong. Hercules knows nothing of Interpol."

I laughed. "Come on, now. He must have discovered your connection with the police. Otherwise it would only be *me* up here."

"I thought so too, but it wasn't that at all. You see, while I was getting ready to meet you and Sarah for drinks, someone knocked at my door. When I opened it, Corry pushed me aside and walked in. With him were the nurse and M'sieu Hegler. He told me at once of an important message he had received from Paris concerning the identity of the person tracing a certain Heinrich Steiner. For two years he had persons trying to discover who it was, and now he knew it was me. Then he went very mad and struck me many times. He wanted to know who else was involved. I said no one. Corry beat me then. At last I told him about my father and how I'd learned Steiner had taken the Brosseau collection and I was seeking personal vengeance. He believed me. They held me down then, on the floor. The nurse gave me an injection. I woke up not knowing who or where I was. I was being put into ski clothes. Corry was to take me skiing."

The conversation ended, leaving us each to our own thoughts. As for me, I vowed we'd both get out of these mountains alive.

For a while we sat in silence, melting snow in our hands and licking at the moisture, totally unaware that the nightmare had really just begun.

Our new threat was the clear sky, for with it came a devastating drop in temperature.

We were hardly on our way again when Monique began to shiver. Trying not to alarm her, I started swinging my arms and flexing my knees, urging Monique to do the same. She tried,

159

then gave up, saying it only wasted energy. I turned her face upward to make sure there were no white patches of frostbite on the skin, then pushed on.

I was increasingly frightened by Monique's deterioration. As before, it became more and more difficult to get her moving again after we had stopped to rest.

Her strength gave out on a hump-backed ridge, a narrow inverted V curving to the east, leaving a dark, empty void on our left. I cradled her in my arms, promising her we were slowly working our way down to where breathing would be easier. Her eyelids were closing, and I shook her gently, then more forcibly. The lips moved, the eyes fluttered open. I was pleading with her now to hang on, but her lips began to quiver. "I can't. I cannot. Please . . . I am so tired. You . . . you must go . . . alone. You have a chance. I cannot go farther. . . ."

I held her to me, telling her over and over that we'd make it. We would get out of here alive, together or goddamn well not at all.

"It is not possible. . . ."

"It is possible! Now c'mon."

The ridge was widening, pushing itself between two silhouetted bluffs ahead. This was the longest stretch we'd made without stopping, and already my mind had slipped away on its own, though my legs kept going. I snapped back to the present and gave the rope a gentle tug, reassuring Monique that all was well. The rope gave. Stunned, I twisted around, jerking it cleanly as I did so. The rope came coiling toward me.

I was yelling for her now, trying to convince myself at the same time that her end of the rope had merely come loose. I knew better.

A single set of tracks led back the way I'd come. Out of the darkness I saw her, crumpled in the snow.

"Monique!"

Her head came up slowly. Her eyes were moist and shining. I watched, paralyzed, as her lips began to move. "I cannot go on, Philippe, I cannot. I must do this. You can't stay with me and die too. Please mon cher . . . I am tired, so very tired."

She was slipping away from me again.

"Monique," I whispered. I was holding her. "Dear God, please, Monique, don't let this happen."

Her eyes closed.

She was gone, Jesus, she was gone.

17

Hypothermia. Freezing to death. It's almost a nice way to go. As the body cools, the shivering begins. Soon the mind is creating its own little diversions to steer you away from the brutal truth that you are dying.

With Monique dead I had collapsed cold and exhausted into the snow, waiting for my turn.

And I knew how it would happen. Hypothermia and I were old friends, in theory if not in practice.

By now I was well into the first stage, shivering, the body's last resort for generating heat. Eventually it would burn up what little energy I had left. Then everything would fall apart. Circulation, respiration, sanity, leaving the heart thumping against the cavity wall, totally unaware that death had already occurred.

Shivering first, then hallucinations.

I could see them clearly now. Lights, crawling up the rock face, only to fade and become a large bed, or was it a cold bath? I couldn't tell which, and yet these visions were as real as the fingers kneading my aching shoulders. Somewhere a voice was saying, "If exposure is allowed to continue, the victim will become irrational, disoriented. He may require physical restraint. . . ."

I sat up. The voice was *mine*.

"Who's irrational? Who's disoriented? Not me!" I screamed back. But the scream turned to laughter and the laughter turned to tears, and I held her against me, rocking back and forth to comfort us both. At last I struggled to free her from her skis and dug a hole in the snow alongside her body. I laid Monique in it and covered her up, sobbing until I couldn't see for the frozen tears. I knelt there and said a little prayer, promising that I would come back for her. Finally I jammed her skis and poles upright nearby, hoping I'd be able to find them again.

From then on my life became a series of stumblings and picking myself up. I was barely conscious of time, of terrain. I missed the sunrise. Thirst plagued me when my fingers would no longer uncurl from around the ski poles.

Illusions kept me going. Monique was one of them. We had a

161

running conversation whenever things got bad. I'd tug on our rope every so often to make sure she was all right. She always tugged back.

Cramps. My bloody legs wouldn't move. It had happened so many times. I leaned forward, flexing my knees till the sharp pain subsided. Resting a moment on my poles, I was fascinated by yet another illusion, a shack, a mountain refuge, perched below me in the middle of nowhere. It was mostly buried in snow, and while my brain was slowly separating the real from the imagined, a door opened.

"Oh, Jesus," I whispered, holding back the tears.

I lay sprawled across the bed on my stomach when the nurse with the steel-blue hair whipped away the cover. With the same easy motion, she plucked the thermometer from between my buttocks and disappeared, leaving me uncovered. I was sure she was retaliating because I had refused a sedative. I'd refused it because I didn't want to sleep. I wanted Agostino. I wanted someone to go up into the mountains and bring Monique down, alive.

My door opened again. I thought it was the nurse coming back, but the voice wasn't hers. It was Agostino's.

"Stay like that and you'll catch your death of cold," he said, tossing the starched white sheet over my backside.

"I'll forget I heard that," I snapped at him. "I've been waiting for you for hours."

"You've only been awake for twenty minutes." He came around beside the bed. He hadn't shaved and his ski outfit looked slept in. "How are you, Stone?"

"Fucking mad," I replied, struggling to turn over, as stiff as the bloody sheet. I made it and lay back. "She's dead, you know. Monique is dead." I was picking on the wrong man, but I had to pick on someone.

He was standing at the end of the bed now, framed in the light from the window directly behind him. "I know. You haven't stopped talking about her in your sleep."

"What day is it?"

"Friday. Afternoon. You were brought down from somewhere near the Fourche refuge early this morning. From what I hear, the refuge is very high up. The guide says you tumbled out of nowhere. You're the talk of the town. They say you must have known what you were doing to survive what you went through. Not many do."

162

"Monique is *dead*," I said again.

His expression didn't change. "How?"

"How? How the hell do you think? They dumped us up there to die, goddammit, and she couldn't make it. I tried . . . Christ, I tried." I could see her now, slipping away from me. I sat up, choking.

"I'm sorry," he said, turning abruptly to the window.

"Is that all you have to say?" I shouted across the room. "You're sorry? You goddamed people out there playing cops and robbers. It's a business, isn't it? But did you ever stop to think who gets caught in the middle, Agostino? Or haven't you been keeping score?"

Agostino whirled around. "You're hurt because Monique is dead, Stone. But who the fuck do you think you are? Do you think you can corner the market on feeling sorry for her? Christ, man, we're all hurt that she's dead. But let me tell you something. Monique Brosseau knew the risks. She accepted them. You, for Christ's sake—you got in over your head. I tried my damnedest to keep you out of it, so don't give me any of that bullshit about being caught in the middle. You drove me nuts!" He was looking out the window again. Over his shoulder I could see the tops of the fir trees rising up toward the white-capped mountains. He glanced at his watch. Something besides me was distracting him.

"I'm sorry," I said, lying down again.

"We're all on edge," he answered without looking around. "For what it's worth, I think you're the gutsiest cockeyed amateur I've ever met. God knows what keeps you alive. Stoney, you have no idea of the risks involved. These people don't just dabble in a few stolen paintings, they're a network. If they want something, they take it, no matter what the cost. In money or lives." He came back and leaned on the end of my bed. "If it makes you feel better, I tried to talk Monique out of this operation when she came through New York on her way to Colorado. I tried to convince her that it was only a matter of time before Hegler discovered who'd been tracking down his past and that he might find out before we cleaned this mess up. I asked her to get out, for personal reasons. The department naturally wanted her in. I didn't. I doubt if anyone could have talked her out of it."

"I'm sorry," I said. I watched him walk back to the window. It was time to change the subject. "How did you know I was going to France?"

163

"I was with Hershel when your second call came through. He does some work for us."

I chuckled to myself. "I might have known. You cover all the bases." Now he was looking at his watch.

"We try."

"Then if you've covered all the bases, what's bothering you?"

He glanced at me over his shoulder. "Nothing. Why?"

"Because you're restless, for one thing. Either that or I'm lousy company." I paused. "Tell me something. How come you sent me off to Montreal if there was any chance of me getting killed."

"We were as amazed as you, Stoney. We figured with Sarah Warden back in the fold and Hercules having this conference on its hands, why would they bother with you? At least for the moment. What clinched it were rumors within Hercules that you were expected in Chamonix. Nesbitt confirmed this, though I still can't figure out how they knew you'd show up. This being the case, why would you be hit at Dorval? Anyway, it happened. I'm sorry."

"But you still could have stopped me. Or had the Mounties do it. Why didn't you?"

There was a chair not far from the window. He picked it up and tilted it against the wall. "Listening in on your second call to Herschel," he said, sitting down, "gave me an idea. You had survived a hit, so I figured what the hell, if he can handle himself that well, why stop him from going to France? After all, Stoney, we weren't sending you."

"Besides, you needed someone up there that Hegler and the boys wouldn't look twice at. At least that's how Monique thought you might have reasoned it. Something akin to desperation, wasn't it, relying on me?"

For the first time Agostino smiled. "True. I had Interpol agents crawling all over themselves down in Chamonix, but no one backing Monique up at Les Pins. You were a risk we had to take. Now, listen, I haven't much time. Did either Monique or your friend Sarah discover where the paintings were hidden?"

"No," I replied, shifting my weight to the other cheek. "Sarah mentioned something about a subbasement. By the way, Hercules doesn't know about Monique's connection with Interpol. Hegler found out that she was the one tracking him down."

"We heard. It was confirmed by Interpol in Paris."

"And your auction. Sarah managed to get her hands on a list of the paintings. But she didn't know when. . . ."

164

Agostino said, "It's tonight."

I pushed myself up on my elbow. "How do you know?"

At first I didn't think he would tell me; then he changed his mind. "We found out from Sarah Warden. She was among a dozen members of Hercules who came down to Chamonix this morning from Les Pins."

I pushed myself up on an elbow. "You're kidding. Down here?"

He nodded. "They were catching the cable car to the Aiguille du Midi, obviously for a day's skiing down the Vallée Blanche. You've heard of it?"

"Yes," I said absently.

"She managed to slip an envelope to an attendant, not knowing he was one of our men. It was addressed to me care of the local police." He smiled to himself. "Marked 'Urgent.' "

"You wouldn't have used the opportunity to get her out of there while you had the chance."

He ignored the remark. "It contained the list of paintings to be auctioned. Several hundred, at least. We're processing them now."

"Was she all right?"

Again the hesitation. "She didn't say. The note enclosed with the list looked as if it was written by a fairly steady hand. She was worried about you. She warned us that you had been taken away in a chopper and wrote down the direction. Monique was missing too. She assumed our friend Hegler had whisked you both away. The envelope came after you turned up."

I lay back again, saying, "I wish you guys had gotten her away from that bunch. But you wouldn't. It's business first." I didn't say it with any rancor.

"I'm sorry. By the way, she also thought the auction would begin in the evening around—" Someone was knocking on the door. He bounded out of his chair.

"Hey," I said as he crossed the room, "what hospital is this?"

"Chamonix General," came his answer from the alcove.

Agostino was back after a hurried conversation in the corridor, looking none too happy. He plunked two pills in a paper cup down next to the water jug on the table beside me. "The nurse said you refused these. Take them," he grumbled, and turned to go.

"I will," I answered, leaving them there. "Why do I get the feeling you're keeping something from me?"

He stopped just short of the alcove and leaned against the wall. "Probably because I am. Sarah Warden's note mentioned something I haven't told you. She thinks her late husband is still alive."

I laughed out loud. "Gerry *alive?* Listen, for God sake, I saw him die."

"Besides, you were at his funeral." He looked at me, then shrugged. "Anyway, eat your pills." And he was gone.

Alone now, I scrunched down under the sheet, listening to feet scurry up and down the corridor. I kept seeing Gerry's body lying in the snow and wondering why Sarah would think that he was alive. Hadn't he said she *thought* Gerry was? Nothing for sure. I was arguing this point with myself when I realized everything was very quiet. I listened. Nothing. I was reaching for the pills when I decided a few knee bends would do me more good.

It wasn't until I was standing that I realized how stiff I was, so for the next few minutes I flexed anything that would bend, then, pulling my hospital gown around me, toddled over to the window.

In the parking lot three floors below, two guys were shoveling snow away from a row of garages while several others fussed around an old car, trying to start it with jumper cables and a spare battery. They weren't having much success, so I hauled myself back into bed.

I must have dozed off, because suddenly Monique was with me. She was slipping. I couldn't reach her. I cried out as I dragged myself forward, our hands almost touching. Then the snow beneath us started giving way, and I screamed.

The next thing I knew, I was sitting bolt upright in bed clutching the sheet. My hands were trembling and I was drenched in perspiration. My throat was parched and I could taste the ointment the nurse had rubbed into my cracked lips. Slowly then I let the sheet go and pulled myself up against the metal headboard. Still shaking, I dumped the sleeping pills from the paper cup and was reaching for the water jug when something flashed against my arm. Startled, I jerked my hand away, hit the jug, and sent it clattering onto the floor.

Sweat trickled into my eyes. I wiped them with the partial sleeve of the hospital gown, then glanced at the window, thinking it might have been a reflection off a pane. Nothing. Feeling better, I leaned out to see where the water jug had ended up, when I noticed something on the wall. It appeared as a round reddish dot and slightly larger than a silver dollar. Even as I

166

watched, the damn thing was on the move again. My way. Not knowing what to do, I rolled to the opposite side of the bed and dropped to the floor.

The light had settled on the pillow. At least I guessed it was a light. But there was no beam, like a ray of sunlight would have, or a flashlight. It just sat there, growing out of thin air.

I watched it start down the bed. Obviously someone was behind it, someone beyond the window, guiding it, aiming it. Then I knew. This was a weapon of some kind. A goddamn beam of light which somehow lined up on target and never missed. An image of Terry Samuels falling to his death flashed through my mind. Wessen!

He was out there somewhere, God knows how far away, sweeping that thing closer and closer. It was waiting for me, there on the end of the bed. But it didn't wait long. Now it was slipping along the sheet, diagonally, hunting me down.

I yelled. It produced more pain than sound. But that didn't stop me from screaming again and again.

The buzzer. The bloody buzzer. It had to be somewhere.

I crawled back and threw the pillow aside. It wasn't there. I looked for the light. It was moving back. The buzzer. Dear God, where was it? The cord. I found the cord and followed it. The buzzer was pinned to the side of the mattress. I yanked it free and jammed my thumb down on the knob.

The light was halfway up the sheet, forcing me against the headboard.

It touched my foot.

The room exploded around me as I hurled myself headlong into the night table, taking it with me to the floor. I hit and lay still along with acres of shattered glass.

The window was completely gone. The room cold. The wall above my head was shredded into bits of torn plaster. Among the bits was the small reddish disk. It was already dropping toward me.

This time I drove myself forward, hitting the floor beneath the bed a second before the night table disintegrated into a shower of debris. I hit the far wall and lay there, waiting to see if the dot would appear above the bed.

But it didn't. Nor could I find it anywhere. I pulled myself up on my knees, only partially aware of the shouts coming from the corridor. Then it was back, scanning the pockmarked wall. In that instant the door on the other side of the room burst open.

167

Two men in coveralls stood in the doorway, their pistols shoved out in front of them.

"Stay back!" I yelled. "For Christ's sake."

The beam was on the move again, gliding toward the headboard. The guy was shouting. In French. I waved him back and pointed at the wall. "Sniper!" I cried. It was picking up speed. He couldn't see the damn thing and stepped forward, his arms still extended. "Get back! No!" I screamed. He looked at me, confused. Too late. I watched, stunned, as the bullets ripped him clear off the floor, driving him back into the wall.

He hit headfirst, the sound of his neck snapping pitched above the deadening thud of his body. The poor bastard hung there a moment and then dropped to the floor, leaving behind a thick trail of blood.

The beam was gone. I pressed myself against the wall, knowing if I so much as breathed the goddamn thing would be back.

"Stoney . . ."

Agostino was standing in the alcove.

"Stay there," I said quietly.

"Are you okay?"

"Yes. But I can't say for how long. It's Wessen, isn't it? He's using some sort of light beam. For aiming."

Agostino swore. "Laser-Lok."

"What's that?" I asked.

"A laser sight. Helium-neon. Strung under a twenty-two-caliber submachine gun. Probably an American one-eighty rimfire. Just line up the beam on the target and pull the trigger. We didn't know the sonofabitch had a laser unit."

The light reappeared. "He's back," I said.

Agostino stuck his head out cautiously, but not far. "Where?"

"Over the bed. Shoulder-high."

"How long can you hold on?"

I laughed. "Ask him."

The agent pulled back. "We need time, Stoney, just a little more time. We've had men all over the fucking place. Scouring the woods, out in the corridor, on every floor. At every entrance. Wessen goes in for the kill as if he owns the place. We thought we were ready for anything. Thank God you were awake. I'm sorry about this."

"Forget it," I said. "Thanks to me, I'm still alive."

"What's he up to now?"

"He's waiting for me to panic. And if he hangs on much longer . . . Oh-oh . . . here it comes. Can you see it?"

"Ya."

"Tell me when it gets around here."

"Where will you be?"

"With any luck, under the bed."

I'd made it, but only just, when he barked, *"Now!"*

I shot out onto the broken glass, lost my footing, and hit the floor. Hands had me by the shoulders, jerking me forward. Plaster shredded off the wall close to our heads as we dived for the floor.

The shooting had stopped.

Agostino sat up, grinning, his face covered with fine dust. "That's what we wanted, Stoney, just one more round from the bastard. Listen."

I leaned against the wall, picking glass out of my nightgown. Thirty seconds went by. Then the echo of a single shot.

"It's over," he said. "Get dressed."

18

Agostino sniffed, then looked at his watch in the light from the stars. I wasn't sure how he could see anything with the wool tuque pulled down almost over his eyes.

Like the rest of us, he wore off-white coveralls over his ski outfit to blend in with the snow. Unlike many, he had no automatic weapon slung over his shoulder. He had warned the men several times in the cable car that Les Pins was not an armed camp. Firearms were to be used as a deterrent, and he wanted no unnecessary gunplay. Then came the last-minute briefing.

There were about forty in this group, police mostly, alpine-trained, from a handful of different agencies. Interpol, the FBI, New Scotland Yard. The French Sûreté, among others. An old Savoyard mountain guide assigned by the local police and I were the exceptions.

We were on the plateau now, at the base of the Grands Montets. Another bunch had already set out for Les Pins on snowmobiles from the Lognan station. The old man and I had to guide these men to the lodge within the hour.

Agostino was watching me. "You're looking a little pasty, Stoney," he said. "Can you handle it?"

"I'm fine," I replied, ignoring a variety of aches and pains.

"Bullshit," he said with a grin. "But I appreciate your coming anyway."

Nothing short of Wessen being on target could've stopped me, despite Agostino's concern over my health and his assurance that Sarah would soon be out of danger.

It wasn't until we boarded the téléphérique to come up here, however, that we had a moment to discuss Gerry Hope-Warden again. Agostino contended that someone had been killed in Gerry's place, leaving me to identify what was left; his clothes could easily have been duplicated. When I was asked to describe Gerry's appearance and mental state before the shooting, my statement to the police had mentioned goggles hooked around Hope-Warden's upper arm in a fashion used by many skiers for safekeeping. And yet the autopsy report, according to Agostino, listed bits of plastic lens in the facial cavity, which meant the victim was wearing goggles when he died. A small point, Agostino admitted, but this is what had started him wondering. Sarah's news gave credence to his hunch. He was waiting for a report from the forensic people in New York. I was asking Agostino why Gerry might have faked his own death when we suddenly clanked into the station and I lost him.

Here on the plateau beneath the Grands Montets, I repeated the same question.

"Easy," he replied, leaning forward on his poles. "He must have learned through the grapevine that sooner or later we'd nail him for murder."

"Murder? You're kidding. Who?"

"A guy called Allan Starkman."

In a way, I wasn't surprised.

The guide and I took the lead. Skiing by moonlight and the stars made Hegler's route seem altogether different, but it was the old guide's uncanny instinct for direction and unseen dangers, such as sudden drops, that finally brought us out from a narrow cut and onto the familiar snowfield.

We were a ragtag bunch of breathless, cursing skiers as we pulled up on the promontory overlooking Les Pins and the lights of Chamonix far below.

"Agostino?" I called out.

"He's coming," said a voice from behind. Others moved

170

aside. Agostino appeared. His tuque was gone and his dark hair and eyebrows were matted with snow. He stopped next to me and leaned heavily on his poles.

I pointed to a dark smudge. "Les Pins. Down behind that outcropping of rock. It's a steep drop of five, maybe six hundred yards."

Agostino wrestled a pair of binoculars out from his coveralls, then lifted them to his eyes. "It couldn't be any steeper than what we've been through," he mumbled. "I can't see any lights." I told him the outcropping was in his way. He shoved the binoculars inside his coveralls. "Let's go."

We left in groups of twos and threes, ten seconds apart. Harrison, a hefty guy from Scotland Yard, took the guide with him. We watched them disappear. Agostino said, "C'mon, Stoney."

We swung in behind the middle shed and dumped our skis. We huddled behind it for a minute while the agent hauled out a pistol. The courtyard was dark. We stepped out to see a shadow pressed against the wall of the first shed. A voice whispered, "Jim? Agostino?"

"Lachuk," he answered. "You're supposed to be with the choppers." I recognized him. He'd helped me onto the plane at Kennedy Airport.

"There aren't any, Jim. The pad's empty."

"Empty?" I said, not liking the sound of it.

Lachuk nodded.

"Where's your team?" Agostino wanted to know.

"Around the corner. I waited here to catch you."

Agostino's head swung to me, then back to Lachuk. "Stay where you are, then. Nail the choppers if they return."

From there we scurried across the open courtyard and dropped into a snowbank not far from the darkened back entrance. Heads popped up a few feet away. I counted eight. I put the missing helicopters out of my mind.

By now the building would be surrounded. Agostino glanced at his watch, murmuring, "Eleven-fourteen."

At eleven-fifteen we burst through the back door. There was no resistance. Les Pins was empty.

I had been racing through the corridors shouting for Sarah when I finally stumbled into my own room on the third floor. There I found the bed made, my clothes hanging neatly in the closet. Even my shaving brush, soap, and razor were beside the basin in the bathroom, just as I had left them.

Harrison, a ruddy block of a man, appeared in the doorway, a walkie-talkie crackling at his side. "Jim has been looking for you, Stone," he said with his clipped English accent. "He's in the main lounge."

He was there, all right, holding court with a dozen others. You could've heard him a mile away.

"I want this goddamn place torn apart. Every inch of it. Hafner's team will go after the subbasement, Bianco's to the office on the second floor. I want every scrap of paper gone over. And who's our safecracker?" He saw me and waved. "Okay, let's go. And if anyone sees Harrison, tell him I'll be on the deck."

Harrison joined us a few minutes later to find Agostino pacing back and forth and me leaning against the railing watching him.

"Reggie," he shouted as the Englishman approached, "where the hell did we go wrong? We've had this place under a magnifying glass for weeks, long before the Hercules members arrived."

I said, "Maybe they got panicky when Wessen didn't show up."

"No way," answered Agostino. "Once a hit's been made, the killer disappears. He's on his own. It's part of the code. Besides, we found an airline ticket in Wessen's pocket for a nine-o'clock flight from Geneva to London."

"They're cunning bastards," interjected Harrison. "Surveillance has been around-the-clock. We've got a crew at the Brévent ski station across the valley who have kept an eye on this place. The daily routine here didn't change, Jim. I'll vouch for it."

Agostino hit the railing out of sheer frustration. "That's your department, Reggie." He swung around to face the Englishman. "What happened when we pulled everyone in to run down Wesson?"

"I didn't touch the Brévent surveillance team, if you remember. The pair reported those tracked vehicles were making their usual trips from the Lognan station and back, picking up members who had been skiing the Montets or elsewhere."

I wanted to know about the staff.

"From here?" asked Harrison. "They were flown out after lunch. They arrived back at Gerhard Hegler's château near Zurich safe and sound."

I glanced at Harrison. "Hegler and Harold Warden didn't want them around for the auction, I take it."

Agostino answered. "That was our theory."

The walkie-talkie on Harrison's hip began to squawk. A voice came through the static calling for him. Harrison, freeing it from the clip, depressed a lever on the side and gave his call sign.

Hafner identified himself, then said, "We've found the sub-basement, Reggie, in back of a storage room. It's empty. Besides, it's too musty and damp here to store paintings, D'you want to come and look for yourself?"

"Fuck it," snapped Agostino, and turned away.

Harrison said, "I'll take your word for it, old boy. Keep looking. Good luck." He signed off.

"We've been faked right out of our jockstraps," Agostino said, without turning around. He was staring at the lights of Chamonix far below us. "Whether those creeps knew it or not, they've faked us good. And do you know what it means?"

"Sure," I replied. "It means the auction never was going to be here."

Harrison started to protest, but Agostino cut him off. "He's right, Reggie, and the answer's tied up in that auction list. Surely those paintings have been traced by now. Get onto Chamonix and raise New York and London. Contact Brévent again and find out what they've been up to. Why couldn't they keep better track of the choppers here. I want to know how they missed spotting sixty or seventy people leaving here, darkness or not. They've got the equipment. I want to know just where those people are right now!"

"Righto," said Harrison, then hesitated. "I'm sorry about the cock-up."

Agostino's face softened. "Listen, don't worry. There's a link missing somewhere here, and we'll find it. Now, I have a hunch Stoney has the answer, but doesn't realize it. We'll stay and thrash it out."

For the next twenty minutes that's exactly what we both did, while pacing back and forth across the deck. He had me recalling everything that had happened from the moment I arrived in the Chamonix Valley. But nothing seemed remotely connected with this place being empty. I knew the auction was something special, but I couldn't say why.

Harrison reappeared on the deck, the walkie-talkie tucked under his arm. He trudged through the snow toward us, at once launching into a long story about the surveillance team having watched the copters make a few runs down to Chamonix in the evenings. They hadn't returned. According to Harrison, this wasn't out of the ordinary. Guests were often ferried down to the casino, and the copters would wait to bring them back. Sometimes it was late.

Agostino swore to himself. "But, Reggie, this isn't any ordinary night. So are they parked down in Chamonix?"

Harrison's face went red. "No, we've lost them."

"Have you any good news?"

"Not really, James. The preliminary report on the auction list came through while I was onto our Chamonix base." He paused. "I've been told this is strictly a preliminary report. . . ."

"Get on with it, Reggie, for Christ's sake," snapped Agostino.

Harrison blushed. "It shows that none of the paintings listed have been stolen, James."

Someone gasped. I wasn't sure if it was Agostino or me. Even in the dull light I saw the veins pop out along his neck. I thought he'd explode, but when he spoke, he showed no sign of anger. "That's not possible, Reggie. We didn't come here- tracking down legitimate art. There has been a mistake."

"At least not reported stolen in the past ten years. This has been confirmed through your Division Twenty-seven and mine through the Yard. The list was immediately telexed to agencies around the world—New Zealand, Canada, everywhere. These reports haven't come in as yet."

Agostino tramped off across the deck mumbling to himself. Coming back again, he said to me, "Do you know, Stoney, with all the technology we have on this earth today, there is no comprehensive up-to-date list of stolen art anywhere? They're working on it, but . . ." To Harrison he added, "They shouldn't have to go back more than a few years, Reggie, maybe not even that, dammit."

Something was ticking away in the back of my mind, two bits of information that hadn't quite meshed together. "Maybe you haven't gone back far enough," I murmured, thinking aloud. They looked at me.

"Go on," said Agostino.

"Why don't you check back, say, to works stolen thirty-five years ago."

Harrison was staring at me as if I'd just taken a turn for the worse. Agostino, on the other hand, was counting backward. "You mean during the war? What made you think of that?"

I thought for a moment longer before replying, "Two people made me think of it. Monique and Hershel Nesbitt, Jim. This may sound crazy, but put their stories together. Let's say Harold

174

Warden did catch up with those five truckloads of stolen paintings and Hegler/Steiner was the officer in charge." It *was* crazy, but I took it one step further. "And suppose the paintings weren't destroyed. . . ."

James Agostino shot me a glance. "Stone," he said, "that's just about the most incredible goddamned thing I've ever heard." Then a grin broke across his face. "Reggie, call down to our Chamonix base and have them contact that Museum and Fine Arts unit. The one left over from World War Two. They still have an office, don't they?"

Harrison nodded. "Yes. Bonn. A token staff, I believe."

"Good. Haul one of those tokens out of bed and read him the auction list. I want some sort of reaction from them in fifteen minutes. In the meantime, you'll find Stoney and me in Hegler's office." Agostino turned to me. "C'mon, maybe we can dig something out of his files."

"Hey, wait a minute," I said. "This was only a thought, Jim. Don't bank your life on it."

He looked at me and smiled. "We have nothing else going for us. Besides, it throws a whole new light on things. What made you think of this?"

We started for the door. "I'm not sure what triggered it," I answered, "unless it was Harrison's remark that none of those paintings had been reported stolen in the past ten years. In the back of my mind I must have thought about Monique and her father's paintings. Hershel once told Sarah about Harold Warden chasing after a convoy of art stolen by the Germans. It just struck me that maybe they had met when Hegler was still calling himself Steiner."

"We'll see," he said as we stepped into the lounge.

Gerhard Hegler's second-floor office was in chaos. Already four agents were busy disemboweling a filing cabinet, its contents spread in small piles on the floor. Boxes of books had been overturned and dumped on the desk, which itself took up half the available space in the small room. Four sets of coveralls and boots had been flung into a corner.

At once Agostino had the agents digging through the files in search of any material dealing with World War Two. Left on my own, I took in the framed photographs covering two walls.

Most were blowups of the valley and the mountains, some in color, many in black and white. On the wall behind his desk Hegler had framed a large color illustration of the Chamonix Valley detailing the principal glaciers, cable lifts, and refuges.

175

These, and the major mountain peaks, had their names printed beside them. I was hunting down the Fourche refuge when Harrison suddenly appeared in the doorway, his ruddy face beaming.

"James, I've just been talking to a chap with the Museum and Fine Arts unit in Bonn. He was absolutely elated when I read him the list. Though he didn't have the file at hand, he swore those paintings were part of a truck convoy the Germans tried slipping through this area. Autumn of 1944. The paintings were written off when the trucks were reported destroyed by the resistance."

Agostino looked at me, then back to Harrison. "Fine, but he'll have to prove it."

"There is more, James. He's sure several of the works belong to the Brosseau collection. He'll confirm the lot within the hour." Harrison chortled. "As soon as he gets out of bed and down to the office."

Agostino's face lit up. "That's the key, dammit." He leaned over and patted my shoulder. "Stoney, thanks." Then, to Harrison: "Reggie, we'll need a roadblock at every exit out of this valley. Local police backed by our people. And Jeanine Gobiel. Where is she?"

"Chamonix base."

"Good. I want her to scratch around for someone in town who remembers the German occupation here. Start with the mayor. He'll probably have some good leads. I want to know what buildings they occupied and which haven't changed much." Harrison wheeled around and disappeared. Back to me: "Now, Stoney, did Monique say anything to you about this region during the last days of its occupation? She did a lot of poking around on her own."

"She told me some, but I don't recall if it's what she dug up or got from you." I tried to think what she had told me. "She talked about the connection between Hegler and Steiner, but that came from you people."

"More?"

"Not much. She mentioned how the Maquis slaughtered anything in a German uniform. One bunch held out for three days before the Maquis killed them all. She described the mood of the Savoyards at the time. How the Germans occupied this region for two years. Then the Savoyards got their own back. That's about it."

The noise in the room was distracting, so we stepped into the

176

corridor. "Now, are you sure she didn't say anything else, Stoney?" he asked quietly. I shook my head. "Okay, then let's back it up. Who were the Germans that held out for three days?"

I shrugged it off. "To be truthful, she just mentioned them in passing. Part of her poking around."

"Where did it happen?"

"Outside Chamonix."

"Where outside Chamonix?"

"I don't know." I tried thinking back to our conversation. "She didn't mention a place, but it was a hotel. Yes, that's what she said. An old hotel. But, Jim, it didn't have anything to do with . . ." I stopped. An *old hotel!* "Jesus Christ," I whispered.

I dragged Agostino back inside the office, where we tripped over agents, scattered papers and files on our way to the large illustration on the wall. We stopped beside it and I jabbed a finger at the Vallée Blanche, once I'd found it, then traced a line between the high ridges and peaks to the Mer de Glace. It took me a moment, but it was there, a small black dot with the name beside it. "That's Montenvers," I said, pointing at it excitedly, "a summer tourist attraction with a great view of the glacier."

He stared at me as if I'd lost my marbles. "So what? I know this area, Stoney. I've studied maps till I can read them in my sleep. Montenvers is government-owned, and as you say, it's a summer tourist attraction, complete with a cog railway. So what?"

"Montenvers was once a hotel."

That stopped him. "Who told you that?"

"Gerhard Hegler. You could see Montenvers from here, in the daylight. With binoculars."

"It's a worth a try," he said, then bellowed, "Reggie!"

Harrison peered around the corner of the door, the walkie-talkie pressed close to his cheek. "I had Jeanine for you, James, but I lost her." The unit squawked. Harrison cursed and thumped it with the palm of his hand. It didn't help. I asked what was the matter. "It needs new batteries," he said to me. "I have some in my kit, down in the foyer."

Agostino cut in. "Reggie, ask Jeanine to check out a place called Montenvers. And second, find out who's got the Startrons." Then to me: "For seeing in the dark." He quickly pointed at the map. "Now, Stoney, you show me how those people got to Montenvers."

"Okay, so Sarah's group arrives at the Aiguille du Midi. See? At this point another cable car runs horizontally to the Italian side of the Alps. See? But they ski down the Vallée Blanche from the Aiguille du Midi, down the Mer de Glace, which passes Montenvers. It would be a short walk to the hotel from the glacier.''

"And if another bunch did the same thing a little later in the day, who'd notice?''

"Sure," I replied, looking at the illustration again. "Hegler had a couple of trusted bodyguards with us who skied well. They might have been local guides who could bring a group each down that run." I pointed to the spot halfway up to the Aiguille du Midi. "Others might have spent a leisurely day cross-country skiing from there to Montenvers. It's a big area out there too. Who's going to notice the odd bunch of skiers?''

"And for those who don't ski at all, the choppers would drop them off on what might look like a regular run to Chamonix, after dark.''

"There's only one trouble," I said. "Our imaginations might be running away with us.''

"James." Harrison was in the doorway holding the noisy walkie-talkie at his side. "I've just talked to Jeanine again. According to the mayor and several others, the Germans occupied many locations. He can remember three definites. The town hall, a small French militia barracks, and your Montenvers.''

The room was cleared, leaving Harrison, Agostino, and me alone. Jim stared at the illustration while the Scotland Yard man told us how the Maquis trapped a group of German soldiers. They were all killed, eventually. In the exchange the building was partially destroyed, but rebuilt after the war with the existing stone.

Agostino was delighted. "Montenvers has to be it, Reggie," he said flatly. "Now, where are those Star-trons?''

"From what I've heard, there is one at the Chamonix base, another with the bunch coming here from Lognan, and the third at Brévent.''

"Good, then I want the guys up there to swing theirs toward Montenvers. They'll be looking for any sign of activity. Lights. Maybe a chopper in back. Speaking of choppers, can you rustle some up on very short notice?''

Harrison scowled. "How short?''

"Thirty minutes.''

The scowl didn't leave his face. "I'll try, James. Mountain Rescue might have some. We have a small Bell, of course.''

"True." Agostino was staring again at the illustration. "I want the choppers up here. They'll have to be flown without lights. And warn the pilots to keep well away from Montenvers. They can land in the courtyard. We'll leave some of our guys here, armed, and fly the rest out. They can keep sorting through every piece of paper they can get their hands on in the meantime." He paused. "And, Reggie, you've been here longer than I have. Pick out those who should stay."

"But, old chap, we don't know for certain about Montenvers." Agostino grinned. "Fair enough. The Star-trons should settle that. Tell those guys at Brévent to hustle their butts. And when the one arrives from Lognan, would you send it down to the deck?"

If we had expected to see anything ourselves from the deck, we would've been disappointed, even using Agostino's binoculars. What we saw in that direction was a solid wall of darkness.

In was a breathless Reggie Harrison who joined us on the deck twenty minutes later. "The lads from Brévent apologize for the delay, but the ridge behind Montenvers cuts off visual observation." He chuckled. "At least that's how they put it. What it really means is that they can't spot the fucking thing from Brévent. So they've caught the cable car over to the next station. Plan Praz. They won't be long setting up."

Agostino was staring into the void. "Dammit, Reggie. You don't set up a Star-tron. You just look through the bloody thing."

"Would somebody please tell me what a Star-tron is?" I asked. "Apart from them seeing in the dark."

Harrison answered. "The brochures call it a 'passive night-vision system.' Actually it's a telescopic lens, only you can see things in the dark with it. The Star-tron amplifies light from any available source, even the stars. You just mount it on a rifle, or better still, a camera, and off you go. It's quite amazing."

The walkie-talkie, which had been cackling quietly to itself, suddenly came to life. "Harrison?" said a feeble voice. "Brévent here. Can you hear me?"

Harrison adjusted one of the knobs and depressed the lever, telling the voice to go on.

"We have Montenvers under observation. Tell Jim, from what we can see, the windows are covered up."

Agostino spun around. "Tell him to quit playing voyeur and search the area for any sign of choppers. Or Sno-Cats. Or any sign of life. I'd even settle for that."

The voice faded, then came back. "I think we have what you're looking for. Reggie. How about three feet of chopper

179

blade sticking out from under a white tarp? Correction. Two choppers. Both mostly covered. And a half-track. Is that good enough?"

Jim Agostino missed Brévent's last question. He was already halfway to the door.

19

The ridge behind us had its beginnings high among the mountains. Its descent from there was rapid, dropping sharply down to the Mer de Glace. As the ridge came forward, it flattened into a plateau that overlooked the spot where the Chamonix Valley and the glacier merged. Back from that junction, several hundred yards below where we were gathering together in the snow, stood Montenvers.

Arriving here had been painfully slow. Reggie Harrison had scrounged a couple of helicopters, French-built Gazelles, whose only drawback was their limited capacity—four passengers plus the pilot.

Hours had gone by. Harrison insisted each shuttle give Montenvers a wide berth so there'd be no opportunity to hear even the faintest sound of approaching intruders. But finally we were there, positioned along the ridge well out of sight of the building below.

As false dawn splashed across the peaks behind us, threatening to expose us all, Agostino stood up. "You'll find the descent to Montenvers a hell of a lot steeper than the final run to Les Pins, so don't get careless." He glanced at his watch. Others did likewise. "It's zero-four-thirty o'clock. At zero-four-fifty exactly, Harrison, Lapierre, Stone, and I will be going through the door at the end of the building. You will be doing the same wherever you've been assigned. Okay, let's move." The silent assault on Montenvers had begun.

The drop was incredible, pitching us down through a series of near-vertical portions where deep soft snow suddenly became hard and wind-packed, its crusted surface breaking against our knees. Other skiers were ahead of me, ghostlike figures gliding through the stillness, disappearing for seconds at a time behind a

180

cascade of flying snow, then emerging farther down the mountain, still intact, still moving.

Montenvers came out of the night, a dark brooding mass of stone planted solidly above the black outline of the glacier. Distracted, I suddenly found myself traveling much too fast and swung away to check my speed. I stopped a few feet short of a covered helicopter. Lachuk was already at work disabling the engine.

I found Agostino, Harrison, and the French Canadian Lapierre crouched well back from the corner of the building. I nodded and was bending down to release my bindings when Harrison touched my arm. The door had opened opposite us. A man stood on the parapet. I had the ugly feeling he was staring at us, but then he moved to one side, fumbled with his ski pants, and urinated in the snow. Finished, he adjusted himself and went back inside. We stood up. I stepped out of my skis and quietly stuck them in the snow beside the others. Harrison was pulling a revolver from his coveralls. Lapierre, having slipped the Sten gun from his shoulder, was wrapping its leather strap methodically around his forearm. Agostino nudged me. "Stay close to us, okay?" Then he turned toward the building.

We were on the parapet now. Agostino reached for the door and yanked it open.

From somewhere came the resounding crash of another door buckling inward. We raced down a short corridor and into the crowded great hall, which erupted into sheer chaos. Pitched above this was the discordant symphony of breaking glass. Around the walls the huge black curtains trembled, then collapsed, leaving behind bare windows with the shutters torn away. In each were men in coveralls smashing away the glass with the butts of their rifles.

The crowd surged around me. I pusned forward, shouting for Sarah. Most were wearing ski clothes. Many were scrambling over one another in a rush for the exits. I recognized those closest to me, faces registering complete shock when they saw me dressed in the coveralls. But I paid little attention as I continued my search for Sarah.

I reached the far side of the room and climbed up on a table crammed with plates of cold cuts. Off to one side was a raised platform with several large paintings leaning against the wall. Above me, crowding the balcony, were more paintings of various sizes. I was climbing down, not having spotted Sarah, when a bullhorn bellowed, "Everyone please remain calm. This is the police. We have the place surrounded."

Agostino and Harrison appeared out of the melee. Jim shouted, "You haven't found Sarah?" I shook my head. "Try up there. Reggie will go with you, to keep you out of trouble. Some of these people might turn hostile when they see who you are."

"Where are you going?" I shouted back.

"Down below. If you find her, let me know." Harrison and I both nodded, and pushed our way toward the main staircase. We found nothing up there but rooms full of tagged paintings and empty crates. We ran back to the stairs.

By now the main floor was littered with sprawled bodies lying facedown, hands clasped behind their heads. Agents stood over them, guarding a room full of powerful men whose lives had just been ruined.

Steps hidden by the main staircase dropped us into a gloom that might easily have passed for a sixteenth-century dungeon. At the bottom we found Agostino and a handful of others flattened against a wall. He spotted us coming.

"Some sonofabitch has pulled the power source down here," he said gruffly, "so we'll have to sweat it out room by room. We joined him. "You didn't find her, Reggie?"

"Not a sign of her, James. By the way, who else do you think is missing?"

"Hegler, Harold Warden, Fleck. Maybe more." He sighed. "Okay, let's spread out. And go real slow."

I stepped in behind Harrison. "Just keep glued to the wall," he warned me, "and if anything happens, drop."

I soon found myself in a damp, cold passage with a high ceiling and a dirt floor. A series of heavy doors led off both sides of this passage, and it became routine for us to flatten ourselves against the cold stone wall, wait while the door was kicked open and the inside probed, before moving on to the next.

By the fifth door along I was anxious to press on. I had a notion to charge back upstairs and find the guy from Arizona, or Joachim Smith. I'd caught glimpses of both stretched out on the floor. Then someone whispered, "Jim, there's one hell of a draft coming out from under this next door. What d'you think?"

I couldn't see who was talking. We were in the dark. I heard Agostino say, "Someone give me the flash. And get that door open." I moved along the wall until I bumped into him.

"And where do you think you're going?" he asked just as someone's boot kicked the door in.

"With you," I said.

He stepped back. Two agents with rifles ducked in. Agostino swore. "Okay, but stay low. And bring Reggie."

We were inside now, pressed against the damp wall. I could feel the rush of cold air on my cheek.

"I don't like it," whispered Agostino, waiting for a few seconds before switching on the flashlight.

The beam flattened itself against the high vaulted ceiling, remained for a moment, then slipped down the end wall. Next it probed the corners and came back along the wall opposite, touching the stone arches. Harrison murmured, "Foundations of the original hotel, most likely. You could wall up truckloads of art down here and it'd never be found. Until you wanted it. On the other hand, it's bloody damp."

The beam stopped. "It's the draft that's bothering me, Reggie. Where's it coming from?"

"Try farther along the wall," I said. The light was moving again. "Keep going."

Almost at once it lit up a round, dark opening.

"Shit! A tunnel!" He whirled around. "Reggie, take these guys and go outside. Find the cog railway and work back along the cliff. Maybe you can cut them off. Hurry."

"What about you, James?"

"Stoney and I will take the scenic route. I'm damn sure they're outside by now."

We eased ourselves by the old turnstile and reached the open double doors at the tunnel entrance. Agostino gave his snub-nose revolver a pat and tossed me the flashlight. "Keep it off, but handy."

The tunnel, blasted out of solid rock, offered little headroom. We found the walkway and broken surface of the walls coated thick with ice. "Watch your step," he warned, and showing none of the caution he expected from the others, bulled his way forward, leaving me to slither along behind.

We'd gone a good fifty yards when the ice beneath our boots changed to packed snow. Just ahead, the tunnel angled to the right. Agostino slowed enough to wave me against the wall. Then, striding quickly forward, his revolver thrust out in both hands, he stepped directly into the walkway. For some reason I half-expected him to disappear in a shower of bits and pieces. He didn't.

Instead, he motioned me into the light. I blinked at the brightness from the tunnel opening. Ahead, just inside the entrance, was a string of snowmobiles lined against the wall. From between two of them a pair of legs protruded. Tracks showed some of the machines were missing.

Agostino remained motionless, the gun still at arm's length. "See who it is, Stoney."

It was Harold Warden.

He was dead.

20

Jim Agostino whipped the old jeep onto Route Blanche, hit the gas too soon, and sent us careening into a snowbank. A wall of white pounded in on us; then the road reappeared in a sort of zigzag fashion as we fishtailed it down the highway. Huddled in the passenger seat, and half-buried in snow, I ignored it all by concentrating on other things, like Sarah's disappearance and why poor Harold Warden was shot, and how come this madman behind the wheel was trying to kill us both while insisting everything was under control.

Everything but the jeep.

And when he finally mastered that, I brushed myself off and shouted, "The least you could've done was hold out for something with windows."

It was true. This wreck, on loan from the Chamonix Department of Public Works, had arrived at police headquarters, Interpol's temporary base, with its plastic windows missing. So was the back flap.

Agostino grinned broadly. "It's just as cold on my side, so what are you complaining about?" I could have started with his driving. At that moment the jeep suddenly veered over on two wheels as we left the main highway and plunged up a narrow twisting road which I would discover led to the Mont Blanc tunnel. "Now, where were we?" he wanted to know.

"Talking about Harold Warden's murder," I replied, leaving it at that.

He had been shot twice through the heart, according to Agostino,

184

probably while pulling a snowmobile suit on over his tux. Nor were there signs of a struggle.

We left Warden there, and grabbing a snowmobile each, rattled out of the tunnel and along the cliffside path which stopped short of the cog railway line. Reggie Harrison and the rest hadn't reached here yet, so Agostino and I continued on alone, following the tracks of the escaping Hercules members. They led us a merry chase down the steep cut of the railway line.

Reaching the floor of the valley, we found four Sno-Cats abandoned in a small wooded area. Nearby were deep tire marks in the snow.

Jim had also been trying to convince me that with roadblocks and patrols sealing off the entire valley, it was only a matter of time before the remnants of Hercules would be flushed out. I'd been trying to convince him that with Sarah as a hostage, the fun might be far from over.

Underneath it all, he must have thought so too, because just before we hit the Route Blanche, he admitted that of any escape route Hegler and Gerry might choose—he was using Gerry's name freely, so sure was he that Hope-Warden was still alive— he'd put his money on the tunnel any day. He was back at it again now.

"Seven miles through it, and they're in another country, Stoney," he bellowed over the high-pitched whine of the engines. "The part of Italy on the other side of the tunnel is pretty much rough-and-tumble. The tunnel itself saves motorists and truckers especially hundreds of miles, and it's always busy." He glanced at his watch without taking his hands off the wheel. "It's just before seven A.M. Busy time. I suspect our roadblock up there is adding to the confusion."

As if on cue, horns began blaring. One moment we could see nothing but forest around us, the next we were rattling across a large open parking lot, itself dwarfed by the sheer magnitude of Mont Blanc.

The honking came from an area off to our right, already jammed with transport trucks and cars funneling toward three tollbooths. I couldn't guess the number. Maybe in the hundreds. Beyond them a huge corrugated shell-like structure of concrete rose diagonally above the darkened entrance to the actual tunnel. Beside this, to the left and embedded in the rock, was a row of tinted glass panels.

"That's what we're after," said Agostino, nodding toward the panels.

*   *   *

Behind the tinted glass was the tunnel's computerized control center with its sophisticated monitoring equipment. Technicians were scurrying around the illuminated terminals, obviously annoyed by all the activity. Agents still wearing the familiar off-white coveralls—Agostino and I had chucked ours in the back of the jeep—stood to one side chatting quietly.

In the middle of the room a smallish dark woman dressed in a trim ski outfit stood with hands on hips. She was talking rapid-fire French to a tall man in his fifties. Just looking at his coarse gray suit started my skin to itch.

"That's Jeanine Gobiel from Interpol, Paris," Agostino mumbled to me from our spot near the door. "She and Monique became good friends." We were moving now in her direction, when she spun around, her wide eyes lighting up her oval face. She waved us over.

The man with her was Auguste Aubert, the superintendent of tunnel operations.

Monsieur Aubert, she told us, was most upset with the delay caused by the police. At the moment, her team of six agents was working with the customs men at the booths. Several others were roaming the parking lot checking cars and keeping an eye out for a gray Mercedes. Agostino frowned at Aubert. "Tell him we're doing our best." She did.

"What's the matter now?" Agostino wanted to know when Aubert frowned back.

"He's worried because the traffic becomes worse at this time of the morning. With the men here changing shifts in about ten minutes, he thinks there will be chaos."

The agent shrugged. "We'll get some men up here once we can free them from the mountain." He looked at me and said, "Pardon me, Stoney, this is Jeanine Gobiel. Jeanie, this is Philip Stone." She smiled and we shook hands. She told me how sorry she was to hear about Monique, then held on for a moment longer as if trying to physically share the burden of all that I'd been through.

"We promise you, M'sieu Stone, that nothing will happen to Madame Warden. We are doing our best to have done with this ordeal as quickly as possible." Again the smile. I thanked her, wondering why Agostino hadn't said it that way.

In the meantime, he had been called to the phone. Left on my own, I wandered over beside a technician seated at a console cluttered with knobs, flashing lights, and toggle switches. High

186

on the wall in front of him was an illuminated panel some eighteen inches wide which stretched the width of the room. Studded with tiny lights of various colors and sizes and running along two inch-wide strips, I guessed the panel represented the actual tunnel.

What also caught my eye was the bank of television monitors installed directly below the panel, whose images changed automatically every five or six seconds and showed different views of the tunnel. I was trying to figure out how the screens were related to the large panel when Agostino called me.

"It's Reggie," he shouted across the room. "They've discovered a goddamn room full of artwork. In the basement, Stoney. Incredible, he says. A *gallery* hidden behind a wall."

I joined him to learn that the crew at Les Pins had found documents linking Hercules members with all sorts of illegal trafficking in stolen art. The routes such works had taken and whose possession they were in now. Names. contacts, minutes of the meetings over the past few days.

"And they haven't even begun to dig into it all yet, Stoney," he said, then glanced at me, sobering. "But there is no news of Sarah. I am sorry. We have half a dozen guys now scouring the parking lot for that gray Mercedes. I promise you, no one will slip her through this tunnel."

"I know," I said. "You're doing everything you can, and I appreciate it. By the way there was a guy called Baglio. He was operating a fleet of boats . . ."

"We know him. He and several others left Thursday afternoon. We didn't want to stop them for fear of screwing up the works. But we'll tie them into this." He grunted to himself. "Reggie also mentioned a collector from Pittsburgh who's ready to sing his little head off."

"That would be Joachim Smith," I said, then paused. "He didn't look the type to take that route."

"It seems he wasn't aware there was murder involved. And he's damn sure most of the others would feel the same way."

"Where is Harrison now?"

Agostino nodded at Jeanine, who looked as though she needed rescuing from Aubert. "He was phoning from the police station in Chamonix, after bringing a bunch down from Montenvers. They're having one hell of a time finding places to hold your Hercules friends." As we started back across the room toward Jeanine, he mentioned that Harrison had brought our skis down

187

with him and we could pick them up at the police station, where he and I had picked up the jeep.

Agostino told Jeanine that Harrison had rounded up eight or nine agents and would be sending them up shortly. She was going to tell Aubert the good news when one of the technicians handed her the phone. She listened for a moment, then said, "James, it is Régis. Someone has reported seeing a gray limousine on the back roads. Near the Les Houches end of the valley."

My heart began pounding in my chest. "Ask him if it's a gray Mercedes. Series Six Hundred."

"We know the car all right, Stoney," Agostino answered. "The problem is, this valley is crawling with expensive cars." He and I were standing near the console, Jeanine closer to Aubert's office. She had the phone up to her ear again, listening, her eyes riveted on Jim Agostino.

The room was silent. Jeanine was nodding into the phone. "Yes," she said solemnly, "I will tell him, Regis." She cradled the receiver. "A gray Mercedes, Series Six Hundred, has just run a roadblock below Les Houches. It is heading down to St. Gervais-Le Fayet." She smiled. "Eh bien, James, we stay here?"

"You bet, Jeanine," he replied. "I want every passenger, every driver, *out* of the vehicles as they reach the the booths. Search them all."

Without a word, Jeanine bolted for the door, taking the two agents with her.

"I don't get it," I said. "Why aren't we going after them?"

He smiled at me. "We are, by sitting tight. Right here. C'mon."

We were outside. There was a commotion at the far booth. We could see a trucker stepping down from his transport, yelling at the driver of the car ahead of him. Several guys in coveralls were running over. Almost at once a crowd was gathering from those parked behind the transport. We were halfway to the first booth when someone started blowing a car horn again.

Agostino had broken into a run. I followed. "This is what Hegler and your friend Gerry were counting on," he yelled. "Total chaos. Throw in a change of shift, and some good timing . . ."

"But what about the Mercedes?"

"A ruse, probably, to distract us. They'd never get anywhere on that road. Too winding and steep. They aren't that stupid. And neither are we."

188

We were passing the second booth when Jeanine came running toward us.

"They're in the tunnel!"

"How did it happen?" Agostino asked Jeanine as we raced back to the control center.

"Someone in a small black Renault bribed the driver in a car near the front of the line with a thousand francs to let him cut in," she said, trying to catch her breath. "The trucker behind them became very upset and complained to a customs inspector. Then the two of them started to argue. One of our agents was on his way over to see what was the problem, but in the confusion, the Renault must have driven off into the tunnel."

We reached the door. Agostino paused long enough to ask if the agent had seen how many were in the car, or if he recognized the driver.

"No," she said as we stepped inside. "It happened so fast. There were two, maybe more in the Renault. The windows were not very clean."

"Was one of them a woman?" I asked, trailing after them, but Jim cut me off. He was pointing at the console, asking Jeanine if the technician could pick up the Renault on the monitors. Aubert had come out of his office. Jeanine shot some French at him, and the superintendent's eyes lit up. He came thundering over, jabbering away excitedly in French. Jeanine loosely translated it as "Yes, he can."

Traffic was held up at this end of the tunnel and the Italian authorities were persuaded to do the same at theirs. At the same time, we began our hunt for the Renault.

With all of us crowded around the console, the technician, under Jeanine's careful guidance, punched up images on the five screens. Fourty cameras dotted the eleven kilometers of tunnel.

The images were coming at us thick and fast as a transport truck popped up on an upper screen, then disappeared, to be replaced by a small panel truck. Often we saw sections of empty road. Or a car would be coming toward us from the Italian side, having slipped through before that end of the tunnel was closed.

These images had been flashing at us about thirty seconds when suddenly I caught a glimpse of something black disappearing from the top-right-corner screen. It was replaced instantly by a transport truck in some other area of the tunnel. I shouted at Jeanine to recheck that particular monitor. She passed this onto the technician, who immediately flipped through the buttons. A green car appeared, then a Japanese-made pickup from the looks of it, then a small black car.

"Renault," the three of us shouted in unison.

Aubert became very excited. As he pointed to that screen, the car swung by and out of sight. Jeanine translated what Aubert wanted us to know.

"He says it is out of range, but we can pick it up on the next camera." Jeanine had no sooner spoken than the same Renault popped up on the lower-left monitor.

It was coming directly at the camera, which gave us a slightly elevated perspective of the car. A metal rack on the roof held assorted luggage.

"I want to see the driver," said Agostino. "Can we move in any closer before we lose him?" The picture widened, showing the driver and a passenger, but the roof cut them off at the chest.

"Tighter," Agostino said patiently. Jeanine countered that by moving in closer we would lose the car too fast. "Fair enough. Then give us a quick look at the driver's window as it passes. That'll give Stoney a chance to identify the driver."

I waited. The windshield filled most of the TV screen. The picture tightened. Part of the side window showed. I saw a face, and the car was gone. "It was Fleck," I said, "it was Fleck." Agostino patted me on the shoulder, then turned to Jeanine.

"Tell Aubert we'll need one of the Tunnel Authority cars. Radio equipped. And, Jeanine, pick out two of your best shooters, along with yourself of course.

Jeanine spoke to Aubert, who lost no time in picking up the phone. He barked a few words, then jabbered excitedly to her. She suddenly kissed him on the cheek. "Aubert has a good idea, James. How about a Tunnel Authority ambulance?"

Agostino beamed. "Tell him he's a genius. Have it brought around to the door here. And one more thing. Get back to the Italian police. Tell them I want a roadblock about a mile in from their entrance. Maybe they could use a heavy piece of equipment. It's not to be on a curve. I want Fleck to have plenty of time to stop." He glanced at me and went on, "Quite possibly there is a hostage involved." Again Jeanine translated this into French.

"M'sieu Aubert tells me there is no problem. The tunnel is perfectly straight."

He turned to me next, looking uneasy. "I can't risk taking you along, Stoney. I'm sorry. Unarmed, you're a liability. Anyway, you speak enough French to get by, and I need a link with the technician here." To Jeanine he said, "Get Stoney a microphone. I want to be in direct contact with him." Then he sprinted away.

Jim Agostino's voice boomed over the room's loudspeakers several seconds before we picked them up on camera. "Just look for a bright red Land Rover, Stoney, because that's us."

"We've got you," I said, trying not to shout into the mike. "We've also picked up the Renault." I asked the technician his name. It was Georges.

"Good," came his voice. "Now, Jeanine says the camera should pick up the distance marker. So where exactly is the Renault?"

I glanced at the screen on the lower left. "It's passing the four-kilometer mark."

"Dammit, that means there's a good two miles separating us. We've just passed the first kilo. Can you figure out how many vehicles between us?"

I spoke a bit of poor French to Georges, who caught enough to understand what I wanted. He punched up a series of pictures carrying us from the Land Rover through to the Renault.

"At least a dozen."

"Okay, Stoney, but I want to stop them before someone's hurt. Or killed. Anyway, keep us posted on what Hegler and Fleck are up to."

At once the ambulance shot across the solid line onto the oncoming-traffic lane. Georges picked up a transport coming the other way on another screen, but I couldn't tell the distance between it and the ambulance, which passed two cars and darted back as the truck blared by.

"Jesus, Jim," I shouted into the mike, "take it easy."

"That's easy for you to say. Besides, these lanes are so damn skinny."

"Okay," I said, "I'll have Georges punch up what's coming." From then on I did my best to tell him when he could pass and when he couldn't.

By the midway point the oncoming traffic had dried up.

"Welcome to Italy," I quipped.

Agostino's voice drifted down from the loudspeakers. "You sure can tell. This section is so damn poorly lit. Jeanine wants to know if you can still see us."

"Yes, but not as well." I checked the monitors. "You've just passed the six-kilometer mark, leaving you about four to the roadblock. There's still a truck and car between you and the Renault, though. You'll have to pass them now. There's nothing coming toward you."

The loudspeakers hissed. Agostino sounded a little garbled. "Anyone in front of the Renault?"

Another screen showed a car loaded down with skis on the roof. I told him. "It's difficult judging distance from here, Jim, but it appears to be about three hundred yards."

His voice again: "What about the roadblock?"

"I can't see anything. I'd feel one hell of a lot better if Jeanine had a word with Aubert." She came on the line. I handed the mike to him. They talked briefly.

"Everything is set, Stoney, but M'sieu Aubert is concered that the car with the skis might get caught between the Renault and the roadblock."

"Stoney, Jim here. Look, keep your eye on the Renault. I'm going to put on the flashers and siren, if we can find the goddamn buttons, and pass this truck and car ahead of us. Fleck and Hegler might think we're an ambulance on an emergency run."

"Hold off a moment, Jim. I don't quite understand it, but one of the monitors has some sort of a break showing in the tunnel wall."

"Those are emergency stations built into the rock. They're scattered along at regular intervals."

"The one on the screen is at kilometer ten." As I watched, what looked like a large piece of machinery was being shifted around inside. Aubert was talking on the phone. In Italian. Then, still holding the receiver, he turned to me and started speaking excitedly in French, pointing at the monitor.

I squeezed the microphone. "Jim, from what I can gather, they've got something to block the tunnel at kilometer ten. Don't pass those other two till you hit nine. That'll give you just over half a mile before the barricade. By then the car with the skis should be out of the way."

"I've just gone by kilometer seven."

My eyes were glued to the Renault. I could see Fleck quite clearly, though in profile. Directly behind him was one of the French bodyguards. I couldn't tell if it was Sarah beside him or not. Nor could I see more than the legs of the person next to the driver. I took it to be Gerhard Hegler. At the moment, I was more worried about Fleck. He'd started checking his rearview mirror.

192

Everything was happening too fast now. A wide view of the Renault in the upper-left screen showed it definitely picking up speed. Beside it the operator had neatly punched up the camera, showing the ambulance passing the small panel truck and drawing abreast of the car. Then the pictures changed as the man at the controls tried to follow what was going on.

I held the mike close to my mouth, waiting for another shot of the Renault. It popped up, lower left.

"Jim," I said quickly, "Hegler's picking up speed."

"Yeah, I know," came his reply over the speaker. "Where's the car ahead of him?"

Lower-middle screen. "From what I can see, about a hundred and fifty yards from the emergency station at kilo ten. But the Renault's catching up."

Agostino's next words were drowned out by the piercing wail of a siren. On the monitor the lights on the ambulance roof flashed against the walls of the tunnel.

The car with the skis was fifty yards from the emergency station. It was slowing. "Come on, come on," I pleaded. "Just keep moving."

The Renault was closing in. Hegler had pulled over into the left lane to pass. Though he was a little distance back, it looked as if both cars would reach kilometer ten at the same moment. Beside me Aubert was shouting into the phone, but I heard nothing for the screaming siren.

Suddenly the car with the skis picked up speed. I could only think that in those few seconds its driver must have figured the Renault was hurrying to clear the tunnel for the ambulance, and decided to get the hell out of there himself.

No sooner had he passed the emergency entrance than a large front-end loader lumbered out, completely blocking off both lanes.

In the upper screen the Renault's nose dropped as the brakes locked, sending up plumes of smoke from all four tires. It was skidding too fast toward the loader, its tail end swinging wildly. At the last moment, the back of the car broke sideways, slamming the length of the Renault solidly against the machine.

Pieces of metal flew into the air, and the car's hood and trunk lid sprang open under the pressure. Before the wheels settled on the road, the doors on the passenger side flew open and two figures tumbled out.

"Sarah!" I lunged toward the monitors, but already I could see it wasn't her or Gerry. Instead, Fleck and the second bodyguard scrambled to their feet and got themselves back behind the car. On the far side, Hegler and the man behind were hauling themselves out the broken windows. The Renault was empty. I grabbed for a phone. If she wasn't here, then where else? In the Mercedes?

I put a call through to Harrison. "Harrison? It's me, Stone." I cupped my hand around the mouthpiece. "We've got Hegler, Fleck, and a couple of others trapped up here in the tunnel. But Sarah Warden isn't with them. I was wondering—"

"What about Hope-Warden?"

A chill went down my spine. "What of him?"

"Isn't he with that crowd?"

"I don't understand," I said. "You mean he really is alive?"

The line clicked and sputtered. Harrison's voice faded, then came back. "These damn French phones. Stone, are you still there?"

"Yes. How do you know Gerry is still alive?"

"Because, old boy, James put a trace on your friend Hope-Warden when he'd heard nothing from the forensic people. It paid off. Interpol in Paris just informed us it's highly likely he passed through customs in Zurich exactly two weeks ago. That would be the day after he was supposedly murdered."

"Then who was driving the Mercedes?"

The line crackled again. "A ski bum. American. He insists some guy offered him two hundred dollars to bomb around the back roads of the valley. Double it if he could reach St. Gervais. He thought it was a joke. Besides, it was more money than he'd seen in months. We stopped him at the second barrier."

"So you'll be going after Gerry."

Harrison hesitated. "For the moment, I'm bringing up reinforcements. And don't worry about Sarah. Hope-Warden won't get far. We have the area virtually locked up. Every road, every exit." He laughed. "We've had men at every cable-car station in the valley. I will warn them immediately to keep an eye out for him, should he decide to make a few runs while we are searching for him in the valley."

Something twigged. I started to speak, but he cut me off. "Believe me, Stone, once we've taken care of Hegler and his friends, we'll roust him out. Cheerio."

"Reggie," I burst out, "that's it. The *cable car!* Reggie . . ." But it was too late. The phone was buzzing in my ear.

Cursing, I dropped the receiver and swung around, aware now of the sound of gunshots pouring from the loudspeakers. Aubert

194

was standing openmouthed before the bank of monitors. I raced over to the console and quickly scanned the TV screens as I picked up the microphone. In one I saw the ambulance with its windshield shattered. Figures crouched down behind it. Knowing I couldn't reach Agostino at a time like this, I put down the mike and grabbed the superintendent with both hands.

"Aubert," I shouted at him, desperately trying to recall a few words of French, "Dites Agostino . . . je . . . vais . . . au téléphérique . . . Aiguille du Midi." I paused, hoping some of it had sunk in. "You got that?" He was staring at me. "Aiguille du Midi, Aubert, for Christ's sake. Dites-lui." He shrugged. "Fuck," I murmured, and ran out to the jeep.

Somebody was on my side. The keys were still in the ignition.

You see the white stucco and wood-frame base of the Téléphérique de l'Aiguille du Midi from the Route Blanche because its cables pass over the highway on its rise up to the first station at Plan des Aiguilles. However, I detoured through town, stopping long enough at the police station to collect my skis and return the snow boots to the poor guy who'd been running around in his socks for the past hour. Unable to find someone who spoke English and fearing I'd miss the first lift, I drove off again in the direction of the Route Blanche.

Within three minutes I wheeled into the téléphérique parking lot. Leaving the jeep where it couldn't be missed, I grabbed my skis and poles and raced for the outside kiosk.

The chubby, pleasant woman behind the wicket spoke better English than I did French. No, I hadn't missed the first lift. They were running behind. It was already eight-twenty. Now, did I want a ticket to the Aiguille du Midi or to Pointe Helbronner, as the télécabine "en haut" was in service today. I settled for Pointe Helbronner and dug a hundred-franc note out of my pocket.

Inside I joined the early-morning crowd filing up the steps to the platform, my heart pounding in my chest. It still seemed incredible to me that Gerry hadn't died; I didn't really want to see them together, no matter what the circumstances.

The line moved slowly. I put on my sunglasses.

I reached the platform. The cable car hung solidly from its support arm. Its doors were open wide. I could see little more than the tops of skis and the backs of heads around me. A few feet farther and I realized the delay was caused by two uniformed police standing by the doors. It wasn't until I was closer yet that I discovered they were checking the men who got on the car

195

against some photographs. Part of Harrison's locking-up-the-valley policy, no doubt.

It wasn't until I had a boot on the cable-car step that one of them touched me on the shoulder. He was smiling. I thought he might have recognized me. Instead, he nodded at my glasses. "Enlevez vos lunettes, s'il vous plaît." I pushed them up onto my forehead, wondering if I should try to explain that I needed help. But what if I couldn't make myself understood? What if they held me up and let the car go? I opted for silence.

They were arguing between themselves, much too fast for me to get the drift of what they were saying. The one who had touched me on the shoulder jerked his head toward the car. The other laughed, then prodded me in the ribs. "Allez-y, m'sieu." I pulled my glasses down, picked up my gear and climbed aboard. In doing so I glanced at the photo in his hand. It was of Gerry Hope-Warden.

I'd worked myself around to the back of the cable car when it finally wrenched itself free of the building and swung out over the highway. There were fifty, maybe sixty of us wedged in together, skis, poles, and all. I was facing the window now, watching us pull away from the valley floor. I'd been wrong. Gerry couldn't have slipped aboard with those two spotting him. Then where the hell was he? I wondered, turning around.

I saw Sarah almost at once, toward the front of the cable car. She appeared tense. Her head was tilted to one side, as if she was listening to someone while staring out the window. I looked at those around her. None was Gerry. But he *had* to be here, so I began studying the men closest to her.

None fit.

The guy on her right leaned forward. Was he talking to her? I couldn't tell. Even with the tuque and sunglasses, it definitely wasn't Gerry Hope-Warden.

Okay, find him.

I scanned the faces farther away from Sarah, thinking Gerry might have insisted they board the cable car separately. But there were too many skis in the way, too many backs, too many people between us. I'd just have to wait until we reached the first stop.

Then what?

I had no plan, no plan at all. But at least I'd found Sarah.

People around me were chattering now. Someone started to sing. Others joined in. The cable car swayed. Bodies shifted. For a moment I lost her. I moved slightly to one side. When I saw

196

her again, she was listening to the man beside her. I couldn't place him, though there was something vaguely familiar.

Suddenly Sarah turned her head and snapped angrily at the guy. As she did, our eyes met and she swayed back against the side of the car.

My stomach muscles tightened. There were two of them. But where was Gerry? Here somewhere. The man with Sarah had his head averted toward the window. I gave Sarah a reassuring nod, then watched again for Gerry among the many faces. I was still looking when the car slowed and slipped into the first station.

The doors opened. The crowd surged forward. I desperately wanted to reach a phone, but there was no way I'd let Sarah and the guy out of my sight.

I remained behind long enough to make sure Gerry wasn't aboard, then, clutching my skis, followed the group toward a sign marked "Direction Aiguille du Midi," ever watchful of Sarah's yellow ski outfit.

From here on I could only hope for a chance to pry her loose from this guy. It seemed logical that he was taking her to meet Gerry, maybe on the Italian side of the mountain. At Pointe Helbronner?

We arrived at the upper platform to find the cables running, but no car. It was probably carrying the operating crew to the top, I reasoned, then waited back against the wall.

Not more than a few minutes passed when out of the clear morning the empty car came dropping toward us. Now it slowed, groaned, and clanked into its concrete slot. An attendant came up the steps near me, pushed through the crowd, and opened the doors. The skiers swarmed on board.

Sarah was among the first, with the singers pressed in close behind her. Her companion didn't seem to mind. He let more by him, then followed. By the time I stepped in, he was standing opposite the door, but facing the window. All I could see of him was the back of his head and tuque, and the tops of his Rossignols. This left Sarah on her own, near the front window. I figured he was giving her a little breathing room. After all, where could she go?

The doors closed. I held back until we'd cleared the building, then, holding my skis close, started to work my way toward her.

The ride was almost vertical. No pylons here. Just a sheer drop of several thousand feet.

Talk stopped. The cabin swayed with its own momentum. Inside my chest, my heart was beating like a jackhammer.

Jammed together as we were, my progress was slow. At last I could almost reach out for her.

Three people to go.

I moved by two of them, trying to make it look as if I was after a better view, then managed to exchange places with the third.

I touched her gently on the shoulder. "Hello," I said quietly. "Don't turn around."

"Philip! Oh, God, Philip. He's—"

"I know," I replied hastily. "I saw him. Are you okay?"

She turned her head and looked at me. Her eyes closed for a moment, then opened. She brought up a hand and brushed it against my cheek. "Stoney, my poor darling, you really don't understand, do you?"

I was about to ask her what I didn't understand when a voice behind me said, "Very touching. Very touching indeed."

I was swept by a wave of nausea.

It was Gerry.

I started to turn when something pushed into my ribs. "No, Stoney. I like you best just looking straight ahead." Sarah turned away in disgust.

"I didn't recognize you, Gerry," I said.

He chuckled to himself. "Nice of you to say so," he replied. "Now, I want you to reach into your pocket carefully and hand me your ticket." I did, and passed it back. "Good, to Helbronner. That was thoughtful of you. One thing more. Are you alone?"

I didn't answer.

"It doesn't matter," he answered. "If anyone comes near us, you'll get it first, Stoney. For now, let's pretend that you two are together. After all, you've been having lots of practice, from what I hear."

Sarah stiffened. "You bastard," she murmured, which pretty well covered what I had to say.

We traveled the rest of the way in silence. When we docked at the Aiguille du Midi station, Gerry insisted we remain where we were until the cable car was empty. The gun, probably in his pocket, never left my side. Neither did he move from behind me. I was putting my sunglasses carefully into my own pocket when he said, "All right, let's go. Sarah, you first. Just follow the others." We each carried our own skis.

Soon we were in a kind of tunnel chiseled out of the rock. Similar to its cousin at Montenvers, the sides were thick with

198

ice. No one talked. Hardly what you'd call like old times. As kids, everyone heard us coming.

We came to a sign hanging from hooks drilled into the rock overhead. One arrow pointed ahead to Vallée Blanche. The other, marked "Télécabine: Pointe Helbronner," sent us off to the right.

The passage was cold, damp, the station at the end ill-lit.

Our skis and poles were secured in the four-seat gondola's outside rack. Two old tight-lipped Savoyards in berets and cloth overcoats steadied it while Sarah climbed in. Then me. Gerry got in and sat opposite us, his back to what little light penetrated this concrete cave from the opening down the way.

The door clamped shut. A push locked the gondola's support arm onto the main running cable. In seconds we were jolted out into the bright sunshine.

Blinking at the harsh light and feeling emotionally drained, I leaned back and covered my eyes with my hand. I heard Gerry say, "Here, try my sunglasses." I ignored him.

"Stoney," he said.

I took my hand away.

At first I saw only the glasses, then the watch on his wrist. It was mine. "Hey," I said, sitting up. But the word died on my lips. The face looking back at me was also mine.

"Jesus," I whispered as he took off the tuque.

I was staring, fascinated, at my own image. The brown eyes, the shape of the mouth, the wide forehead. Not perfect, but the likeness was uncanny. The hair too had been lightened, to match mine. Scars left by the cosmetic surgeon's knife were still visible around the mouth, where the nose had been reshaped, and more about the eyes. Several small Band-Aids on his face covered what I guessed were the worst scars. But for all that, it was me.

His revolver was out in the open now, aimed at my chest. He was smiling. I found myself wondering if I smiled the same way.

"You've been slowly taking me over," I said at last. "That's what it's been all along. First my voice, now the rest of me." Beside me Sarah made a little noise in her throat. She took my hand in hers. I went on.

"The deposits in my New York bank account. They were for you. Philip Stone, the newest patron of the arts, makes his debut at the Chamonix Casino. At the Les Pins conference." I laughed to myself. "But I wasn't supposed to make it this far, was I? The Philip Stone who registered at the Majestic should have been *you.*"

199

In the silence that followed, Sarah squeezed my hand. "Stoney," she whispered, "I knew nothing of this until we arrived at Montenvers. Nothing. I heard rumors last night that Gerry was still alive." Again silence. At last she said, "But why, Gerry? Tell me that much, at least."

"Because your husband killed Allan Starkman," I said flatly, "that's why. He must have heard that the police had enough evidence to indict him for first-degree murder." I looked at Gerry. The smile had gone. "That's premeditated murder, isn't it?" I was embellishing what I'd picked up from Sarah and Agostino. "Ask him why, Sarah. And he'll tell you he tampered with your car the night you had a rendezvous with Allan at the motel near . . . where? Harrison?"

Gerry broke in. "I went to reason with him. He'd been threatening to expose Hercules, at least the inner core, and we couldn't have that."

"And you also heard rumors he was having a torrid affair with your wife. And you couldn't have that, either."

He went on as if he hadn't heard me. "Starkman opened the door when I knocked. I barged in and closed the door. I saw logs burning in the fireplace, an ice bucket chilling a bottle of wine." He was talking directly to Sarah now. I thought about jumping for the gun, but he broke off, telling me not to try it. I settled back and listened to him, aware of Sarah's grip tightening on my hand.

He told us that while promising Starkman he might be considered for membership in the inner core, he couldn't get his mind off the fireplace, the wine, the covers folded back on the double bed and what could have gone on had Sarah been there.

I glanced at Sarah. She sat rigid, her eyes fastened on the window beside her.

According to Gerry, Starkman had become unreasonable. He demanded that Gerry make a place for him within the inner group, and put it in writing. Gerry refused. They didn't work that way, he told Starkman, but he would convene a special meeting and the kid could try to convince the others that he should be allowed to join. Starkman accepted this, in exchange for not exposing the Hercules operation. He also boasted of having told Sarah everything about how Hercules functioned.

"It was crazy," Gerry went on. "Here I was dealing with a punk who had one more demand. He wanted to go on having an affair with Sarah. I told him he was nuts." Gerry hesitated. He looked at Sarah. "What I didn't tell him was Gerhard and the others were in favor of putting a contract out on him. I'd argued against it. Hercules wasn't in the business of killing people.

"Well, I was leaving it at that. I had come to reason with the guy and let him know that if I ever caught him sniffing around my wife again, I'd kill him. I told him, and walked to the door. That's when he began taunting me about what Sarah and he had done together. Graphically. And how would I like to hear a tape recording of them making love? I turned and slugged him. He fell down between the beds, still talking like that. Then I saw him reaching under the bed. He said he had the tape right there on the machine. I . . . went for the poker by the fireplace and brought it down on his head. I hit him again and again and again."

Gerry stopped. I watched Sarah's head turn toward him. Her eyes were full of tears.

The gondola swayed in a fresh breeze. I found myself looking down at a broad basin of snow wedged between the rising peaks. From what I could see, we were a third of the way across the bowl. I could only hope that help would be waiting for us at the other side.

It was Sarah who asked him to go on.

Having come to his senses, Gerry had wiped the poker free of his fingerprints with a towel from the bathroom, tossed them both in the fire, and left. Once clear of Harrison, he'd phoned Gerhard. A meeting was set up that night at Hegler's penthouse suite in a building facing Central Park. Hegler picked five trusted men who would swear that Gerry had been present all evening. Only Hegler and Gerry knew what had happened.

According to Gerry, Gerhard Hegler began to worry more and more about the investigation into Starkman's death. He was afraid it might spill into Hercules' activities, which would be disastrous. When at last Hegler learned from his contacts that Gerry was indeed one of the prime suspects, they concocted the plan to kill Gerry off. But whose place could he take?

"I had suggested you, almost from the start," Gerry was saying now quite matter-of-factly. "I described you to Gerhard. He agreed you'd be perfect. I hadn't seen you for fifteen years, so there was no sentimental attachment. Your affair with Sarah seven years ago still irked me."' He paused and smiled at me. "She is still in love with you, Stoney. She's never stopped."

I squeezed Sarah's hand. I didn't want her to interrupt. Letting him talk kept his mind off the gun. She let the remark pass.

201

"You must have been overjoyed when you found I'd chucked everything," I said, encouraging him to go on.

Gerry nodded. "True. But I knew that before I suggested you. I've kept tabs on you."

"For the past seven years."

He put on my smile. "Yes, for the past seven years."

Sarah could restrain herself no longer. "And you have no twinge of conscience, no regrets?" Her eyes searched his. "Gerry, for heaven's sake, take a *look* at yourself. People have died because of you and Hegler."

"People like Monique." I said softly, "and your father."

Sarah caught her breath. "Oh, God, no!"

"Monique never made it out of the mountains." I nodded at Gerry. "Your father never made it out of Montenvers. He was shot to death in the tunnel."

The barrel of the revolver wavered. "Gerhard must have killed him," he said. "We had snowmobiles there to bring members down after the auction. When the roof fell in, we made it to the tunnel. My father got that far and refused to leave his paintings. Gerhard told us to go on. He'd bring my father."

Sarah said, "Why would he kill him?"

"Because my father would have told the police everything. He'd destroy what was left of Hercules."

"What would have happened to the paintings?" I asked.

"Over the next couple of weeks those paintings which were sold would've been flown at night over the mountains to Switzerland. By helicopter. Then shipped through normal channels to their new owners. No questions asked. The rest would have remained at Montenvers."

Sarah wanted to know how they got there in the first place.

It seemed that his father had tracked down Hegler and the five trucks during the war, confronting him at an overnight stop at a small inn near Albertville, about thirty-five miles past Grenoble. Warden was wearing civilian clothes. He told Hegler, whose name was Steiner then, that the slightest nod would bring the Maquis down on top of them. Hegler called his bluff, saying that if the Maquis were around, they wouldn't have waited for a nod. He then produced a pistol. Under threat of being shot, Warden told him who he was. Hegler thought he might be interested in the contents of the trucks. Warden was mesmerized by them.

Hegler was very hospitable. Over drinks he told Harold Warden how he had been convoying paintings and art treasures into Germany for Hitler. Knowing the war was lost, Hegler had

202

planned to keep this shipment for himself. Harold Warden, the prisoner, listened.

The German officer explained how he had spent the last eight months in charge of Montenvers, one of several transfer points for such art en route to Germany. During that eight-month period Hegler's contingent of a dozen soldiers had brought up bricks from old buildings leveled in the valley by the Germans' initial invasion. Using these bricks, he and his men sealed off an area in the musty old basement of Montenvers. Hegler had it specially ventilated for storage and installed heaters connected secretly to the electrical line from the cog railway system's main terminal. That way there would still be power in the off season.

Gerry then told us the rest of the story.

"That night Hegler offered my father a deal," he said. "In exchange for his own life and a share in the collection, Dad was to help Hegler get established when the war ended. Of course my father's international reputation would give Gerhard the credibility he needed. When the time came, Hegler would make the contact.

"In his mind, I'm sure my father only went along with Hegler to save his life and planned to report all this to Paris later.

"When the paintings arrived at Montenvers the next day, by the railway, my father was there too. He and Gerhard and the soldiers got the goods inside just before the Maquis attacked. The five trucks left empty in the valley were destroyed. Then Montenvers was under siege.

"My father must have been scared shitless. I think he had a breakdown. Anyway, Gerhard got him out of there through the sightseeing tunnel and down onto the glacier. Then he turned him loose."

I interrupted at this point. "I'd heard all the Germans were killed after three days."

Gerry smiled. "All but Gerhard. He left my father and went back to make sure the paintings were hidden safely and the entrance bricked up. When the Maquis finally stormed Montenvers in the dark, Gerhard knifed the first one coming through the tunnel and switched clothes. He was the only one who escaped."

It seemed that Harold Warden's return to the Dordogne was a nightmare. Mostly he was terrorized by his own conscience, torn as he was between his duty to reveal what took place and a passion to keep such a treasure secret. He chose to remain quiet. Later Steiner showed up in Paris, introducing himself as Gerhard Hegler.

"After the war, Dad and Gerhard heard about Les Pins being for sale. They bought it. From there they could keep an eye on Montenvers. Each fall when it closed for the season, the pair would slip over after dark and spend hours caring for the paintings, which explains why my father was constantly away during the winter." He stopped talking and leaned back. "I'm boring you both, I'm sure."

"Not at all," I said. "It's fascinating. But I would appreciate it if you'd put your sunglasses back on. It's like staring in the mirror. By the way, who did your face?"

Gerry laughed. "I suppose I can tell you. A doctor by the name of Hauser. He operates a private clinic outside Zurich." The damn smile again. "Hauser owes much of his fine art collection to Hercules. He returned the favor with a six-hour operation. Common stuff these days, cosmetic surgery."

I said, "You provided him with a recent photograph, of course."

The smile was getting on my nerves. "Of course. We sent a young woman up to the Laurentians to take one of your cross-country ski classes. She photographed you from every angle."

"Good for her," I replied. "And your little scars?"

"Soon they'll hardly show. Anyway, I'll spread the word around that I—you—had a face lift."

Sarah asked about the brown eyes. "Yours are blue."

"Simple. I wear corrective lenses, like some people wear contact lenses." He glanced at me. "What's the matter?"

"Nothing," I said. But there was something. Out of the corner of my eye I'd noticed the ridge off to my right was getting closer, meaning we'd soon be docking. If there was any activity going on at the Pointe Helbronner station, a rescue attempt, I didn't want Gerry to turn around and notice it. I had to distract him just a little longer.

He was trying to pull his tuque on with one hand. When he couldn't, he shoved it in his pocket. I said, "There is something that bothers me in all this, Gerry. Why did you choose me? Surely you weren't seeking revenge for something that happened between Sarah and me seven years ago?"

He grunted. "Don't flatter yourself. We needed someone in a hurry. Someone whose background I knew well. Someone I could replace easily. I began to create the new Philip A. Stone. Gerhard worked out the bank account so I'd have money right away and we gave you a reputation within Hercules. He also planned the details of my death in the Laurentians. I don't know who died in my place. I left you that note telling you Sarah was in trouble because I knew you'd go after her. I just wanted you both at the funeral and to be seen together. I heard she phoned you. Once in New York, you'd both be brought here, where you, Stoney, would vanish and I'd take your place. But Sarah bolted. When it didn't look as if she'd budge out of Colorado, we had to take desperate measures. I wanted her here. To be seen by members of Hercules. A contract was out on you, but the catch was, you had to disappear. Logically. When the pair at Dorval missed, things worked out for the better. You came here instead of going back to the Laurentians."

I settled back against the seat. Over his shoulder now I could see the station still some distance away. Keep him talking. But how? Sarah must have caught on, because she too leaned back and murmured aloud, "I must be stupid, Gerry, but I fail to see how ¡you and Gerhard managed to get control of such an old establishment as the Hercules Foundation."

Gerry spent the next few minutes detailing exactly how it was done. He wás obviously proud of such a manipulation.

The foundation had begun during the depression in the thirties,· when many New York art-gallery owners formed a loose association to help each other during the hard times. They called it Hercules. After World War Two, private collectors associated with it because it kept them in close touch with the art world. Then came the museum curators, for the same reason. But the Hercules Foundation proper didn't blossom until the fifties, when the price of paintings soared. The foundation needed reshaping to deal with this new popularity—and power. Gerhard Hegler, a born administrator, was voted in as general manager at a salary of one dollar a year. He would keep his own art-consulting business.

Two years ago, Gerry told us, he heard about a sculpture from India which, though stolen, had found its way into a private collection in Texas. The Indian government's protest to the American administration had fallen on deaf ears. Because the U.S. was not signatory to the particular UNESCO convention, nothing illegal had occurred on American soil.

"I heard rumors at the time that Gerhard had something to do with the transaction," said Gerry. "I'd been pretty close to him over the years, so I confronted him with it. It turned out he had been handling assignments for museums and so on that weren't so legal. He told me about them, saying he could use a younger partner. We brought in others we could trust. The Hercules Foundation was a perfect cover. Only a small percentage know the operation exists at all. Most don't really want to know how the foundation obtains works for them.''

We were getting closer now. I could see the station clearly. Gerry must have sensed this, because the barrel of his revolver moved up to point at my face.

"We'll be getting off together and heading down the Italian side, Stoney. I don't want any trouble. Or I'll shoot Sarah first. Then you.''

"So there'll be two of me running about the Italian country-side,'' I quipped.

Gerry fidgeted with the revolver. "Not for long, I'm afraid. Before we joined the line for the run up here, I made a phone call. I arranged for the same helicopter that brought me in from Switzerland yesterday to pick us up just beyond the Pointe Helbronner station. Needless to say, you won't be on board when we land.'' He stuffed the gun in his pocket but kept his hand on it. "You see, Stoney, we all had contingency plans.''

I considered telling Gerry how far Hegler's got him, but I didn't bother. Instead, I said, "I'm happy for you.''

We stood in silence at the base of the Pointe Helbronner station and dropped our skis onto the hard-packed snow. We were to put them on, then ski several hundred yards along the right to meet the helicopter, which as yet hadn't arrived.

At the moment my stomach was a tangle of knots. We were *alone*. I hadn't expected that. No police, no one. No gondolas had followed us. I stepped into my ski bindings and looked around, cursing myself for not having left Agostino a written message.

From here the world was certainly below us, with the ridge Gerry had mentioned, to one side of us, dropping away in one long plunge toward the Vallée Blanche. My view to the other side was hampered by the station, though I could see some broken slopes out beyond the far end of the building.

By the time I'd slipped my hands through the leather straps on the ski poles, I knew exactly what I must do. Gerry's first priority was having me dead and buried. Obviously there couldn't be two Philip A. Stones running around anyone's countryside, and that was our trump card. I had to separate the three of us, and the only way to do that was to ski off the ridge, forcing him to follow. We both knew he was the better skier, and from here I couldn't tell just how steep a drop it was off the ridge. I had gotten only a glimpse from the gondola; it didn't look totally vertical.

Both were risks I had to take. Besides, I was hoping it might give Agostino and his friends enough time to catch up with us.

Gerry was already waiting. I took a deep breath and started toward him. As I passed by Sarah, who was fussing with her poles, I whispered, "Get to a phone," and continued on a pace or two, to stop on Gerry's left side. This put me between him and the ridge itself, which was a good dozen yards off.

We waited for Sarah. I took a deep breath and glanced at Gerry Hope-Warden. He looked ridiculous, aiming his pocket at me. I wondered how long it would take him to yank the gun free, or would he just fire through the material?

Sarah had pulled up on Gerry's other side. Her head was tilted to one side as if she were listening to something. Gerry asked her what was wrong.

"I can hear it. The helicopter."

I thought she was fooling, but now I could hear it too. Instinctively we all looked up. Then it came to me, rather stupidly, that she was using the sound of the copter to distract Gerry.

I reacted by jamming my poles down and driving my skis toward the ridge. I was aware of a scuffle going on behind me, but I didn't stop until the tips of my skis were pointing out over the ledge.

Below it, the drop now seemed almost vertical.

I glanced behind me.

Gerry was coming, his powerful strides driving him forward. I held back long enough to see Sarah struggling to her knees, then hurled myself off the lip.

For one brief moment I sensed a feeling of weightlessness; then my skis sank deep into the snow and dragged me in after them.

Many times since, I've tried piecing together exactly what happened on the mountain that morning, but I can't. Not fully. A medical friend says it's natural. You can live and experience appalling moments, but later the brain will erase the memory of what terrified it.

The pain I remember. The pure physical pain of muscles strained beyond their limit, of lungs burning up for lack of oxygen. Of exhaustion from dropping down pitches so steep that my speed went unchecked. God only knows how I stayed up. Fear helped.

I plunged on, aware of Gerry dogging me from behind. From the top of the world I soon found myself dwarfed by peaks and ridges high above me as my skis suddenly clattered across boiler-plated snow that made my teeth rattle. Great ugly outcroppings of rock appeared. Without checking my speed, I dodged between them, hoping to put Gerry off my trail. But coming out the other side I didn't have to look behind to know he was still there. He was biding his time. Minutes later I shot over a rise to see a sight I'll never forget.

The glacier of the Mer de Glace spread out below me, the damnedest upheaval of snow and ice imaginable. Frozen geysers pressured up from beneath formed mounds of ice several stories high. And crevasses. Deep, treacherous. Christ, now I knew why Gerry had bided his time. But before stuffing me down one of those bloody holes forever, he'd have to find me.

I didn't see the first crevasse until I came over the rise too fast. It was directly ahead of me, so I cranked my aching legs into a snowplow to brake my speed and veered away.

Tracks. Ski tracks. I was in them. I remembered the group from the cable car. With a guide? You *need* a guide to survive the Mer de Glace. Crevasses appear, shift, and heal overnight. If I could keep in the tracks . . .

They dropped me deeper into the icefield. I wanted to reach two mounds not far off. Another crevasse was on my left. I was almost by it when something heavy slammed into my thigh, driving my legs out from under me.

I was lying in a heap on my stomach, tangled up in skis and poles, my head lower than the rest of me. I felt fuzzy. My leg was numb. I turned my face to the side so I could breathe.

My hands were under me, pinned there by the pole straps. I started working them free, when I began to slip. I hung on. The motion stopped. I lifted my head slowly.

Ten feet away was the opening of the crevasse, longer than me and twice as wide. I was in a kind of funnel that sloped down to it. I was moving toward it again. Only a few inches this time. "Gerry," I called out. "For Christ sake, Gerry . . ." The bastard didn't answer.

I freed my hands by easing them slowly out of the gloves. Worried about my leg, I worked a hand down my side and touched my thigh. The fingers felt something warm and wet. Moving my head around carefully, I saw the hand was covered with blood. I'd been shot. It didn't surprise me.

"Gerry!" He was near. I sensed it. I tried twisting around to

208

look for him, but it started me moving again. Six inches. A foot. Oh, God. I tried going limp. Another few inches and I stopped.

Hardly able to breathe, I hung on till I had my wits about me. Knowing if I ever broke loose I'd be gone, I snaked a hand down into the solid snow, got whatever grip I could with my fingers, then did the same with the other hand. Then I began working my body around. Sweat was running into my eyes. I took my time. Finally my skis and boots were below me. I started inching upward, moving my legs only when my fingers were holding fast above.

My chest caught the upper edge of the slope. I gave one more heave to put me up on the flat at last and lay still, wondering if he'd mercifully left me here to bleed to death.

My eyes were closing when something nudged my shoulder. It was the tip of a ski.

"I was hoping you wouldn't make it," said Gerry.

I shook off an urge to laugh and slowly lifted myself up on one arm. He was moving back from me, along the edge of the funnel, the gun pushed out in front of him.

The muscles tightened along his neck. "Stoney . . ."

I looked away. "Don't tell me you're sorry. Spare me that much." I heard the click of the hammer. Somehow I had to prolong the agony. "What happens? After."

"I'll cover over the blood, then mess myself up. Cut my face."

I was listening to every word. Something was happening to him. I don't think even he was aware of it, but his voice was changing to sound like mine.

"Then what?"

He gazed at me over the sight on the barrel. "I'll say I had a fight with Gerry Hope-Warden and he tripped and fell down a glacier." It was my voice now. "Once I leave here, I won't know which crevasse you've gone into anyway, even if I'm brought back up to look for you. Me. So how could I tell anyone else?"

A breeze ruffled his hair. I said, "You've forgotten about Sarah."

The smile was me. "No problem. She'll be back to her old distraught self after this. I'll get to her. Comfort her. Even her own psychiatrist in New York will agree she was off the wall. I'm planning to get her into a clinic in Zurich, then she'll spend her convalescence in Chamonix. It will take time, but who

209

cares?" I could've told him it wouldn't work on her now. She wasn't the Sarah he'd known.

A numbness boiled through my body. The muzzle came up a little higher. I dropped my eyes. "Get it over with," I whispered hoarsely. I saw it then. A small red disk the size of a silver dollar sliding across the snow. It stopped on Gerry's boot and started up the leg of his blue outfit. I began shaking. I watched it move to his shoulder, then pause. The gun wavered. I couldn't breathe. His lips moved.

"Gerry, drop the gun. Drop the fucking gun, Gerry." He noticed the red disk. I watched him bring a hand back and try brushing it away. "Gerry!" I screamed, "drop—"

I heard the distant sound of popping champagne corks. Stunned, I watched as Gerry's eyes went as big as saucers. The arms and revolver went up as he was driven backward. I screamed again and threw myself sideways.

I lay there feeling the cold snow against my cheek.

Moaning. I thought it was me. But it wasn't. I looked back into the crevasse.

Gerry was there, lying on his back, spread-eagled on the slope. Most of his chest and left shoulder were covered in blood. It was all around him.

My leg was stiff. My own blood was seeping into the snow. Forgetting it now, I got my legs and skis and the rest of me around, pushed my chest over the edge, and reached out. I couldn't touch him. I pushed myself even farther and tried again. Not good enough. "Hold on, Gerry," I whispered. Jesus, hold on. "Gerry!" The head moved. Then the whole body started slipping toward the crevasse. I pushed my hand farther. "Gerry, your good hand. Push it back. I'm here." The hand started to move. "Yes, yes. A little more. Easy. Oh, Christ, not too fast." Our fingers touched. "Don't move," I whispered. I inched myself down. My fingers closed around his wrist.

We lay still. He was having trouble breathing through his mouth. "Gerry, help me. I want to pull you this way. Easy, just easy."

The head moved to one side. "I can't, Stoney." His body stiffened. He slipped, taking me with him. I clawed at the snow with my free hand.

"Gerry, goddammit, relax. I can't hold you." I struggled to dig in my boots and skis. My stomach was sliding. His arm jerked, trying to pull free. I was crying now. He was pleading with me to let him go. I couldn't. I felt my legs giving out. I

210

yelled at him. Another jerk and his hand was free. "Gerry!" I screamed, watching helplessly as the distance between us widened. He was moving faster, trailing blood behind him, trying to roll over on his belly. More than his shoulder had been shot away. I called out. His face came up. I was looking at myself, at my nose, my mouth, my pain. I closed my eyes. When I opened them again, he wasn't there.

I lay still, unable to move. Then a voice. Arms were around me. It was Sarah, dragging me back from the edge. She said I was bleeding, and I slumped back, exhausted. Once when I came to, she was fussing with my leg. When I looked away from the sun, I saw a figure skiing down the mountain, his legs splayed wide. But I couldn't stay awake long enough to see who it was.

When I woke up, Sarah.was holding me. She had been crying. I asked how she got here. She had followed us down, she said, after calling the police. Another face came into view. It was Agostino.

He shook the snow and ice from his hair. "Sorry I couldn't hit him any sooner, Stoney. I had to sort the pair of you out."

I shivered. "I'm just as glad you waited. Of course, if I'd seen that little red disk on my shoulder, I wouldn't have brushed it off so casually."

Agostino grinned at me. "That's what I was counting on." He turned to Sarah. "You're some woman, Sarah Warden. Thanks for everything. Your call saved Stoney's life. He owes you one."

Sarah blushed. "I've owed him one for a lot longer than just today."

"Listen, if you two are finished, I'd like to ask a few questions. First. You got Hegler?"

"Ya. Well, bits of him. One of our bullets hit the gas tank."

"And Monique?" asked Sarah.

Agostino took a deep breath. "We'll find her. We owe her a lot. Mountain climbers are up there now. And choppers. They're working back from where you were found, Stoney. Your marker should still be there."

"And what about the Brosseau collection?"

The agent didn't answer for a moment. "It's intact. We'll find some way of sending it back to Oradour-sur-Glane. Maybe as a permanent collection. There's a new town, I hear, beside the old."

Sarah eased me back onto the snow and stood up. I asked if there was anything I could do. No, she said, walking away.

We watched her sit with her head on her knees, arms wrapped around her legs. I shifted my rump to ease the dull pain in my leg. I said to Agostino, "I hope you're planning to get us out of here?"

"Oh, yes," was his only comment. He hadn't taken his eyes off Sarah, but I knew his thoughts were somewhere up past the Fourche refuge. Sarah's were either there or down the crevasse. Probably both. Mine were.

"How?"

"Chopper." He looked at me and grunted. "Reggie's sending it up, along with a friend of yours. God knows how he did it, but he's conned the ride. It's Bo Jacobs."

"Bo!" I exclaimed. "The sonofabitch. What's he doing? He hates flying."

"He's here, all right. We knew all about him from Monique's reports. He told Reggie he couldn't just sit around the ranch knowing damn well that you'd be knee-deep in cow chips." He nodded toward Sarah. "Will she be all right?"

"Yes," I said, "she'll be fine. What about you?"

"I'm okay," he said quietly. "By the way, Stoney, that money in your account is clean. It's yours."

I thought of my camera sitting on the shelf in the Montreal pawn shop. "It'll come in handy," I replied.

We talked awhile longer. It took my mind off the pain. I learned that the person killed in Gerry's place had most likely been a bum picked up on the Main in Montreal, then promised a wild old time in the Laurentians. Later, I wondered aloud why after all these years Hegler and Warden had decided to turn their paintings loose.

"They were beginning to show signs of deterioration, Stoney. At least that's what Reggie got from Joachim Smith. Both Hegler and Warden knew it had to be done. It broke Warden's heart long before the bullets got him." He paused, then added, "We'll have a mountain rescue party up here as soon as you leave. To get Gerry's body." He grunted to himself. "Funny, he's already had his funeral."

Sarah was tying her hair back from her face. We watched her stand up.

Agostino said, "Do you think Hope-Warden really would've shot you like that?"

212

The answer didn't come right away. "I don't think he really wanted to."

Sarah was coming back.

"That isn't what I asked."

She stood with her hands on her hips, her head tilted to one side, then sat down close beside me. I could smell her perfume. She looked at us both and said, "I think I hear a helicopter? Can you?"

Yes, we could.